PEKOE MOST POISON

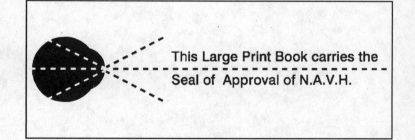

This Large Print Book carries the
Seal of Approval of N.A.V.H.

TEA SHOP MYSTERY, BOOK 18

PEKOE MOST POISON

LAURA CHILDS

WHEELER PUBLISHING
A part of Gale, Cengage Learning

Farmington Hills, Mich • San Francisco • New York • Waterville, Maine
Meriden, Conn • Mason, Ohio • Chicago

LIBRARY OF CONGRESS CATALOGING-IN-PUBLICATION DATA

Names: Childs, Laura, author.
Title: Pekoe most poison / Laura Childs.
Description: Waterville, Maine : Wheeler Publishing Large Print, 2017. | Wheeler publishing large print hardcover | Series: A tea shop mystery
Identifiers: LCCN 2016059301 | ISBN 9781410497468 (hardback) | ISBN 1410497461 (hardcover)
Subjects: LCSH: Large type books. | BISAC: FICTION / Mystery & Detective / Women Sleuths. | GSAFD: Mystery fiction.
Classification: LCC PS3603.H56 P45 2017b | DDC 813/.6—dc23
LC record available at https://lccn.loc.gov/2016059301

Published in 2017 by arrangement with The Berkley Publishing Group, an imprint of Penguin Publishing Group, a division of Penguin Random House LLC

Printed in the United States of America
1 2 3 4 5 6 7 21 20 19 18 17

ACKNOWLEDGMENTS

Special thanks to Sam, Tom, Allison, Amanda, Lesley, Danielle, Roxanne, Bob, Jennie, and all the amazing people at Berkley Prime Crime and Penguin Random House who handle design, editing, publicity, copywriting, bookstore sales, and gift sales. Heartfelt thanks, too, to all the tea lovers, tea shop owners, bookshop folks, librarians, reviewers, magazine editors and writers, websites, broadcasters, and bloggers who have enjoyed the Tea Shop Mysteries and have helped to spread the word. You make this all possible!

And I am especially indebted to you, dear readers. You have embraced Theodosia, Drayton, Haley, Earl Grey, and the rest of the tea shop gang (even mad-as-a-hatter Delaine!) as family. For that, I am eternally grateful and pledge to bring you many more Tea Shop Mysteries!

1

Palmettos swayed lazily in the soft breeze, daffodils bobbed their shaggy heads as Theodosia Browning stepped quickly along the brick pathway that wound through a bountiful front yard garden and up to the polished double doors of the Calhoun Mansion. Pausing, she pulled back the enormous brass boar's head door knocker . . . nothing wimpy about this place . . . and let it crash against the metal plate.

Claaaang. The sound echoed deep within the house as the boar's eyes glittered and glared at her.

Turning to face Drayton, her friend and tea sommelier, Theodosia said, "This should be fun. I've never visited Doreen's home before."

"You'll like it," Drayton said. "It's a grand old place. Built back in the early eighteen hundreds by Emerson Calhoun, one of Charleston's early indigo barons."

"I guess we're lucky to be invited then," she said. Their hostess, Doreen Briggs, also known to her close friends as "Dolly," was president of the Ladies Opera Auxiliary and one of the leading social powerhouses in Charleston, South Carolina. Theodosia had always thought of Doreen as being slightly bubbleheaded, but that could be a carefully cultivated act, aimed to deflect from all the philanthropic work that she and her husband were involved in.

A few seconds later, the front door creaked open and Theodosia and Drayton were greeted by a vision so strange it could have been a drug-induced hookah dream straight out of *Alice in Wonderland.* The man who answered the door was dressed in a powder blue velvet waistcoat, cream-colored slacks, and spit-polished black buckle boots. But it wasn't his formal, quasi-Edwardian attire that made him so bizarre. It was the giant white velvet rat head perched atop his head and shoulders. Yes, white velvet, just like the fur of a properly groomed, semi-dandy white rat. Complete with round ears, long snout bristling with whiskers, and bright pink eyes.

"Welcome," the rat said to them as he placed one white-gloved hand (paw?) behind his back and bowed deeply.

8

At which point Theodosia arched her carefully waxed brows and said, as a not-so-subtle aside to Drayton, "When the invitation specified a 'Charleston rat tea,' they weren't just whistling Dixie."

It was a rat tea. Of sorts. Drayton had filled her in on the history of the quaint rat tea custom on their stroll over from the Indigo Tea Shop, where they brewed all manner of tea, fed and charmed customers, and made a fairly comfortable living.

"Seventy-five years ago," Drayton said, "rat teas were all the rage in Charleston. You see, at the advent of World War Two, our fair city underwent a tremendous population explosion as war workers arrived at the navy shipyard in droves."

"I get that," Theodosia had said. "But what's with the rats specifically?"

"Ah," Drayton said. "With the increased populace, downtown merchants were thriving. Because they were so frantically busy, they began tossing their garbage out onto the sidewalks, which immediately attracted a huge influx of rats. The local public health officials, fearing some kind of ghastly epidemic, quickly spearheaded a 'rat torpedo' campaign. Volunteers were tasked with wrapping poisoned bait in small folded bits of newspaper and sticking them in alleys and crawl spaces."

Theodosia listened, fascinated, as Drayton continued his story.

"These rat torpedoes were so effective," Drayton said, "that prominent society ladies even held fancy 'rat teas' to help promote the campaign."

"And the rats were eventually eradicated?" Theodosia had asked.

"Charleston became a public health model," Drayton said. "Several major cities even sent representatives to study our method."

The blue rat at the door was still nodding to them as Theodosia and Drayton stepped inside the foyer. Here, they were greeted by a second rat wearing a pastel pink coat. This rat was equally polite.

"Good afternoon," pink rat said.

"I feel like I've been drinking to excess," Theodosia said. "Seeing pink rats instead of pink elephants."

"This way, please," pink rat said to them in carefully modulated tones.

They followed him down a long, red-tiled hallway where oil paintings dark with crackle glaze hung on the walls and the hum of conversation grew louder with each step they took. Then pink rat turned suddenly and ushered them into an enormous sunlit parlor where fifty or so guests milled about and a half-dozen elegant tea tables were carefully arranged.

Pink rat consulted his clipboard. "Miss Browning, Mr. Conneley, you're both to be seated at table six."

"Thank you," Drayton said.

"Do I know you?" Theodosia asked pink rat. Her blue eyes sparkled with curiosity and her voice was slightly teasing. She was a woman of rare and fair beauty even though she'd be the first to pooh-pooh anyone who told her so. But with her masses of auburn hair, English rose complexion, and captivating smile, she certainly stood out in a crowd.

"I don't think so, ma'am," pink rat said as he spun on the heels of his buckle boots and hastened off to escort another group of guests to their table.

"Who *was* that?" Theodosia asked as her eyes skittered around the rather grand room, taking in the crystal chandelier, enormous marble fireplace, gaggle of upscale-looking guests, as well as tea tables set with Wedgwood china and Reed & Barton silver. "He sounded so familiar. The rat guy, I mean."

"No idea," Drayton said as he regarded the table settings. "But isn't this lovely? And what fun to stage a madcap homage to the rat teas of yesteryear." Drayton was beginning to rhapsodize, one of the most endearing qualities of this debonair, sixty-something tea sommelier, while Theodosia was suddenly fizzing with curiosity. Why had she been invited when she had just a nodding acquaintance with Doreen Briggs? And who were these white rat butlers, anyway? Professional servers shanghaied from a local catering company? Or actors who'd been hired to wear costumes and playact a rather bizarre role?

These were the kind of things Theodosia wondered about. These were the things that kept her brain whirring at night when she should have been fast asleep.

"Drayton!" an excited voice shrilled. Theodosia and Drayton turned to find Doreen Briggs closing on them like a five-foot-two-inch heat-seeking missile. She charged up to Drayton, rose on tiptoes to administer a profusion of air kisses, and then flashed an enormous smile at Theodosia. "Theodosia," she said. "So good of you to come." Doreen gripped her hand firmly, pumped her arm. "Welcome to my home."

"Thank you for inviting me," Theodosia said. "And I must say, you have a very lovely home."

"It is cozy, isn't it?" Doreen said. Her green eyes glinted almost coquettishly; her reddish-blond hair cascaded around her face in a forest of curls that didn't seem quite natural for a woman in her late fifties.

"We're thrilled to be here," Drayton added.

Doreen, who was stuffed into a pastel pink shantung silk dress with a rope of pearls around her neck, waved a hand that was festooned with sparkling diamond rings, and said, "Don't you think this is jolly fun? The rat tea theme, I mean? Aren't my liveried rats just adorable?"

"Charming," Theodosia responded. Truthfully, she thought the rats — she'd seen at least four of them chugging officiously around the room — were a little strange. But this was a woman who supported the arts, gave money to service dog organizations, and was on the verge of bequeathing a sizable grant to Drayton's beloved Heritage Society, so she was willing to cut her a good deal of slack.

"Where's Beau?" Drayton asked. "He's certainly here today, isn't he?" Beau Briggs was Doreen's husband, a self-professed

13

entrepreneur who owned apartment buildings in North Charleston and was a partner in the newly opened Gilded Magnolia Spa on King Street.

Doreen pushed back a strand of frizzled hair. "He's around here somewhere. Probably bending the ear of one of our guests, talking about one of his pet business projects." She put a hand on Theodosia's arm and said, "Isn't it cute when men work themselves into a tizzy over business? I love how they think they're masters of the universe when it's really we women who run things."

"And a fine job you ladies do," Drayton said.

"Aren't you the most politically correct gentleman yet," Doreen fawned. "You'll have to indoctrinate Beau with some of your fine, liberal ideas." She managed a quick sip of air and said, "We're sitting right here." Then she waved a chubby hand. "Your table is right next to us."

"I'm looking forward to meeting your husband," Theodosia said. She'd heard so much about the man who'd helped create Gilded Magnolia Spa. Magazines had run full-color spreads, health and beauty editors had rhapsodized about it in articles, and the ladies-who-lunch types, who shopped at

Bob Ellis Shoes and Hampden Clothing, had been exchanging whispers about the spa's gold foil facials and amazing electrostim lifts.

"I imagine Beau will pop up any moment," Doreen said as she glanced around the room. Then her face lit up and she cried, "There he is." She waved a hand as bracelets clanked. "Beau!" Her voice rose higher. "Yes, I'm talking to you, hunky monkey . . . who do you *think* I'm waving at like a crazy lady? Get over here and say hello to Theodosia and Drayton."

Beau Briggs, who was forty pounds overweight, with slicked-back red hair, the jowls of a shar-pei, and perfectly steam-cleaned pores, came huffing over to join them.

"Dolly," he said. "What?" His pink sport coat was stretched around his midsection, the gold buttons looking about ready to burst and go airborne. Theodosia decided Beau might partake of his own spa's skin care regimen, but not their low-cal smoothies and fruit salads.

"These are the people I was telling you about," Doreen said. "Theodosia and Drayton. They run that lovely Indigo Tea Shop over on Church Street. You remember, they bake those chocolate chip scones that you adore so much?"

15

Beau turned an expectant smile on them. "I hope you brought some along?"

Doreen gave him a playful slap. "Silly boy. You know our caterers are handling the scones and tea sandwiches today. Theodosia and Drayton are our guests. They're here to partake of tea, not serve it."

"A respite," Drayton said, trying to be jocular.

"Then sit down, sit down," Doreen said as all around them guests began taking their seats. "Oh!" She spun around to position herself at the head table, all the while looking a little scattered. "I suppose it's high time I get this fancy tea started." She glanced down, looking slightly perturbed. "Now, where did I put my silver bell?"

The tea turned out to be a lovely affair, albeit a trifle strange. The rat theme continued as everyone took their places and more liveried rats came scurrying out of the kitchen. They carried steaming teapots in white-gloved hands, pouring out servings of Darjeeling and Assam tea. By the time silver trays overflowing with cinnamon and lemon poppy seed scones arrived, Theodosia was well past her initial surprise. In fact, she was able to sit back and enjoy herself as Drayton did the heavy lifting, chatting merrily with all the guests at their table, most of whom she had only a nodding acquaintance with. Then again, Drayton was a stickler for politeness and decorum. And tended to be a lot more social than she was.

Let's see now, Theodosia thought after they'd gone around the table and made hasty introductions. The two blondes, Dree and Diana, were on the board of directors for the Charleston Symphony. The woman in the fire-engine red suit . . . Twilby . . . Eleanor Twilby? . . . was the executive director of . . . something. And then . . . well, she just wasn't sure. But the crab and Gruyère cheese quiche she was digging into was incredibly creamy and delicious.

Doreen turned in her chair and tapped Theodosia on the shoulder. "Having fun?" she asked.

Theodosia, caught with a bite of food in her mouth, chewed quickly and swallowed. "This quiche is incredible!" She really meant it. "I'll have to get the recipe. Haley would love it." Haley was her chef and chief baker back at the Indigo Tea Shop.

"Carolina blue crab," Doreen said in a conspiratorial whisper. "From a caterer that's brand-new here in Charleston and making quite a splash. We even tapped them to cater all the appetizers for our grand opening party at Gilded Magnolia Spa next Saturday."

"You have quite a large group here today," Theodosia said. "Are most of them spa customers?"

"It's a sprinkling of all sorts of people," Doreen said. "Spa members, media people, a few friends and neighbors, some business associates." She raised a hand to one of the rat waiters and said, "We're going to need a fresh pot of this orange pekoe tea for Beau." And to Theodosia: "It's his favorite."

"One of Drayton's recommendations?" Theodosia asked.

"Oh, absolutely," Doreen said. "I consulted with Drayton on all the teas we're serving here today. As usual, he was spot-on."

"He's the best tea sommelier I've ever encountered. We're fortunate to have him at the Indigo Tea Shop."

"Watch out someone doesn't try to steal him away," Doreen said. She turned, held up Beau's teacup for the waiter to pour him a fresh cup of tea, and said, "Just set the teapot on the warmer, please."

The pink rat leaned forward, set down the teapot, and, in the process, the edge of his sleeve brushed against one of the tall white tapers.

"Watch the . . . !" Doreen cried out as the candle wobbled dangerously in its silver holder.

But it was too late.

The burning candle bobbled and swayed for a couple more seconds and then tipped onto the table. It landed, flame burning bright, right in the middle of an enormous, frothy centerpiece. As if someone had doused it with gasoline, a ring of dancing fire burst forth. A split second later, the decorator-done arrangement of silk flowers, pinecones, twisted vines, and dried moss was a boiling, seething inferno.

As the guests at Doreen's table began to scream, two people leapt to their feet and began beating at the crackling flames with linen napkins. Their efforts just served to fan the flames and set one of the napkins on fire. It twisted and blazed like an impromptu torch until the person waving it suddenly dropped it onto the table.

Beau Briggs, as if just realizing they might all be in mortal danger, suddenly jumped to his feet, knocking his chair over backward. "Somebody get a fire extinguisher!" he yelped as flames continued to dance and scorch the tabletop. Now everyone from his table was jigging around in a fearful, nervous rugbylike scrum, while people from other tables were rushing over to shout suggestions. Doreen, no help at all, put her hands on her head and let loose a series of high-pitched yips.

"Somebody do something!" a woman in a black leather dress screamed.

At which point Theodosia grabbed the teapot from her table, elbowed her way through the gaggle of guests, and poured the tea directly onto the flames.

There was a loud hiss as an enormous billow of black smoke swirled upward. But the tea had done the trick. The fire had fizzled out, leaving only the remnants of a singed and seared centerpiece swimming in a brown puddle of Darjeeling tea.

"Thank you," Beau cried out. "Thank you!"

"Good work," Drayton said to Theodosia, just as blue rat arrived, fumbling with a bright-red fire extinguisher. He aimed the nozzle at the table and proceeded to spray white, foamy gunk all over the remaining plates of food.

"Stop, stop," Beau yelled at the rat. He lifted his hands to indicate they were all fine, that the danger was over, even as a few tendrils of smoke continued to spiral up from the charred centerpiece.

"Goodness," Doreen squealed, nervously

patting her heart with one hand. "That was absolutely terrifying. We could have . . . all been . . ." She spun around toward Theodosia, a look of gratitude washing across her face. "Thank you, my dear, for such quick, decisive thinking."

"But your tea party's been ruined," Theodosia said with a rueful smile. "I'm so sorry." The head table, which had looked so elegant and refined a few minutes earlier, was now a burned and blistered wreck. The ceiling above was horribly smudged.

"We'll salvage this party yet," Beau said. Undeterred, he pulled himself to his full height and raised his hands, like a fiery evangelist, ready to address the upturned, still-stunned faces of all his guests.

"I don't know how," Doreen muttered.

"My dear friends," Beau said. "Please pardon the inconvenience." He pulled a hankie from his jacket pocket and mopped at his florid face as a spatter of applause broke out. He acknowledged the applause with a slightly uneven smile and continued. "Even though everything is firmly under control, I think it's best that we finish our . . . ahem, that we adjourn to . . ." Stumbling over his words, he halted mid-sentence as a tremendous shudder ran through his entire body. It shook his shoul-

21

ders, jiggled his belly, and made his knees knock together. Then his eyes popped open to twice their normal size and he let out a cough, razor sharp and harsh. That cough quickly became a series of coughs that racked his body and morphed into a high-pitched, thready-sounding wheeze.

Doreen, looking properly concerned, held out a glass of water for her husband. "Please drink this, dear."

As Beau struggled to grab the water, his hands began to shake violently. He managed to just barely grasp the glass and lift it shakily to his lips.

"I just need . . ." Beau managed to croak out.

But just as he was about to take a much-needed sip of water, his head suddenly flew backward and he let loose a loud choke that sounded like the bark of an angry seal. The water glass slipped from his hand.

Crash! Shards of glass flew everywhere.

"Beau?" Doreen said in a small, scared voice, as if she sensed something was catastrophically wrong.

Beau was waving both hands in front of his face now, gasping for breath and hacking loudly. "Wha . . . bwa . . ." He fought to get his words out, but simply couldn't manage it.

At least five sets of hands stretched out to help him, all holding water glasses. Instead of grabbing one of the glasses, Beau struggled to pick up his cup of tea. He managed to get his teacup halfway to his lips before his right hand convulsed into a rigid claw and the cup slipped from his grasp. As it clattered to the table, he clutched frantically at his throat. Eyes fluttering like crazy as they rolled back in his head, he managed a hoarse groan. Then, as if made of rubber, his legs gave way completely.

Bam! Beau dropped to the floor like a sack of potatoes, smacking his forehead on the sharp edge of the table on his way down.

In a frenzy now, screeching for help, Doreen bent over and tried to grab him. But Beau was so heavy and unwieldy that all she managed to do was bunch his shirt above his jacket collar. "He's not breathing!" she screamed. "Does anyone know the Heimlich maneuver?"

One man from a nearby table immediately sprang to his feet and came flying around to help. He knelt down directly behind Beau, wrapped his arms around his chest, and pulled him halfway upright. Then, locking his hands under Beau's sternum, the man pulled his arms tight, making quick upward thrusts.

Beau's eyes flickered open, then turned glassy as white foam dribbled from his mouth.

"It's working, it's working!" Doreen cried. "He blinked his eyes."

"Thank goodness," Drayton said. He sank into his chair as the Good Samaritan continued to thump and bump poor Beau Briggs.

"Is he coming around?" Doreen asked in a tremulous voice as Beau's head jerked back and forth spasmodically and then lolled to one side as if his neck were made of Silly Putty.

"His color's looking better," the skinny woman in black leather cried out. "His face isn't purple anymore."

"That's good?" Doreen asked. Then, as if to reassure herself, said, "That's good."

Meanwhile, the man who was still administering the Heimlich maneuver was struggling mightily and beginning to lose steam. "If I could just . . ." he grunted out, trying to catch his breath. ". . . Dislodge whatever he's got caught in his throat. Try to get him breathing on his own." He pulled and thrust harder and harder, his own face turning a violent shade of red. "Where's the ambulance?" the man gasped. "Where are the EMTs?"

"On their way!" the pink rat cried. "I can

24

hear sirens now."

"Can somebody take over here?" the Good Samaritan gasped.

A man in a white dinner jacket sprang into action. He employed a different technique. He bent Beau forward and thumped him hard on the back. But nothing seemed to be working. Beau's eyes, open wide but unseeing, looked like two boiled eggs. His bulbous body was as limp and unresponsive as a noodle.

"I don't think that technique is going to work," Theodosia said in a quiet voice.

Drayton heard her and frowned, his eyes going wide with alarm. "Why would you say that? What do you think is wrong with him?"

"You see that white foam dribbling from his mouth?" Theodosia said. "You see his pale, almost waxy complexion? I think he's ingested some sort of poison."

"Poison!" Doreen suddenly screamed at the top of her lungs. "Don't drink the tea! The tea is poison!"

2

Bone china teacups crashed rudely into saucers, most of them shattering instantly as guests dropped their cups in terror. People bent forward and spit out their tea as blind panic ensued. Even bits of scone and shortbread were spit discreetly into cloth napkins.

Meanwhile, Beau hadn't given up the ghost quite yet. His body began to shake as he suddenly launched into a cataclysmic fit. Gold buttons popped off his jacket and shot through the air like tiny, deadly missiles. His arms flailed about, his feet drummed the floor so hard one leather loafer flew off and sailed across the room, whacking some poor woman in the head.

"Grab him, grab him!" Drayton shouted. "We've got to hold him down."

"Shove something in his mouth so he doesn't swallow his tongue," another man yelled out.

26

The woman in black leather poked at Beau's mouth with a silver spoon, then jumped back, fearful.

More frantic suggestions rang out from the crowd that had gathered around him.

"Don't let him crack a rib."

"Ambulance is coming."

"Try to sit him up straight."

Nothing worked, of course. Beau Briggs was caught in the violent throes of some deadly paroxysm. His head lolled, his eyes glazed over, and more white foam dribbled out the sides of his mouth as everyone gathered around in a macabre circle to watch.

Finally, Beau let out a single garbled choke, something on par with a guttural *gwack,* and gave one final, fatal shiver. Seconds later he lay unnaturally still.

"Oh no, no no no!" Doreen lifted up her arms as if imploring the intercession of some heavenly force. "He's not moving! Somebody *do* something!"

One of her fingers snagged in her long strand of pearls and ripped them hard. A tiny snap sounded and then her precious Akoya pearls tumbled down the front of her dress.

"My husband! My pearls!" Doreen

screamed. She looked like she was ready to faint.

Theodosia leapt for Doreen and wrapped her arms tightly around the woman's upper body, pinning her arms down to her sides. "Doreen, calm down," she said. Then she glanced over her shoulder and briskly called out "Chair" to Drayton. He immediately slipped a chair behind Doreen. "Sit down," Theodosia commanded. Doreen finally closed her mouth and sat down hard.

"What about him?" Drayton gestured to the body of Beau Briggs, which lay contorted on the floor. His pink jacket was covered with black ashes and white foam, his meaty face twisted into a death's-head grimace.

Theodosia grabbed two linen napkins off her table and carefully placed them across Beau's face.

"That's it?" one of the female guests asked, her face its own mask of horror. "That's all we can do?"

"You could say a prayer," Theodosia said as she became aware of the press of curious onlookers all around her.

Blue rat poked his head next to Theodosia's, jostling her roughly with his snout. "Anything I can do to help?" he asked. His voice sounded muffled inside his mask.

Theodosia looked at him tiredly. "Yes. You can take off that stupid rat head and get the EMTs in here fast."

Two EMTs did come rushing in, bringing along a clattering gurney and a portable respirator. In fact, all activity seemed to kick into hyperdrive. More guests pushed forward and their voices rose to create a wall of sound like the drone of a thousand bees. Two uniformed police officers shoved their way in and stood behind the EMTs, watching as they attempted to resuscitate Beau. Phones began to ring and buzz. A few surreptitious photos were snapped.

"Okay, everybody move out of the way right now," a voice called out. "Show's over. Officer Bowie, Officer Jepson, let's get cracking here. I want a twenty-foot perimeter set up. Push everybody back, string up some tape, and arrest anyone who doesn't cooperate."

Theodosia glanced up to see who was shouting out orders. And saw rushing toward them a tall, intense-looking man in a flapping raincoat. He looked cool and calm and seemed to possess a no-nonsense attitude. She decided this was good. He was exactly what was needed right now.

The young man in the raincoat knelt down

29

next to Beau's body. "Any luck?" he asked one of the EMTs who was working on him. The EMT shook his head slowly. It was clearly over for Beau.

"Oh no," Doreen moaned. She popped up from her chair to see what was going on with her husband, basically leaning against Theodosia for support.

"I'm sorry," the young man said to Doreen.

"Who are you?" Doreen asked in a shaky voice.

"I'm Detective Pete Riley," the man said. "And you are . . . ?"

Doreen's chin quavered. "He's m-m-my . . ."

"Your husband?" Riley asked, not unkindly.

Doreen bobbed her head. She didn't seem to be tracking particularly well.

"I'm very sorry," Riley said again. "But perhaps you and your friend could give me a little space?" He looked directly at Theodosia. "Could you take her . . . somewhere?"

"Certainly," Theodosia said. As Riley's eyes met hers there was a flash of recognition. *He knows me?* Then she thought, yes, of course. This young detective had come into her tea shop a few months ago with Detective Burt Tidwell, the head of

Robbery-Homicide. Though she had no clear recollection that the two of them had ever been properly introduced.

Detective Riley didn't waste any time. He rounded up the people who'd been seated at Beau Briggs's table and set about questioning them. Theodosia, burning with curiosity, tried to edge her way back over to where the interrogation was taking place so she could listen to what was going on. Which, basically, was that everyone was coming across as either indignant or uncooperative.

A big guy by the name of Reggie Huston, who claimed to be Beau Briggs's business partner, wanted no part of the questioning.

"Why are you talking to me?" Huston asked in a belligerent tone. "When you should be questioning all these other yahoos."

The woman in black leather kept firing her own questions back at Riley. "What are you going to *do* about this?" she snapped. "What happens next?"

And a few other people, a tall man in a finely tailored suit, and another couple, seemed rude at best.

"What's going on?" Drayton asked. He'd pushed his way through the throng of people who were buzzing about angrily, to be close to Theodosia.

"The detective in charge just questioned all the people who were seated at the head table," she told him. "Not that they gave him any substantial information. Now he's working his way through the people who were sitting at the nearby tables."

"That's us," Drayton said, looking nervous. "But we were guests, purely observers. We don't really know what happened."

"But maybe one of those guys does," Theodosia said. She nodded toward the rat servers who were now lined up against the wall, looking like some kind of perp walk that you'd see on an episode of *Law & Order.* "You see that young guy on the end?"

"The one with the spiky hair?" Drayton asked.

"That's the one. Doesn't he look nervous to you? Evasive, almost?"

"He's probably just scared," Drayton said.

"Scared, yes. But he also looks like he wants to say something. You see how he's chattering away with the guy next to him?"

Drayton nodded. "Uh-huh."

"I've been watching the two of them," Theodosia said. "Whenever one of the police officers asked a question, they clammed right up. It struck me as . . . suspicious."

Drayton lifted a single eyebrow. "You know, Theo, you have a very active imagination and are slightly suspicious of everyone. You're always imagining there's a bogeyman hiding out there in the woods."

"Yes," Theodosia said. "But this time there really could be."

Some thirty minutes later, it was Theodosia's turn to be questioned.

Detective Pete Riley fixed her with an earnest gaze. "I'm told you're the one person who uttered the word *poison*. Why did you make that call? How did you know?"

"I didn't know for sure," Theodosia said. "In fact, I still don't know. I just made an educated guess." She noticed that Detective Riley's eyes were very blue. Cobalt blue. She shook her head, trying to focus. "Was it poison?" she asked. "Was it the tea?"

"The tea?" Riley shook his head. "No, I don't believe so. The emergency medical techs tell me that the condition of the victim's mouth and throat was not consistent with any sort of toxin that the victim might have ingested. But obviously we need to get the crime scene guys out here. And then transport the victim to the lab and run a series of tests."

"And an autopsy," Theodosia said. "You'll need to do an autopsy." She stopped, drew a breath, and said, "Because we're looking at . . ."

Riley finished the sentence for her. "Murder. Yes, I'm afraid that's right."

"Murder!" Doreen suddenly screamed from where she was standing ten feet away. Her eyes crossed as she stumbled backward and pretty much collapsed into the arms of the man standing next to her.

3

It was an impromptu Sunday brunch held on Drayton's back patio. He'd called Theodosia at nine o'clock Sunday morning and invited her over. By eleven o'clock they were enjoying cream scones along with one of his famous mushroom and Brie cheese omelets. Earl Grey, Theodosia's long-limbed dog (what she'd come to think of as a Dalbrador, since he looked a bit Dalmatian and a little bit Labrador), and Honey Bee, Drayton's King Charles spaniel, lay at their feet, enjoying the sun, ever hopeful for shared tidbits.

Drayton's patio was modest at best, with gray flagstones and overflowing pots of pink bougainvillea. But the rest of his backyard was a veritable jungle. Tall thickets of bamboo, beds of furry green moss, and large twisted Taihu rocks served as the perfect backdrop for Drayton's enormous collection of Japanese bonsai trees. There were windswept trees that had been tamed and twisted into shape, elegantly pruned junipers and oaks, and even miniature bonsai forests that had been painstakingly trained to grow, and even flourish, in small, flat containers.

As Theodosia knew it would, their conversation turned to Beau's bizarre death yesterday afternoon.

"I've reversed my opinion," Drayton said as he sliced his cream scone in half and dabbed on a puff of Devonshire cream. "You *do* need to get involved. Poor Doreen is simply frantic with worry."

"I don't think my involvement is one bit necessary," Theodosia responded. "I have the distinct feeling that Detective Pete Riley is quite capable of handling this. Or certainly his boss, Detective Tidwell." She took another bite of omelet. It was delicious. Drayton prided himself on using locally sourced, cage-free eggs, claiming they were superior in taste.

"In fact," she continued, "I'm surprised Tidwell himself didn't show up last night. This is the kind of wacky, pseudocelebrity type of murder that he dines out on."

Theodosia had a somewhat storied history in dealing with Detective Tidwell. She'd been present at a crazy smash-and-grab robbery at Heart's Desire late last year where Tidwell had been the investigating officer. They managed to figure a few things out together, and he was also a frequent drop-in visitor at the Indigo Tea Shop.

"I wondered about Tidwell's involvement myself," Drayton said. "Which is why I asked one of the uniformed officers about him yesterday. It turns out that Detective Tidwell is in absentia."

"Where's he run off to?"

"He's currently attending some sort of homeland security seminar in New York City. So the Briggs case has landed squarely in Detective Riley's hands."

"Good," Theodosia said with approval. "Because Detective Riley struck me as being a fairly smart cookie. I'm sure he'll be able to handle this . . . this mess."

Drayton tilted his head at Theodosia and his furry brows raised up a few millimeters. He was giving her *vexed.* Or maybe it was *indignant.* Either way, Drayton had a way of making Theodosia feel as if she'd committed some horrible faux pas. Like she'd sliced her scone improperly or held up her pinky finger whilst sipping tea.

"It's not working," Theodosia said finally.

Drayton gazed across his teacup at her. "Whatever do you mean?"

"I'm talking about the look you're giving me. I know that look. It means you want something. That you're trying to lob a ball squarely into my court. Even though I have no idea what you want."

"When you put it that way . . ."

"Hmm?"

"I was thinking that perhaps you could *talk* to Doreen," Drayton said. "I know she'd welcome your concern and sympathy."

"That's what you want?" Theodosia asked. "For me to talk to her? And do what . . . lend a sympathetic ear?"

"Well." Drayton's teacup made a delicate *clink* as he set it down in the saucer. The distinctive ring of fine bone china. "Perhaps you could listen to her as well."

Theodosia knew something was brewing and it wasn't just another pot of oolong tea. "And what would I be listening for?"

"When I spoke with Doreen this morning . . . Excuse me, let me rephrase my words. When Doreen woke me up at the crack of dawn, babbling hysterically, she asked if I knew anyone who could help her."

"Help her," Theodosia repeated. "And, please don't let this be the case, but you immediately thought of me?"

"Yes, I did," Drayton said. "And don't sound so surprised. Isn't it obvious that the poor woman needs someone to serve as a savvy advocate?"

"What exactly do you want me to advocate?" Theodosia really was playing hard to get.

"I think you have a fairly good idea," Drayton said. And now his words and manner had taken on a stiff, almost formal tone. "You know how *resourceful* you are, how very *perceptive* you can be. Especially in light of yesterday's . . . dare we call it . . . murder?"

"I think you could definitely venture out on a limb and call it murder," Theodosia said. "Because I don't think Beau Briggs choked to death on a piece of Juicy Fruit gum."

"No, he did not. In fact, you voiced a not-so-subtle hint about that yesterday."

"When I said that Beau might have been poisoned?"

"Precisely," Drayton said. "You see how intuitive you are? How your hypothesis was spot-on?"

Theodosia leaned forward in her chair and eyed Drayton warily. "Are you asking me to go on the offensive and help solve Beau Briggs's murder?"

Drayton lifted his shoulders in a casual shrug. "Don't act so surprised. It's not like

39

you haven't done this before." When Theodosia let out a deep sigh, he said, "You're very good at this, Theo. You are spookily clever when it comes to ferreting out clues and making smart, logical deductions."

"I still don't know why you're so fired up to have me involved. May I remind you, *you're* the one who's always warning me *not* to get involved in any kind of murder, disaster, or crazy scheme. You're the autocrat of good sense."

"This time there are extenuating circumstances."

"What are you talking about?"

Drayton hesitated. "It's really difficult to say."

"I'm sorry, but you're going to have to explain yourself," Theodosia said. "Because you're acting very mysterious and it's starting to worry me."

Drayton touched a hand to his bow tie. "There's a quid pro quo involved."

"And that would mean . . . what, exactly?" Theodosia couldn't quite fathom what Drayton was talking about. Why was he talking in circles when he was usually direct to the point of being blunt?

"As you know, Doreen Briggs is thinking about awarding a rather sizable grant to the Heritage Society," Drayton said. "She's in the middle of what you might call the decision process." The Heritage Society, a sort of hybrid museum–historical society, was Drayton's baby. He sat on its board of directors, and Timothy Neville, the organization's octogenarian director, was one of his oldest and dearest friends.

"You mentioned that grant to me a couple of days ago," Theodosia said. "But I imagine that Beau's untimely death might certainly delay Doreen's decision."

"That's not exactly right," Drayton said. "Now circumstances have conspired to make it all a tad more complicated."

"How so?"

"Doreen was very impressed with your cool head and quick thinking in yesterday's impossible situation."

"That's nice. I was happy to help, even though there was no earthly chance of reviving her poor husband." Theodosia took a sip of tea. "Now, what else? Tell me why you're dancing around as if you're just learning the tango."

Drayton grimaced. "Doreen made it quite clear to me this morning that if you and I didn't assist her in a sort of . . . well, let's call it a private investigation, then . . ."

"Wait a minute." The reason for Drayton's nervousness suddenly clicked into place for

41

Theodosia. "Are you telling me that if we don't help Doreen, she won't come through with your grant?"

"I'm afraid that's it in a nutshell."

"She's holding a *grant* over your head?" Theodosia said. "Seriously?"

"Yes." Drayton was so embarrassed he did everything but hang his head.

"Then I'd say Doreen is being horrid and petty. In fact, I'm pretty sure an attorney would categorize her request as plain old extortion."

"Could we just call it *arm-twisting* and be done with it?" Drayton said. "That doesn't sound quite so illegal or threatening."

"Blackmail," Theodosia spit out. She reached for a second scone and then decided against it. Her brain was spinning and the extra sugar wouldn't do her any good at all. "I take it this grant is important to the Heritage Society?"

"I would deem it highly necessary for continued sustainability."

"You want to give that to me in English?" Theodosia asked. Drayton's speech sometimes went from formal to florid.

"Yes . . . well," he said. "You know how the stock market has pogoed up and down the past couple of years? And how interest rates have been at an all-time low?"

"Tell me about it. My 401(k) is gasping for breath."

"Obviously this rather dire financial situation has affected everyone," Drayton said.

He was clearly uneasy talking about money, so Theodosia decided she'd better jump in and pull the rest of the story out of him.

"You're telling me that the people who have been the Heritage Society's loyal supporters, your contributors and benefactors, aren't getting a decent return on their investments like they have in the past," Theodosia said.

"That's correct."

"And so their charitable giving has dropped off. They're not writing the large checks anymore."

"They're not." Drayton paused. "Some of them aren't writing any checks at all."

Theodosia leaned back in her chair and gazed at the two dogs who were lying on the patio, still patiently waiting for crumbs to drop. She took a scone, broke off two pieces, and gave them their goodies. Both dogs swallowed once — *gunk* — like hungry crocodiles that didn't bother to chew. "Your situation does sound serious," she continued. "So I take it the Heritage Society is desperate for Doreen's infusion of cash?"

"I'm afraid we are."

"Oh my," Theodosia said. She knew she was being subtly shanghaied. Still, a part of her wanted to resist. Who was Doreen Briggs to make Drayton jump through hoops? To make her jump through hoops? "I'm not sure what I can do," she said finally.

"The truth of the matter is, you may not be able to do much of anything to help Doreen," Drayton said. "But at least you could give it a shot."

"And if we investigate Beau's death privately, if we unlock a few clues, Doreen may repay our good efforts by writing a check?"

"That's exactly right."

"It's an absurd proposition on her part," Theodosia murmured. She wanted to rail against the idea of being coerced, but hated the idea of letting Drayton down. He was one of her best friends, after all. She sighed deeply. "I suppose if I just . . ."

Drayton gazed at her expectantly. "Yes? Was that a yes?"

Theodosia set down her teacup. This was one of the strangest requests she'd ever received. And to have the future of the Heritage Society riding on her investigational smarts was ridiculous. Preposterous even. On the other hand . . . she'd been right smack-dab in the middle of things when Beau had given up the ghost. She had a nodding acquaintance with the detective in charge. And, truth be told, she was . . . let's just say, sublimely curious.

Theodosia stared across the table at Drayton, who seemed to be waiting on pins and needles.

"When did you tell Doreen we'd drop by?" she asked.

Drayton consulted his watch, an antique Piaget that perpetually ran five minutes late. "Twelve o'clock," he said. "We can just make it if we hurry."

4

Theodosia didn't much like the idea of being strong-armed. On the flip side of the coin, she had to admit she was keenly interested in Beau Briggs's murder. It wasn't every day that some poor rich dude dropped dead right before your very eyes. Correction, make that right in front of at least fifty pairs of eyes. And even though all those people had been witnesses, the murder weapon, motive, and killer hadn't been one bit obvious.

Which made this case interesting, bordering on . . . well, tantalizing.

"Excuse me," said a police officer who was stationed at the front door of Doreen Briggs's ginormous home. "I'm afraid that Mrs. Briggs is not accepting visitors right now."

"We're not visitors," Drayton said. "We're friends. Doreen is expecting us."

The officer, whose name tag read PAR-

46

NELL, consulted a list and said, "Steele?"

"No," Drayton said.

"Huston?"

"Let me look at that list," Drayton said. He pointed to his name. "There. Drayton Conneley. That's us."

Parnell looked relieved. "Okay, then."

"Excuse me," Theodosia said. "Why exactly are you stationed at the front door?"

Officer Parnell smiled. "I'm here to make the family feel safer. Mrs. Briggs is worried there might be an attempt made on her life, too."

"Of course," Theodosia said. She threw Drayton a look that clearly said, *Doreen Briggs is one crazy lady.*

Doreen was sitting in a purple velvet chair in an overheated library that was stuffed to the rafters with leather-bound books. Looking morose, she was sniffing into a white lace hankie while sipping amber liquid from a heavy cut glass tumbler. She had on a black silk dress, enormous diamond earrings, and her hair looked like a basket of curly fries. Perched in matching straight chairs opposite her were two people who looked to be in their early twenties, a young man and a young woman. Theodosia figured they must be Doreen's children.

47

"Drayton," Doreen exclaimed when they walked into the room. She didn't get up, but extended an arm, like a deposed queen receiving visitors. "Thank you for coming."

Drayton leaned forward and patted her hand. "Of course, dear lady. How are you holding up?"

"Terrible." Ice cubes rattled in Doreen's glass as she took a sip of amber liquid. Then she focused a wan smile on Theodosia. "And, Theodosia. I had a conversation with Drayton this morning and he shared so much about you. Not just what a clever tea entrepreneur you are. But how smart and intuitive you are." Doreen tapped the side of her head with an index finger. "How you have a sixth sense at reading people, at understanding human nature."

"Sometimes I can," Theodosia hedged.

"As you might imagine, I am in desperate need of your help," Doreen said. "I've talked to the police until I'm blue in the face and all they do is take notes, nod their collective heads, and blather on about an investigation. But I don't believe they have a single idea as to where to start looking." Her voice rose. "I don't believe they've even *started* looking."

"Started looking for what exactly?" Theodosia asked. She wanted to be crystal clear about Doreen's expectations.

"For Beau's killer, of course!"

"You're sure that your husband was, in fact, murdered?"

Doreen's eyes bulged. "What else could it be? You yourself said he was poisoned."

"I said it looked like poison. But I'm not a doctor or a medical examiner. Lab tests need to be done . . ."

"They've *been* done," Doreen screeched. "I received word from Detective Riley this morning. It turns out you were spot-on with your assertion. My poor Beau was poisoned!"

"Mother," said the young man. "Please don't get overly excited. It's not good for your heart."

"You're getting yourself all worked up," the young woman warned.

Doreen waved a hand dismissively. "Drayton, Theodosia, this is my son, Charles, and Beau's stepdaughter, Opal Anne. They've been a great comfort to me in my time of need."

"Thank you, Mother," Charles said. He was dark haired, slim, and seemed preternaturally quiet. Then again, Doreen probably never let him get a word in edgewise.

"And so has . . ." Doreen looked around with slightly bleary eyes. "Where on earth

49

did Starla run off to now?"

"You asked her to get some more ice cubes," Opal Anne said. She was young and pretty with brown doe eyes. Theodosia figured she was probably just a year or two out of college.

"Oh, right," Doreen mumbled.

"Starla is a family member as well?" Theodosia asked politely.

"These days I certainly feel like I am." A woman with short, dark, spiky hair, and a hard expression on her narrow face was staring directly at them. She held a silver ice bucket in bony, fidgeting hands. Theodosia recognized her as the skinny woman who'd worn the leather dress at yesterday's rat tea. Today she wore a tight black sweater and a matching pencil skirt.

Doreen waggled her fingers in a come-hither gesture. "Starla. Thank you."

Starla handed Doreen the ice bucket and flashed a cool smile at Theodosia and Drayton. "Hello there."

Doreen hastened to fill them in. "Starla Crane is our PR guru. She owns the Image Factory here in Charleston."

"Nice to meet you, Miss Crane," Drayton said.

"Perhaps you've heard of us?" Starla asked. "My firm specializes in image con-

50

sulting and public relations strategies." She glanced at Doreen, who was busy shoveling ice cubes into her glass. "We also handle crisis management."

"And you think this particular situation — Doreen's situation — warrants crisis management?" Theodosia asked. She'd spent a number of years working at a marketing firm, so she was quite familiar with public relations and the management of brand images. She'd also never heard of the Image Factory and wondered if it might be a one-person shop.

"Doreen is well-known in Charleston's philanthropic world and social community at large," Starla said in a slightly hectoring tone. "As such she needs to maintain a flawless image of taste and decorum. This incident . . . the smooth presentation of this incident . . . needs to be handled with kid gloves."

"I'm sure Doreen's image is and always will be impeccable," Drayton said.

But Theodosia was studying the almost-anorexic Starla Crane. She decided Starla had that high-strung, pushy attitude that self-absorbed career women sometimes affected. It made her wonder how good Starla really was when it came to public relations and media relations. Because the people who were generally the most skillful tended to be congenial and highly empathic. Starla, on the other hand, seemed nervous, contentious, and inner-directed. Then again, you never knew. She could turn out to be an absolute whiz.

"As you can see," Doreen said, "Starla really knows her business, which is why I asked her to sit in today."

"Fine," Drayton said. "Then we should get started."

"Excuse me," Starla said. "What are we doing exactly?"

"I mentioned to Doreen that Theodosia here is an excellent problem solver," Drayton said. "So she's agreed to talk to Doreen. To ask a few questions and see what she can come up with."

Starla's upper lip curled. "You're an investigator?"

"Not at all," Theodosia said. "I'm merely trying to sift through what we already know."

"A cool, calm voice of reason," Drayton added.

"Interesting," Starla said in a tone so flat it was clear she wasn't one bit interested.

Theodosia pulled a chair up close to Doreen, then reached over and took the glass from her hand. Passed it over to Drayton. "Let's get started," she said.

Doreen bobbed her head. "Okay."

"The police obviously asked you a lot of questions yesterday."

"You have no idea."

"Because something strange happened. Between the time the centerpiece caught fire and your husband collapsed on the floor, *something* happened."

"I guess," Doreen said in a small voice.

"And there were any number of people who were clustered around Beau," Theodosia said. "During the tea, right after the fire, and just before his collapse. It appeared as if they were all trying to help him. But any one of them could have caused his death."

"Maybe it was the tea?" Doreen said.

"And possibly it was something else," Theodosia said. "Poison doesn't necessarily mean tea — I'm sure it can be administered in many different forms."

"I don't know what that would be," Doreen said.

"Well," Theodosia said, "we don't expect you to solve this crime, just to help point the way with your best recollections."

Doreen snuck a glance at her empty glass. "I'm not sure I understand."

"Let's approach this from a slightly different angle," Theodosia said. "There must have been someone — either a guest at your table or a person who was in the immediate vicinity — who wanted your husband dead."

Doreen winced. "You're talking about motive. I hate to think about that."

Theodosia glanced over at Drayton.

"You have to think about this," Drayton said to Doreen. "It's absolutely critical. Don't you want Beau's killer apprehended? Don't you want justice?"

Don't you want to award the Heritage Society a nice fat grant? Theodosia thought to herself.

"I guess," Doreen said.

"Tell me about the people who were sitting at your table," Theodosia said.

Doreen frowned. "Well, there was Reggie Huston, Beau's business partner. And then Starla, of course. And our neighbors Honey and Michael Whitley and Robert Steele."

Theodosia had pulled a pen and paper from her handbag and was jotting down names. "And at the surrounding tables?"

"It's difficult to remember," Doreen said.

"Charles and I were sitting at table three," Opal Anne said. "Along with some financial people and new spa clients." She glanced at Theodosia. "If I looked at the guest list, I'm pretty sure I could give you their names."

"That would be great," Theodosia said. "Thank you." She focused on Doreen again. "There must have been someone who was deeply angry or offended by something Beau had done. Perhaps someone who'd lost a good deal of money in a business deal? Or someone who felt they'd been cheated in some way?"

"Is this absolutely necessary?" Starla asked.

"Yes, it is," Drayton said, without bothering to look at her.

Theodosia tried again. "There must be someone who was angry with your husband."

"Are you asking me to put together an enemies list?" Doreen asked. She looked heartsick as she squirmed around in her chair, anxiously twisting the rings on her fingers. "Because I'm not sure Beau had any enemies. I mean, everyone pretty much *adored* him." She started leaking tears. "He was sweet and smart and generous to a fault. Just ask anyone."

Theodosia knew for a fact that not everyone had loved and adored Beau Briggs. After all, someone had murdered the man in plain sight of fifty guests. That required the skill and cunning of a stone-cold killer.

Someone who possessed confidence and chutzpah beyond belief.

"Just relax and think about it," Theodosia said in a soothing voice. "Try to recall what your husband might have been involved in lately. Maybe a new business venture? Real estate or investments?"

"Tell her about the money," Opal Anne said.

Doreen shook her head. "She doesn't want to hear about that."

"Yes, she does." Opal Anne turned to look at Theodosia. "Don't you?"

"I guess maybe I do," Theodosia said, wondering what this cryptic exchange was all about. "Why don't you tell me about the money, Doreen?"

Doreen hemmed and hawed, but finally the truth began to spill out. Turns out Beau had made more than a few terrible investments. And that the money he'd lost or squandered hadn't really been his to lose. It had belonged to Doreen. Had come, in fact, from Doreen's family fortune, a rather sizable amount that she'd inherited from her father and grandfather.

"You see why she's so upset?" Opal Anne said. She reached over and squeezed Doreen's hand. "Poor thing."

"It's embarrassing," Doreen said. "Even if

Beau wasn't the brightest bulb on the tree when it came to money, I still loved him." She waved a hand in front of her face as tears sparkled in her eyes. "Loved. You hear what I just said? I'm already talking about him in the past tense. How awful."

"Of course it's awful," Drayton said.

"Luckily, he didn't fritter away my entire fortune," Doreen said. "There's still plenty of money left for all of us to be quite comfortable." She smiled at Drayton. "And for me to support a few museums and charities that I hold dear. It's just that now . . ." She sniffled. "I have to make these difficult decisions all by myself." She cocked her head and eyed the empty whiskey glass that was sitting on a side table.

"Would you like me to fix you a cup of tea?" Theodosia asked.

Doreen sighed deeply. "I suppose that would be nice. Do you know where the kitchen is?"

Theodosia and Drayton were already up and moving.

"I'm sure we can find our way," Drayton said.

5

"What do you think?" Drayton asked once they were in the kitchen behind closed doors.

Theodosia glanced around. "The kitchen needs serious updating, for one thing. The range is a Hotpoint from 1975; the refrigerator is basically one step up from an icebox."

"I was referring to Doreen. Her story."

"I know what you meant," Theodosia said as she stepped into a rather large, well-lit pantry. She began opening and closing cupboard doors, looking for a tin of tea. "The fact of the matter is, Doreen doesn't have a story because she doesn't have a clue."

Drayton stood at the pantry door and looked in. "You don't think there's anything to be gleaned here?"

"No, I don't. Remember what I said earlier about letting the police handle this? Well, I was right. Only, God bless the

Charleston police if they can pull even one useful tidbit of information out of Doreen. No wonder they asked her a few questions and then went on their merry way. I think they'll have a lot more luck talking to the other guests. Even if they interview snappy Starla out there, who, by the way, should be fitted with a muzzle."

"You're not going to give up just like that, are you?" Drayton asked. He sounded almost desperate.

Theodosia pulled open another cupboard door and peered in. "Drayton, I know your grant for the Heritage Society is on the line here, but I don't know what more I can do."

"You could keep talking to her. I can tell that Doreen likes you. She trusts you."

"You want me to string her along? Give her the impression that we can be of some help in her husband's death?"

"No, that wouldn't be fair. I guess what I meant was . . ."

"Holy crackers!" Theodosia suddenly shouted. She'd been searching a cupboard when her eyes landed on a bizarre black-and-yellow box. As the impact of what she was seeing clanged around inside her brain, she took a giant step backward.

"What's wrong?" Drayton asked.

"Come over here and take a look," Theodosia hissed.

Hesitantly, Drayton tiptoed over.

"Middle shelf," she said.

Drayton peered tentatively into the cupboard, as if fearing something horrible might pop out at him. When he saw what had startled Theodosia, he said, "Dear Lord!"

There, on the middle shelf, surrounded by a clutter of spice tins, was a box of orange pekoe tea. Sitting next to the tea was an open box of rat poison.

Drayton's face blanched white. "You don't suppose . . . ?"

"I don't know what to think, but it's very creepy." Theodosia studied the box again. Just so there was no mistaking its intended purpose, the box carried a cartoon drawing of a dead rat on it. The rat was lying on its back, its stiff little legs sticking straight up in the air.

"Why on earth didn't the police find this yesterday?" Drayton asked.

"Maybe because the police weren't prowling through the cupboards looking for Doreen's box of stale tea bags?" Theodosia said. "I mean, they pretty much had their hands full, interviewing all the rat servers as well as the guests. And, I suppose, the people who looked the most suspicious."

60

Drayton folded his arms and leaned against the opposite cupboard. "Did you think some of the guests looked suspicious?"

"After finding this box of poison, I think everybody's a bit questionable. Especially the caterer and kitchen workers."

"But those people were all busy baking scones and arranging tea trays."

"So maybe the killer was one of the white rats."

"Do you know how ridiculous we sound?" Drayton asked. "Talking about poison and white rats?"

"Yes," Theodosia said. "We sound like something out of *Grimm's Fairy Tales.* Cue the gnomes and foxes, send in Hansel and Gretel." She shook her head as if to clear it. "We have to tell the police about this box of poison."

"You're referring to the somewhat indifferent officer who's standing outside the front door? The one tasked with guarding our lives?"

Theodosia shrugged. "At least it's a place to start."

But when Theodosia showed Officer Parnell the rat poison in the black-and-yellow box, he let out a surprised gasp. Then he took

61

off his cap and scratched his thinning blond hair.

"Is that poison?" he asked, even though there was also an ominous-looking skull and crossbones on the package.

Theodosia wanted to say, *No, it's Cap'n Crunch.* Instead, she said, "X-Terminate Rat Poison, if that label is to be trusted."

Officer Parnell was still playing catch-up. "Isn't poison what killed the man who . . ." He gestured toward Doreen and company, who were still in the library.

"Bingo," Theodosia said.

"Then this is like a clue," Parnell said.

"Maybe even an important clue," Drayton said. He was standing at the stove, heating a kettle of water.

Theodosia favored Parnell with a quizzical smile. "Excuse me, Officer Parnell, but what is it you do exactly? I mean, in your official capacity with the Charleston Police Department?" She figured he was either a meter reader or data entry guy. Because he certainly wasn't firing on all cylinders like an experienced beat cop would.

"Two days a week I play Officer Pugsly Pup," Parnell said, sounding pleased. "I wear a furry dog costume and go around to all the elementary schools. Teach kids basic safety skills."

"That explains it," Theodosia said.

"I guess I'd better call this in," Parnell said. He was still gazing with trepidation at the box of rat poison.

"Call it in to Detective Pete Riley," Theodosia said. "He's in the Robbery-Homicide Division. Then have someone from crime scene drop by and pick up the rat poison." She held up an index finger. "But don't you touch it."

"I won't, ma'am."

"And you probably shouldn't mention this to the folks out there in the library, either," Drayton added. He gestured at Theodosia. "You want to hand me that box of tea?"

Very carefully, Theodosia plucked the box of orange pekoe off the cupboard shelf and handed it to Drayton.

Parnell's eyes got big. "You're going to drink that?"

"Of course," Drayton said. He was plopping tea bags into teacups, adding steaming hot water. "You can test it yourself if you'd like."

Parnell shook his head. "No way."

"Now, listen to me," Theodosia said to Parnell. "That box of poison needs to be analyzed in your crime lab. Some kind of toxicology test needs to be run to see if it might be the same type of poison that killed

Mr. Briggs yesterday."

"Okay," Parnell said. "Got it."

Theodosia turned toward Drayton. "You're sure that tea is okay?"

Drayton lifted one of the teacups and took a quick sip. "Not great tea. A little on the bakey side, but it will have to do."

"That's not what I meant," she said. "I don't want you to gack out and go boom!"

"I know exactly what you meant," Drayton said. "And it's fine." He picked up his tea tray and inclined his head toward the swinging door. "If you could?"

Theodosia pushed open the kitchen door for Drayton. "You need some help with that?"

He slid past her, teacups rattling on his tray. "You just stay on top of Officer Pup there."

"Will do."

But as Theodosia listened to Parnell talking to whoever had answered the phone at Robbery-Homicide, a million questions swirled in her brain. And she wondered — if a woman was crazy angry at her husband for frittering away a small fortune, would she seek revenge by taking matters into her own hands?

That notion not only shocked and scared Theodosia, it made her a lot more interested in investigating Doreen Briggs. And the entire Beau Briggs murder.

Yes, she knew she'd just told Drayton there really wasn't much to go on. But, holy crap, look what just popped up!

6

"Doreen had a box of *rat poison* in her cupboard?" Haley asked.

"I'm afraid so," Drayton said.

Haley leaned back in her chair and shook her head, her long blond hair swishing like a curtain. "Whoa." Then, "Do you think it's the same poison that killed her old man?"

"We have to wait for the results of the lab tests," Theodosia said. She sounded calm as she said it, but really had a case of the jitters. Could Doreen be a killer? A clumsy killer at that? Well, they'd know soon enough.

"Still," Haley said, "a box of poison is beaucoup creepy."

"What's creepy is that Beau's death was premeditated murder," Drayton said. "Somebody came to that rat tea, either as a guest or server, and left as a full-fledged killer."

Haley nodded. "I guess Doreen's tea

didn't go quite as planned. It wasn't a hale and hearty tribute to the rat teas of yesteryear."

"It was well-intentioned," Drayton said. "And started out pleasantly enough."

"But ended with a bang," Theodosia said. "If you could have seen that poor man . . ."

Haley held up both hands as if to ward off a vampire attack. "No way. Please don't tell me any more about it. I don't want some awful image of a man in his death throes implanted in my brain. I don't need that. Especially today. Mondays are always super busy and then the week just gets crazier as we go along. It always feels like we're on some kind of wild log flume ride."

"Haley," Theodosia said, "if you need help in the kitchen we can always hire . . ."

"An assistant?" Haley said.

"Yes, of course."

"No," Haley said. "I would hate that. You know I would." Haley was young, in her early twenties, and still thought she could do it all.

"You'd still be in charge," Theodosia said. They'd broached the subject to Haley several times before and she'd always rejected it. Haley was a brilliant chef and baker, but she was also a tough little martinet.

67

"No matter who you hired, they'd still have their own ideas and notions about how to do things," Haley said. "And I'm just not ready for any sort of change, okay?"

"By *change* you mean *compromise,*" Drayton said.

Haley surprised them with a grin. "Yeah, I guess."

"Okay," Theodosia said. "Whatever makes you happy. Whatever *keeps* you happy."

"Working with you guys makes me happy," Haley said. "I love our little threesome. Our work family. It's perfect. We all have our jobs to do and we do them really well."

"I sometimes think we put too much on your shoulders though," Theodosia said.

"I'm not complaining. I'm really not." Haley looked nervous. "Could we please just drop the subject?"

"Of course," Theodosia said. She glanced at her watch. "In fact, we'd better get cracking. Like you said, Mondays are busy."

"Lots of Church Street shopkeepers will be coming in for takeout," Drayton said. He furrowed his brow. "Perhaps I'll brew some Chinese Keemun today. And definitely a pot of Pussimbing Garden Darjeeling. That's nice and brisk and always goes over well."

"What are our morning offerings?" Theodosia asked Haley.

"Well, the strawberry scones you guys have been nibbling. And I've got pans of apple scones and orange blossom muffins in the oven."

Drayton bounded to his feet. "Excellent."

They got busy then. Drayton draped the dozen or so tables with linen tablecloths and added napkins, silverware, teacups, and water glasses. Theodosia followed him around and put out sugar bowls, creamers, and crystal vases filled with pink tea roses.

"Don't forget the tea warmers," Drayton said.

"I have them right here," Theodosia said. These were made of heavy glass with an indentation in the center to accommodate a small vigil light.

"And should I light a fire in the fireplace?"

"I think . . . yes," Theodosia said. It was still early spring and mornings were cool, bordering on chilly. How nice for her tea shop guests to come tumbling in and be able to inhale the rich, fruity aromas of brewed tea and enjoy the crackling warmth of a fire.

"Here's a dozen scones to start you off with," Haley said. She set a glass pie saver piled high with scones on the front counter.

"Thank you, Haley," Theodosia said.

Haley stood there, looking like she wanted to say something more. Finally, she said, "It sounds like you guys are kind of involved in this thing with Doreen. Why'd you go back there yesterday . . . I mean, really?"

"For one thing, we just wanted to *talk* to Doreen," Drayton said. "We didn't set out to poke around in her kitchen cupboard and find a box of poison. We were there to offer our sympathy."

Haley cocked her head at him. "So now you're a grief counselor?"

"Haley deserves to hear the truth," Theodosia said to Drayton.

"Wait a minute," Haley said. "What's going on?"

"We went to Doreen's because Drayton thought we could do a little subtle backgrounding on the folks who might be involved in her husband's murder," Theodosia said. "He thought we could help Doreen out."

"You mean, like, investigate?" Haley asked.

"No," Theodosia said.

"Yes," Drayton said.

Haley held up a hand. "Are you guys sure you want to get involved in this? Because it seems to me that Doreen just became a prime suspect."

"She could be," Theodosia said.

"And the thing is," Haley said, "involvement in this type of crime is the exact kind of thing Drayton is always warning us to stay away from."

"I can change my mind, Haley," Drayton said. "I'm not that rigid."

"Yes, you are," Haley said. "I can set my watch by it. As a matter of fact, I *count* on you to be rigid."

Theodosia gazed at Drayton. "She's got you there." Drayton prided himself on his formality and slightly stilted manner.

"You know what?" Haley said. "It gives me chills to know the two of you were at that stupid tea. I mean, what if the murderer was someone right there in the family? Or, worse yet, what if something had gone haywire and one of *you* had been poisoned?" She looked stricken. "What then?"

"I don't think . . ." Theodosia began. And stopped abruptly. Haley made a good point. A very good point.

Just as Haley had predicted, it was a busy morning. Shop owners from up and down Church Street popped in for their morning cuppa, neighbors strolled in for tea and scones, and even a few tourists found their way to the Indigo Tea Shop, intrigued by the indigo-blue canvas awning hanging over the antique bow window.

Theodosia dispensed tea, scones, Devonshire cream, and good humor to all her guests who were seated at tables. In between, she ran to the front counter and packaged up scones for takeout. With a long, black Parisian waiter's apron draped around his neck, Drayton stayed busy brewing tea. His nimble fingers plucked the various tea tins from their shelves, then carefully measured out the exact teas requested by guests. Those teas (depending on the blend and country of origin) were brewed in Brown Betty teapots, Japanese *tetsubin,* English floral teapots, and Chinese teapots, and then hustled to waiting customers.

Late morning, when Theodosia found a few moments to breathe, she ducked behind the celadon-colored velvet curtain to see what Haley had planned for lunch.

Haley looked up from the counter where she was buttering slices of bread, two at a time. "You want the menu, don't you?" She looked almost dwarfed beneath her tall white chef's hat.

"Or you can just give me a hint." Theodosia was always impressed that Haley could whip up so many delicious treats in their postage stamp–sized kitchen.

"No, no, I'm all set." Haley set down her knife and picked up an index card. "Let's see. You already know about the strawberry and apple scones. And the orange blossom muffins. Okay, so we have fruit compote, tomato bisque soup, shrimp salad tea sandwiches, stir-fry chicken, and lemon tea bread."

"It all sounds lovely," Theodosia said.

"Oh, and I just took a call. Teddy Vickers phoned from the Featherbed House B and B. He says he needs four takeout lunches for some of their guests who want to take a day trip to Sullivan's Island."

"You want me to help package up those lunches?"

"Already did it," Haley said. She tilted her head to indicate four indigo-blue bags sitting on a shelf. "All you have to do is pop them in a shopping bag and hand them over when Teddy's guests show up."

"You're a wonder, Haley."

Haley picked up two wooden spoons, did a little twirl, and smacked the lid of a kettle as if it were a snare drum. "Aren't I just?"

The pace of this Monday's lunch felt just right to Theodosia. Not so busy that they were overwhelmed, but not slow and draggy, either. In fact, she'd just jotted down what she figured would be her last luncheon order when the front door opened and Opal Anne stuck her head in. The girl looked tentative and a little apprehensive. As if she didn't know what to expect.

"Are you busy?" Opal Anne asked. "Because I can come back later if you're . . ."

"Don't be silly," Theodosia said, hurrying over to greet her. "Please come in. Have you eaten lunch yet?"

"Not really." Opal Anne was dressed in a black cashmere sweater and camel-colored skirt. She looked like she'd just escaped from an upscale private girl's school.

"Then kindly sit down and let me bring you something," Theodosia said. "What kind of tea do you like?"

Drayton smiled over at Opal Anne. "Perhaps something with a hint of fruit? Peaches and ginger?" He held up a purple tea tin. "Indian spice?"

"Indian spice sounds great," Opal Anne said.

"Coming right up," Drayton said.

"Let me run this order in to Haley and grab us a couple of scones and tea sandwiches," Theodosia said. "But you go sit. Take that little table right there by the fireplace. I'll be back in a jiffy."

When Theodosia returned a few minutes

later, with luncheon plates for both of them, Opal Anne was sipping her tea and looking around expectantly. Whatever it was, the cardamom and spices in the tea, or the warmth of the fire, she seemed considerably more relaxed.

"Your shop is absolutely charming," Opal Anne said, her face practically lighting up as she spoke. "I can't believe I've never been here before."

"Well, now that you're no longer a stranger, we can welcome you back anytime you want," Theodosia said. She gently pushed a plate in front of Opal Anne. It held two tea sandwiches, a scone, and a pouf of Devonshire cream. "Please, help yourself."

But the girl was still looking around, taking in the cozy environs of the tea shop.

"What's all that on your highboy over there? Oh, I see. You sell all sorts of jams and jellies and honey, don't you? And I adore the wreaths on the walls. They're so squiggly and fun. Are they made from grapevines?"

"Vines that I picked and dried at my aunt Libby's plantation," Theodosia said.

"And then you decorated them with ribbon and fancy teacups."

Theodosia waved a hand. "The teacups are a snap to find at tag sales around the county."

"But how clever. I mean this *place* is so adorable. You must love it here."

"I do," Theodosia said, and she meant it. "I love it more than anything."

"Have you always done this? Owned a tea shop, I mean?"

"No, I started out in marketing, playing that game for a number of years. But the pace was a little too intense, a little too twenty-four/seven for me."

"So now you work here twenty-four/seven," Opal Anne said, laughing.

"I do, but now I work for myself."

"That's the most important thing, isn't it?" Opal Anne said. "You have to find your passion and go for it." She picked up a tea sandwich and then paused. "I graduated with a major in business administration, but I'm still trying to figure out my passion in life."

"How old are you, if you don't mind my asking?"

"I'm twenty-two." She took a bite of her sandwich.

"You've got time."

"I know." Opal Anne laughed. "But I'm getting antsy."

They chatted casually as they ate their lunches, never mentioning Doreen or the dearly departed Beau. But once they were finished, Opal Anne got down to business.

"I have to apologize for Doreen's theatrics yesterday. She's still overcome with grief, so it's difficult for her to think straight."

"That's only natural," Theodosia said. "Beau's death was a terrible shock to her. To all of us, really."

"The good thing is, she's a fairly tough and resilient lady."

"I can see that," Theodosia said. "Which means she'll get through this. It won't be easy, but she'll come out the other side. Maybe even stronger than before." *Just as long as she's not a poisoner who ends up doing time in prison.*

"You're very perceptive," Opal Anne said.

"Thank you. But I have a feeling you didn't just come here to flatter me. Or have lunch."

Opal Anne looked down at her hands and said, "I have some rather unpleasant information that I think you should know about."

"Concerning . . . ?"

"Reggie Huston, Beau's business partner at Gilded Magnolia Spa. Maybe you noticed him? He was sitting at her table the day of the tea."

"Okay." Theodosia had a fleeting recollection of the man named Reggie. Perhaps they'd been introduced the other day? Then again, maybe not.

"I'm fairly sure that Reggie's been embezzling money from the company," Opal Anne blurted out.

7

Didn't this just *come zinging out of the blue,* was Theodosia's first thought.

"Even though the spa's only been open for a few months?" she asked.

"Reggie Huston works fast," Opal Anne said.

"And you came to this conclusion . . . how?"

Opal Anne ducked her head, as if talking about Reggie was painful. "For one thing, I know Reggie. He's a guy who drives a Porsche and an Audi, enjoys expensive golf vacations, and fancies a very luxe lifestyle. He doesn't come from money, so the money has to come from somewhere. I'm guessing he's using Gilded Magnolia Spa as his own personal bank account."

"I see." Theodosia leaned back in her chair. "Do you have any idea how much . . . ?"

"How much money he's managed to

abscond with?" Opal Anne lifted her shoulders. "I don't really know. I don't even know if Reggie's guilty for sure. I'm only making an educated guess. Trying to connect the dots and put it all together. But I work out at the club on a fairly regular basis — do Pilates and spin classes — so I hang around, talk to the trainers, shoot the breeze with the spa managers." Her brows knit together. "I hear things."

"Have you questioned the bookkeepers?"

"No," Opal Anne said. "Reggie's outsourced all the bookkeeping and accounting. Anything related to finances seems to be a deep dark secret."

"What does Doreen know about this, if anything?" Theodosia asked. "Is she aware of Reggie's larger-than-life lifestyle?"

"Doreen doesn't have a clue. She likes Reggie, considers him an okay guy. Last night she even mentioned that she might want to step in and run the spa along with him." Opal Anne shook her head. "Then Reggie could really suck her dry. Doreen's idea of running a business would mean breezing in at eleven o'clock, waving at the hired help, and then going out for a two-hour lunch with the girls. She'd expect the spa to operate by itself and for cash money to come pouring in."

"That sounds fabulous," Theodosia said. "How do I get in on that?"

"Exactly."

Theodosia got serious then. "Do you think Reggie could have killed Beau? To kind of . . . get him out of the way?" There really wasn't a delicate way to phrase it.

"If Reggie was desperate enough, yes. I think he could have killed my stepdad. Especially if Beau was starting to suspect that Reggie might be embezzling money."

"Did Reggie and Beau have any kind of partnership agreement?"

"Nothing beyond the usual," Opal Anne said. "But it just seems incredibly suspicious to me that Reggie was blithely siphoning money from his business partner. And then . . . boom . . . that partner is suddenly murdered. How convenient."

"Do you think Beau suspected that Reggie was bleeding him dry?"

Opal Anne looked disheartened. "Who knows? You heard Doreen yesterday. Beau wasn't the wealthy, hotshot businessman his public persona made him out to be. Even *I* didn't know how bad things were, and he was my stepdad!" She snuffled loudly and went on. "Apparently Beau was throwing lots of Doreen's money at several really bad investments. So he might not have realized that Gilded Magnolia was running at a deficit." She dabbed at her eyes. "And we've got the grand opening party coming up this Saturday. Some party that's going to be."

"Doreen seems very angry about Beau's bad investments," Theodosia said slowly.

"She's furious with him." Opal Anne placed both hands flat on the table and stared at Theodosia. "But she didn't kill him. I know what you're thinking, that Doreen might have snapped and decided to get rid of him. To put a stop to his spending once and for all. But she's not that kind of crazy. She's a good person, a kind person. And she loved Beau very deeply."

Theodosia reached over and placed her hand on top of Opal Anne's hand. "I'm sorry you had to go through this. That you had to watch your stepdad collapse and die like that."

"Thank you," Opal Anne said, her voice getting hoarse and her eyes reddening even more. "This is like living some awful nightmare. I'm not trying to be obsequious or anything, but you've been the only bright spot in this whole thing. You and Drayton."

"I'm just not sure how much we can help," Theodosia said. She felt like a louse for hedging her words like that.

"Doreen has faith in you." Opal Anne

pulled a hankie from her bag and wiped tears from her eyes. "And so do I. We loved Beau, you know. We loved him with all our hearts."

"Okay, now I feel like a complete rat," Theodosia said.

"What's the problem now?" Drayton asked. He was standing behind the front counter, searching the floor-to-ceiling shelves for a missing tin of Tieguanyin oolong tea. It was a small tin, because the tea was expensive, almost sixty-five dollars a pound.

"I upset Opal Anne. She's pretty sure we're looking at Doreen as a prime suspect."

"And she's right. Unfortunately."

"Yes, but I still don't want to hurt the girl's feelings. She's suffered enough."

"It's a murder investigation," Drayton said. "Feelings are going to get trampled. Drat, where *is* that tea?" He looked positively owlish as he peered over his tortoiseshell half-glasses, scanning the shelves.

"She also opened my eyes about Beau's partner in Gilded Magnolia Spa."

"Mmm?"

"Opal Anne thinks that Beau's partner, Reggie Huston, is siphoning money away from the spa."

"Which one was Reggie Huston?" Drayton asked.

"The guy sitting across from Opal Anne at the tea. I think he was wearing a white dinner jacket."

Drayton straightened up. "Yes, I do remember him. Lovely jacket. And he paired it with a brown-and-cream paisley Drake's bow tie. Very stylish."

Theodosia was mildly amused. "You actually remember his bow tie?"

"It isn't the kind of detail one would forget."

"I forgot."

"Your interest lies in other areas." Drayton squinted, stretched upward on tiptoes, and reached over his head. "There you are, you little dickens." He grabbed the wayward tea tin and bounced it once in his hand. "Gotcha."

"Opal Anne thinks we're completely off base with Doreen."

"Perhaps she's right," Drayton said. "I hope she's right."

"Because if Doreen was guilty, the Heritage Society wouldn't receive a penny of that grant money."

"No, it would not. But the very idea of Doreen being involved in her own husband's death makes me heartsick." Drayton cocked his head. "Do you think she's guilty?"

"I don't think we've gathered enough information yet to make any sort of judgment call."

"It certainly sounds like Reggie Huston needs to be investigated, though," Drayton said. "Maybe you should pay a visit to this fancy spa."

"I'm definitely going to do that," Theodosia said. "And we need to keep looking at Doreen. She's not off the hook yet."

Drayton sighed. "I probably won't get a decent night's sleep until she is."

Just when Theodosia thought afternoon teatime was going to be fairly quiet, Bill Glass came clumping in. He was the cigar-smoking, gum-chewing, snarky publisher of a local scandal rag called *Shooting Star*. Everyone professed to despise the magazine, but nobody seemed to object when colorful photos from their party, charity ball, or fancy barbecue were splashed across the front page for everyone to see. And be jealous of.

"Hey there, tea lady," Glass called out. As usual, he was dressed in a shabby khaki jacket, baggy slacks, and scuffed boots. He had a scarf and two cameras slung around his neck and wraparound sunglasses pushed up on his forehead. Theodosia thought

85

Glass looked like a cross between a Himalayan trekker and a disreputable reporter.

"Hello, Bill," Theodosia said, not bothering to look up. Maybe if she ignored him he'd go away? But Glass was imbued with a keen ability to annoy, so he bellied up to the counter and grinned at her.

"Hey," he said. "I hear you were at that rat tea thing. Care to share the dirty details with me?"

"Not on your life." Theodosia busied herself with a pot of tea as she sensed Drayton stiffen next to her.

"Come on," Glass said. "How about you sneak me inside the Calhoun Mansion? I hear you've got an inside track with the old lady. Thing is, I'm trying to put together a story about the death of Beau Briggs — my readers are nuts for these wacky society murders — and I'd kill to get some snaps."

"Why do you persist in asking me for favors when I always say no?"

"Probably because you say no so nicely?"

"Mr. Glass, you are incorrigible."

"That's good, huh?" Glass said. "That means I'm persistent?"

"Not exactly," Theodosia said. "But you are consistent. I'll give you that much."

"But will you give me a scone?"

Theodosia threw up her hands. "Yes. But

only if you stop pestering me."

"Make the order to go," Drayton said in a gravelly voice.

"Yes," Theodosia said, lifting the top off her glass pie saver. "You have to take your scone and kindly leave the tea shop."

"Honey," Glass cackled, "I'll take it any way I can get it."

"He's like a jackal or a vulture, isn't he?" Drayton said when Glass had finally left. "Circling the carcass, scavenging for any bits and crumbs."

"The man's got a nose for nasty news, that's for sure," Theodosia said. "I just hope he doesn't find out that we're involved with Doreen."

"Who would tell him?"

"Um . . . maybe Doreen herself?" Theodosia said.

Drayton touched a hand to his mouth. "You could be right. Doreen does love to blather on a bit. Perhaps we should warn her not to talk to Bill Glass."

"Call me crazy," Theodosia said, "but if Glass showed up on her doorstep, that might give her an even bigger impetus to pour out her heart to him."

8

At two fifteen the front door whapped open and the bell above it *da-ding*ed like crazy. Theodosia, who was just pouring a cup of tea for Mrs. Beckman, and Drayton, who was brewing a pot of Dimbulla for a ladies' tea group, both stopped what they were doing and looked over.

Starla Crane had come crashing in like an unwelcome guest at a private party. Her bright eyes roved the tea shop hungrily, her mouth seemed permanently downcast, and a pair of nasty wrinkles were etched between her brows. Wrinkles that would eventually get deeper if she didn't learn to adjust her attitude.

Theodosia finished pouring tea and hurried over to greet her.

"Good afternoon, Starla," she said pleasantly. "Are you here for afternoon tea?"

"I need to talk to you. Like, immediately." Today Starla wore a tightly belted black leather trench coat. A bright purple dress peeped out at the neckline and hem.

"Sure." Theodosia set her teapot down on the front counter, threw a knowing glance at Drayton, and said, "Please follow me. We can talk privately in my office." The last thing she wanted was for Starla to cause a disturbance in the tea room.

Theodosia slipped behind her desk and sat down, then indicated for Starla to take a seat in the upholstered chair across from her.

"Would you like a cup of tea?"

"No," Starla said. "I don't drink tea. I don't like tea."

Theodosia managed a polite smile. *Oh, so it's going to be like that. Fine. Go ahead, little girl, say your piece.*

Starla glanced around Theodosia's office, taking in the stack of boxes, floppy straw hats, tea magazines, and wreaths that hung on the walls.

"I'm sure you're good at what you do," Starla began. "And I'm very good at what I do as well. So I'm going to ask you to stay out of my business."

"I wasn't aware I was in your business," Theodosia said.

"I've put together a carefully crafted press release regarding Beau Briggs's untimely death as well as the future of Gilded Magnolia Spa."

"Okay."

"I am also writing a press release to announce Mr. Briggs's funeral and am engineering a plan for Doreen's eventual reentry into society."

Theodosia leaned back in her chair. "You make it sound as if Doreen's gone into formal mourning, like Scarlett O'Hara in *Gone with the Wind*. When six months are up, she's allowed to wear a short veil that no longer covers her face. After a year she may attend social functions, but only if they involve a relative." She chuckled, pleased with herself, pleased with the twitch of annoyance that appeared on Starla's face.

"You don't get it, do you?" Starla sputtered. "For your information, I'm pushing Doreen to take over the running of Gilded Magnolia Spa."

"Really?" Theodosia said. "*Really?* She's going to work hand in hand with Reggie Huston?"

"Yes, why not?"

Theodosia gave Starla a cat-that-swallowed-the-canary smile. Obviously, Opal Anne and Starla hadn't gotten together to compare notes. Opal Anne hadn't told her about Reggie's incompetence and free-spending ways.

"From what I've heard," Theodosia said, "there seems to be some financial impropriety going on over there."

Starla was completely taken aback. "Who said that? Who's spreading nasty rumors?"

"Perhaps you should check with the spa's CPA firm. Oh, wait a minute, you're not an officer of the company, so you can't do that. Well, no matter, there's a good chance the state attorney general will be stepping in to audit their books."

"Are you serious?" Starla leapt to her feet. "Where are you getting this information? Who's been feeding you lies?"

Theodosia fixed Starla with a level gaze. She didn't raise her voice, but she was firm. "Miss Crane, don't ever try to tell me what is or isn't my business. Don't you dare try to insert a wedge between Drayton and Doreen. And I'd appreciate it if you never set foot in my tea shop again."

Starla clenched her fists tightly and glowered at her. "I will *never* come in here again." She was practically spitting she was so mad. "This place is corny and too old-fashioned for words!"

"That's your opinion and you're entitled to it," Theodosia said. She stood up and walked to the door that led out to the back alley. "But since you feel so strongly, I think it's best you leave immediately." She yanked open the door. "Via the back door."

"Where did Starla fly off to?" Drayton asked a few minutes later. It was late afternoon and the tea shop was empty. Haley was rattling around in the kitchen; Drayton was straightening up out front.

"She left," Theodosia said. She'd just set a box filled with jam and scone mixes on the counter and was sorting through it. It was time to restock her shelves.

"Did you offer her tea?"

"She declined."

"Then what did she want?" Drayton asked.

"She asked us to stay away from Doreen."

Drayton's entire body gave an almost seismic jerk and his head snapped toward Theodosia. "She did? Seriously?" He considered this. "Who does Starla think she is, anyway?"

"I don't know," Theodosia said. "The grand pooh-bah of PR, I guess."

"So you sent her packing out the back door?"

"Why not? The girl was hissing and spitting like an alley cat."

Drayton glanced sideways. "Does it seem

like Doreen has a rather strange cast of characters gathered around her?"

"Drayton," Theodosia said, "I think we all do." She picked up her box, dropped it next to the highboy, and placed two packages of scone mix on a shelf. She stared at the display for a few seconds, not really seeing it, and then went back to her office. The idea of calling Detective Riley had been pinging in her brain all day long. Now she decided she couldn't wait any longer. She wanted to know, *needed* to know, about that rat poison. On top of that, she was dying to find out how the investigation was coming along. Or if they'd made any progress at all.

Theodosia went into her office, dug out the business card Riley had given her, and dialed his number. It took a few minutes to get through his gatekeepers, but finally she had him on the phone.

"We know each other, you know," was the first thing Riley said to her. "And not just from this past Saturday."

"We do?" Theodosia said. But there was a smile in her voice. He was, after all, a very attractive man.

"I stopped by the Indigo Tea Shop once. With Detective Tidwell. You served us tea and the most delicious scones I've ever tasted in my life. Coconut cherry, I think.

They brought tears to my eyes."

"We had apple scones today," Theodosia said. "I think there might be a couple left."

"Miss Browning, it's all I can do not to jump in a squad car and rush over there, lights and siren."

"That's very flattering, Detective Riley."

"Pete. You don't have to be so formal, you can call me Pete."

Perfect, Theodosia thought. "Okay, then, Pete, I was wondering if your lab has already analyzed the poison that Beau Briggs ingested?"

There was the briefest hesitation and then Riley said, "We've run an initial battery of tests, yes."

"I'm also wondering if the rat poison I discovered yesterday in Doreen's kitchen cupboard was the same type of poison that killed him?"

"That was a good catch. Finding the rat poison."

"Thank you," Theodosia said. "It made for a startling find. So you can see why . . ."

"To put your mind at ease, it was not the same poison that killed Mr. Briggs."

Theodosia was both surprised and a little relieved. "So he drank something else?"

"There was poison in Beau Briggs's system, but it wasn't from anything he drank."

"Excuse me," Theodosia said. "I'm confused. Then how did . . . ?"

"Have you ever heard of an L-pill?" Riley asked.

"No, should I?"

"Probably not. I hope not anyway. During the Cold War, it's what the air force, bless their hard little hearts, used to issue to U-2 pilots. It wasn't a pill per se, more like a small metal disk with a very sharp pin."

"What were they supposed to do with it?" Theodosia asked. "Swallow it?"

"Nothing quite that simple. The pin contained a lethal dose of cyanide. If shot down and captured, the pilots, who were essentially spies, were supposed to pull out the pin and scratch their own skin."

"Are you serious? They really issued something like that? It sounds positively inhumane. It's basically a . . . suicide pill. Though I guess not technically a pill."

"I guess the air force didn't have a lot of faith that American pilots would hold up under Soviet interrogation."

"Wait a minute." Theodosia's mind was whirling like an out-of-control gyroscope. "So what are you telling me? That somebody scratched cyanide into Beau Briggs's skin?"

"That's probably what killed him, yes."

Theodosia let Riley's words rumble

through her brain. "That sounds preposterous. Like something out of an old spy novel."

"Doesn't it?" Riley said. "But it's not, of course. This particular poison, with this type of delivery system, is highly effective. It works in about ten to fifteen seconds. And it's almost always fatal."

Theodosia thought back to when Beau was waving his hands above the flaming centerpiece with everybody clustered around him, trying to help. Then, some ten to fifteen seconds later, maybe a little more, he started to completely wonk out. Wow.

"Poison through a scratch in his skin?" Theodosia was shocked, but a little relieved that he hadn't died from drinking poisoned tea.

"That's what we're tentatively calling cause of death right now," Riley said. "But I'm no medical examiner. Obviously, our people are working with toxicology experts and will be running additional tests. So any new results could possibly skew our initial thinking."

"Have you ever encountered this type of thing before?" Theodosia asked.

"Never."

"Where would you get something like

that? The poison-needle thing, or whatever it was."

Riley sighed. "I don't know. I'm going to have to figure that out. Find a contact or source. I ran a search on poisons in the FBI's database as well as Interpol's. There's not a lot out there. There are databases on wanted persons, fingerprints, DNA, firearms, even radiological and nuclear materials. But poison only seems to pop up when it has to do with the KGB or the Russian Mafia."

"Holy cats," Theodosia breathed.

"Keep this on the down low," Riley said. "I shouldn't have told you as much as I did. I'm only sharing information with you because you were such a great help in finding that rat poison yesterday."

"Even though the poison that killed Beau Briggs was different from the rat poison," Theodosia murmured.

"That's right."

"But it still doesn't eliminate Doreen Briggs as a suspect, does it?"

"No, it does not. But please don't repeat any of this. Again, I'm only being candid with you because I know you're a personal friend of Detective Tidwell."

Theodosia smiled. "Yes, he is rather a good friend. Thank you, Detective Riley. I

97

appreciate your candor."

"Pete. And I really do plan to stop by your tea shop for some of those scones."

"I look forward to seeing you."

Theodosia set down her phone and thought for a few moments. Hmm. A completely different type of poison. It wasn't what she'd expected to hear at all. In fact, it sounded as if the murderer — whoever he or she was — was also a rather skilled assassin. She shook her head and frowned. It felt like she'd just boomeranged back to square one.

Drayton was swishing out the last of the teapots when she went back into the tea room.

"I just talked to Detective Riley," Theodosia told him.

"What did he have to say? Is there any news about the poison?"

"Yes, but I'm not supposed to tell you."

"Tell me anyway."

"It wasn't the exact same poison," Theodosia said. "The poison that killed Beau was different from the rat poison."

Drayton's face dissolved from a knot of worry into a big smile. "That's wonderful. Doreen's been cleared, then."

"Not so fast. All it means is Doreen didn't

drop a spoonful of rat poison into her hubby's teacup. She still could have *scratched* his skin with a lethal dose of cyanide."

"What!"

So Theodosia had to tell Drayton all about the L-pill and the U-2 pilots.

"That's awful," Drayton said. "But Doreen wouldn't do that. She couldn't do that."

Theodosia stared at him. "Because the poison delivery is just too sophisticated for her?"

"That's right."

Theodosia made a face.

"Okay, I'll indulge your skepticism for about one minute," Drayton said. "*Why* would she do that?"

"For one thing, Beau was hemorrhaging money. Money that came from Doreen's own personal fortune. She admitted as much to us, and then Opal Anne basically hammered home the same thing."

"If Doreen *did* kill her own husband, then why bring us in to investigate?" Drayton asked.

"I don't know," Theodosia said. "To set up a direct conflict with the police? To hopefully steer us in the wrong direction? Because she's incredibly clever and manipulative?"

"I'm not sure any of that makes sense," Drayton said.

"Maybe it's not supposed to. The other thing to consider is . . . if Doreen was furious at Beau, if she thought he was robbing her blind, she could have hired someone to do the job for her."

"You mean a contract killer?"

"Think about it," Theodosia said. "Doreen was the one who chose this fanciful rat tea theme, hired the caterer, and dreamt up the rat disguises."

"Maybe . . ." Drayton began. He was beginning to see her point.

Theodosia snapped her fingers. "We need to find out who the caterer was. And who provided those rat costumes. That could possibly lead somewhere."

"Don't you think the police already questioned those people?"

"Probably, but the police tend to be awfully forceful," Theodosia said.

"As opposed to your subtle charm? Yes, when you put your mind to sleuthing, you are very skillful." Drayton paused. "I suppose I could drop by Doreen's house tonight," he said slowly. "Ask a few questions, find out who handled the catering and things."

"Good. Just be careful."

Drayton touched a hand to the side of his face. "From what you're telling me, the smoking centerpiece could have literally served as a smoke screen for murder."

"It was a perfect diversion."

"And how many people were clustered around Beau's table to greet him? And then help him?"

"As I recall," Theodosia said, "there had to be a dozen or more."

"Beau being a popular guy," Drayton said.

Theodosia shook her head. "Not anymore he's not."

9

Theodosia had long since decided that Earl Grey was the perfect roommate. He didn't smoke, play loud music, or hog the TV remote. How could he? He was a dog. A lovely Heinz 57 mix that she'd found huddled in the alley behind her tea shop one rainy night. She'd rescued him, fed him, cared for him, and loved him.

Now he was the one constant in her life. Boyfriends had come and gone, some departing reluctantly, some kicked to the curb so fast they didn't know what hit them. But Earl Grey occupied a major place in Theodosia's heart and in her home.

Her home. That was a source of pride as well. A few years ago, Theodosia had made the leap into home ownership and bought a small, quirky little cottage in Charleston's historic district.

And what a charmer it was — a classic Tudor-style English cottage that was asymmetrical in design with rough cedar tiles that replicated a thatched roof. The front of the building featured arched doors, cross gables, and a small turret. Lush tendrils of ivy curled their way up the walls.

Inside was just as cozy. The foyer featured a brick floor, hunter green walls, and antique brass sconces. The living and dining rooms had beamed ceilings and polished wood floors. Her own chintz and damask furniture, blue-and-gold Aubusson carpet, antique highboy, and tasty oil paintings had added the perfect touch.

Now, as Earl Grey stared at her with limpid brown eyes, Theodosia said, "Yes, I told you we're going for a run and I meant it." She'd just pulled on a fleece hoodie and was tying her shoelaces.

Earl Grey's tail thumped with enthusiasm. "Ready?"

The dog jumped to his feet.

Together they tore through the kitchen, out the back door, and down the back alley. It was full-on dark now, so they were mindful of their footing on the inlaid cobblestones. Then, popping out on Concord Street, a cool breeze suddenly snapped in from Charleston Harbor, carrying a beckoning hint of salt and endless ocean.

Down to White Point Garden they ran,

that green space right at the tip of the peninsula, where tulips and crocuses were just starting to burst through damp sod. Ancient cannons stood like sentinels in the same spot where a hangman's gallows had once dispatched unruly pirates. Fog swirled in, lending an ethereal feel, and Theodosia could hear the mournful toot of ships far out in the churning harbor.

Earl Grey tugged at his leash, wanting to walk right along spits of damp sand and oyster-shell fill, the waves lapping at their feet. Theodosia had once found an ancient shark's tooth buried in these crushed shells, but that had been two decades ago. Now the only sharks around Charleston were old-money politicos in three-piece business suits.

Forty-five minutes later, they strolled down Meeting Street, their run practically concluded, their cool-down walk made all the more picturesque by the presence of enormous mansions and wrought-iron streetlamps that dispensed little puddles of yellow light.

When Theodosia and Earl Grey dashed in the back door of their home, the phone was ringing.

Theodosia snatched it off the hook. "Hello?"

"You're needed on a mission of mercy," came Drayton's pleading voice.

Theodosia dropped the leash and unsnapped Earl Grey's collar. "What's wrong? Who's in trouble?"

"Me. I'm at Gruenwald Brothers Funeral Home."

"How on earth did you end up there?" Theodosia opened the refrigerator door, grabbed a bottle of spring water, and kicked the door shut again. Twisting off the top, she took a couple of good glugs, waiting for Drayton's explanation.

"I'm not entirely sure," Drayton said slowly. "One minute I was at Doreen's house, biting into an overdone crab cake, and the next thing I knew, we were standing in the basement of a funeral home debating the merits of an ugly bronze casket they keep calling the Alhambra model."

"Kicking the tires, huh?"

"So to speak. But we've run into a horrible snag."

Theodosia didn't say a word.

"Are you still there?" Drayton asked.

"Yes." She took another swallow of water and said, "What's wrong? One size does not fit all?"

"Theodosia, rarely do I impose upon you to this magnitude, but tonight I truly require your assistance."

"You want me to come over there and help pick out a casket?"

Drayton's response sounded almost pained. "I want you to come over here and be the voice of reason."

When Theodosia pulled up in front of Gruenwald Brothers Funeral Home, freshly showered and wearing non-jogging attire that consisted of black slacks and a lightweight tan suede jacket, the place looked plainly deserted.

She studied the exterior of the funeral home from where she sat in her Jeep. It was large and rambling, bordering on spooky. A fine place for Lurch to get a job as caretaker. Or perhaps as a receptionist?

Except when she knocked on the front door, the receptionist who greeted her was a plump middle-aged woman with wavy brown hair and a cheery smile.

"I take it you're joining the Briggs party?" she asked.

"That's right," Theodosia said.

"Won't you please come in?" The woman opened the door to reveal a tastefully done gray interior. Gray chairs, gray carpet, gray wallpaper. The only spark of interest consisted of two enormous floral bouquets, one

106

sitting on the front desk, another on a side table. Theodosia noted that the bouquets consisted of traditional funeral flowers — decorous carnations and unassuming lilies.

"Our showroom is just downstairs," the woman said as she led Theodosia around a tricky corner and then down a long, narrow staircase. "Here you go." She stopped in front of a door and smiled broadly, as if picking out caskets was the most wonderful thing in the world. Which maybe it was to her.

The Gruenwald Brothers showroom reminded Theodosia of a basement rec room from the nineteen seventies. Cheesy wood paneling, beige indoor-outdoor carpet, knobby red glass lamps. But instead of the requisite foosball table and dartboard, the room held two dozen caskets. They sat on metal stands and seemed to gleam wickedly under pinpoint spotlights that were hidden in the white-paneled ceiling.

Drayton caught sight of her and came rushing over. "Theodosia. You came."

"You didn't give me much choice," Theodosia murmured. Glancing around, she spotted the usual suspects — Doreen, Opal Anne, Charles, and Starla. They were perched on uncomfortable-looking funeral folding chairs and had sour expressions on their faces. Two people she didn't recognize were also sitting with them. "Who are those two?" she asked Drayton.

"Neighbors. Honey and Michael Whitley."

"Why are they here?"

"Who knows?"

"And you say the group is deadlocked?" Theodosia glanced over at the wall of caskets. To her they all looked pretty much the same. Sure, a few caskets had silver fittings instead of brass geegaws, but they all served the same basic purpose: place the deceased inside, then place the casket in the ground. Harsh, yes. But those were the cold, undeniable facts.

"*Deadlocked* is a terrible choice of words," Drayton said. "But yes. The group, such as it is, can't seem to agree on one single casket model."

"How about Doreen?"

"Don't ask. She's in the middle of a Chernobyl-style meltdown."

A roly-poly man in a black three-piece suit came striding forward to greet Theodosia.

"Hello," the man said in hushed tones, extending a pudgy hand and arranging his face in a mournful smile. "I'm Frank Gruenwald. One of the Gruenwald brothers. Welcome."

"I understand we're at a stalemate," Theodosia said. She didn't see much point in dancing around. The sooner she got right to it, the sooner she could go home.

Gruenwald nodded in the direction of Opal Anne and Starla, who were locked in an argument that consisted mostly of hisses and snarls. "The two young ladies seem to be at loggerheads."

At that exact moment, the Whitleys popped up from their chairs and hurried over to introduce themselves.

"We're Honey and Michael Whitley," Michael said, matching hushed tones with Gruenwald. "We own the B and B right next door to Doreen's home. The Scarborough Inn."

"Sure," Theodosia said. "Nice to meet you." The Whitleys were both well-fed, well-heeled-looking fifty-year-olds. Honey had honeyed hair and a Palm Beach tan; Michael wore a seersucker suit and had the whitest teeth Theodosia had ever seen.

"And of course you're well acquainted with Doreen, Opal Anne, Charles, and Starla," Drayton said.

Starla suddenly turned and stared red-hot bullets at Theodosia. "Why is *she* here?" she asked in a menacing voice that sounded like it was right out of a Freddy Krueger movie.

"I invited her," Drayton said. "As such, we shall now proceed with the decorum and dignity that Mr. Briggs deserves for his final send-off."

Starla made a hissing sound, like a cobra getting ready to spit venom. Opal Anne just smiled.

Theodosia, feeling uncomfortable at stepping into such a heated family argument, cleared her throat and said, "I take it you folks have managed to narrow this down to a few good choices?"

Opal Anne spoke up immediately. "I prefer to go with the more basic Lancelot model. The gray finish just seems more solemn and refined."

"No, no, no," Starla said. "We need a much more ornate model." She jumped to her feet and faced the group, as if she was about to make a major marketing presentation. "I hope you people realize that I have convinced two television stations as well as several members of the print media to cover the funeral this Thursday. Which is why I feel we need something fairly dramatic. A casket that is more . . . dare I say it . . . presidential?"

Frank Gruenwald smiled broadly. "You've just described our Pendergast to a T," he said, stepping over to a gleaming black casket decorated with polished brass fittings. He swooped an arm toward it, like a model showcasing a pop-up camper on *The Price Is Right.*

"What do you think, dear?" Drayton asked Doreen.

Doreen hunched her shoulders and shook her head. "I wa, I wa, I wa . . ."

Drayton patted her arm. "That's okay, we'll figure it out."

"I still think the Alhambra is absolutely stunning," Honey Whitley said.

"Wait. Who are you again?" Theodosia asked.

"Next-door neighbors," Drayton whispered.

"Right. Well, is there any chance of a compromise?" Theodosia asked. "A meeting of the minds?" She peered at the gallery of stone faces and wondered what she'd gotten herself into. It was a good thing these people weren't delegates to the United Nations. They'd let the world crumble, burn, and explode into a gaseous mess before one of them grudgingly gave in. "Maybe we could select a coffin that feels both refined *and* presidential?" She turned to Gruenwald. "You must have something like that."

Gruenwald cupped a hand under his chin and tried to look deeply thoughtful. "Now

111

that you mention it, we do offer the rather elegant Exeter. A popular choice with businessmen." He cleared his throat. "Well, at least it is with their *families.*" He managed a rueful smile. "But I'm afraid we only have last year's model in stock."

"That's not a problem, is it?" Theodosia asked. "I mean, a casket's not like a car. You don't need serious add-ons like Wi-Fi or antilock brakes." She could almost hear Drayton's strangled groan as she said it.

"No, no," Gruenwald hastened to explain. "The Exeter is quite handsome and well equipped. Burled cherrywood, pleated fabric, very roomy and luxurious. Unfortunately, it's not on display at the moment. We have it tucked in our storage room."

"I think we should take a look," Theodosia said. "I mean, what could it hurt?"

They all trooped out of the showroom, down a narrow corridor, and into a dingy storage room. Back here, the ceilings were lower, the lights dimmer, and the caskets stacked three and four high. For some reason, it reminded Theodosia of an image she'd once seen of an ancient, underground burial chamber, maybe one tucked deep beneath the narrow streets of Rome or Paris.

"This is the Exeter," Gruenwald said, doing his arm wave again.

They all stared at the casket with its fancy brass fittings in the form of winged birds. Or maybe they were just lumpy fish.

"Can we see the interior?" Opal Anne asked.

Gruenwald nodded. "Certainly." He undid the latches, and lifted the lid with a flourish. As it rose to reveal a plush, pink interior, the hinges uttered a low creaking sound that made everyone give an involuntary shudder. Gruenwald pretended not to notice. "As you can see, the Exeter also offers an excellent padded lining."

"Is it silk?" Starla asked.

"Well, no," Gruenwald said. "It's a poly blend, but still very fine quality."

"It looks quite handsome," Drayton said. "I think this might be a good compromise."

"Doreen?" Theodosia said.

"I ba . . . I ba . . . I ba . . ."

"I could throw in a sateen pillow at no additional charge," Gruenwald offered.

When no one said anything more, Theodosia jumped in to close the deal. It was akin to yelling *Sold!* at a fast-moving horse auction. "Then we all agree? It's a unanimous vote for the Exeter?" She figured everyone would say yes just so they could escape this dark hole and get back up top with the living. She was right. Still weeping and hiccupping, Doreen managed to whip out her American Express Gold Card and hand it over to Gruenwald.

Back upstairs in the lobby, Theodosia huddled with Opal Anne. Honey and Michael Whitley had struck an odd chord with her. She wasn't sure why they'd come along tonight and no one else seemed sure, either. She decided to get the story from Opal Anne because, of all the attendees tonight, Opal Anne struck her as being the most sane.

"Tell me about the Whitleys again?" Theodosia asked.

"They own the Scarborough Inn right next door to Doreen's home," Opal Anne said.

"So the Whitleys are family friends?"

Opal Anne rocked a hand back and forth. "Sort of. They started getting chummy with Doreen when they first made an offer to buy her home."

This was news to Theodosia. "When did this happen?"

"Oh, maybe a few months ago," Opal Anne said. "Honey and Michael are a very enterprising couple. They figure if they can buy the Calhoun Mansion from Doreen and turn it into a B and B adjacent to the one they already own, they'll have a lock on available guest rooms in the Historic District."

"Would they really?"

"They'd certainly be dominant." Opal Anne peeked at her watch. "I'm sorry, I have to be going. I have a date." She gave a sad smile. "Unless he's already stood me up."

"About Doreen's house," Theodosia said, unwilling to let it go. "She's not interested in selling, is she?"

Opal Anne shrugged. "You tell me. Doreen couldn't even pick out a simple casket tonight. The poor woman can't figure out what music the organist should play at Beau's funeral." She sighed. "Right now it seems like anything and everything is up for grabs."

As they walked out into the cool night air together, Theodosia wondered if that also included Gilded Magnolia Spa.

10

"You stopped at the farmer's market," Drayton said when he saw the armload of pink tulips that Theodosia had carried in.

"I felt the need to brighten the atmosphere after all the doom and gloom of last night," Theodosia told him.

"Let me help you." Drayton grabbed all three bunches of flowers and laid them gently on the counter. "I want to thank you again for coming to my rescue."

"No problem."

"Ah, but it was a problem. One you resolved rather handily."

"Did you think the Whitleys were somewhat strange?" she asked.

"Strange in what way?" Drayton was assembling an assortment of colorful teapots and quilted tea cozies to carry them through the day. "Oh, you mean like it's a little early to break out the seersucker?"

"No, I meant like the Whitleys didn't

exactly seem like Doreen's best buddies," Theodosia said. "I had the feeling they might have bullied their way in last night."

"All I know is that they offered to come along for moral support."

"What's interesting is that the Whitleys are trying to buy Doreen's house."

Drayton frowned. "I didn't know that. Seriously? Doreen never mentioned anything of that nature to me."

"Opal Anne told me all about it last night. Apparently the Whitleys are looking to expand their B and B empire. If they buy Doreen's home, they'll be kingpins in the Historic District. Or something like that."

"That sounds vaguely suspicious," Drayton said.

"Tell me about it," Theodosia said. "The Whitleys were not only guests at the rat tea, they sat at the same table as Doreen and Beau."

"You're giving me chills," Drayton said. "It's like another suspect suddenly materialized out of thin air."

"Two suspects. Working in tandem. Trying to get Doreen to sell her home."

"Do you think the police know about the Whitleys?"

"Are you kidding?" Theodosia said. "*We* didn't even know about the Whitleys until last night."

While Drayton busied himself fixing tea —
orchid plum and vanilla chai to start the
day with — Theodosia pulled her Shelley
Chintz teacups out of the cupboard.

"Fancy," Drayton said. "Are you expecting someone special?"

"All our guests are special," Theodosia
said, smiling.

"I couldn't agree with you more."

"I'm going to check in with Haley," Theodosia said. "Then grab the crystal vases
from my office. Can you finish up out here?"

"Count on it."

"Haley?" Theodosia said. "Are you in
here?" She waved a hand in front of her face
as she stepped into the kitchen. "It's so
steamy I can barely see you."

"That's because I'm making lentil soup,"
Haley said. "I was going to do bone broth,
but I figured that would scare everybody
off."

"You figured right. Let's leave the trendy
food to the trendsetting restaurants."

Haley flashed a crooked grin. "And you
don't think we are? Trendsetting, I mean?"

"I think we were out there on the front
lines of the comfort food revolution," Theodosia said. "Serving the kind of sweets and

118

savories that make people feel all happy and warm."

"Then you're going to love today's menu."

"Okay."

"Raisin scones, cranberry bread, and banana muffins."

"And for lunch?"

"Citrus salad, lentil soup, mushroom quiche, and strawberry cream cheese tea sandwiches. With apple nut squares and peanut butter cookies for dessert." A bell *ding*ed on the stove and Haley bent to grab a pan of banana muffins. "What do you think?"

"I feel lulled into oblivion already. I'm ready to grab my blanket and take a nap."

Back out in the tea room, a few customers drifted in for early-morning tea. Theodosia delivered pots of steaming hot tea and fresh-baked scones to their tables, as well as small glass bowls in the shape of dainty slippers that were filled with Devonshire cream.

When she stepped behind the counter to grab some fresh-cut lemon slices, Drayton said, "Let me ask you something. Why would somebody want Beau dead? Let's think about that for a minute."

"I once read a newspaper piece . . . or maybe I saw it on the Internet . . . about criminal motive," Theodosia said. "Anyway, according to this CIA expert, there are three main motives that lead to a major crime."

Drayton lifted an eyebrow. "And what would those be?"

"Revenge, political ideology, and financial gain."

"Beau Briggs wasn't exactly a political animal, so it either has to be revenge or financial gain."

"Do you think there's a last will and testament floating around somewhere?" Theodosia wondered. "You know that old saw — where there's a will, there's a relative."

"I asked Doreen about that," Drayton said. "She told me that she inherits everything."

"That's because she owns everything," Theodosia said. "She probably purchased the Calhoun Mansion herself. And we know she controlled the purse strings — or tried to anyway. So it stands to reason she would be the major beneficiary."

"So nobody stands to gain from Beau's murder."

"I didn't say that. The way I see it right now, several people stand to gain." Theodosia ticked them off on her fingertips. "Doreen gets rid of a severe drain on her financial resources . . ."

Drayton grimaced. "I knew you were going to say that. Who else?"

"The business partner, Reggie Huston, if Opal Anne is to be believed. With Beau gone he probably plans to take over the running of the spa all by himself."

"Okay."

"And now the Whitleys have entered the picture."

"Because now that she's a widow, Doreen might not want to rattle around all by herself in a big old house."

"Exactly," Theodosia said.

"Moving on to revenge," Drayton said. "Do you think someone might have been trying to get back at Beau?"

"If someone was angry with him, it would have to be over something major. A huge personal or financial reason. Doreen hasn't mentioned anything like that." Theodosia tapped a finger against the counter. "Then again, she may not *know* anything."

"She's coming in today. We can quiz her."

"Wait," Theodosia said. "Doreen's coming here?"

"She called bright and early, right before you arrived. Wanted to thank us for all our good help last night, said she was bringing in that list you wanted."

"How'd she sound?" Theodosia asked.

"Amazingly rational."

"Glory be."

As Tuesday morning turned into a whirl-wind of customers and phone calls, Theo-dosia's brain continued to tick along, too. In between packaging up bags of scones for takeout and writing down luncheon reserva-tions, she said, "My brain keeps circling back to the rats, Drayton. You know, the costumed waiters from the catering com-pany."

"Crispin's Catering," Drayton said. That's the outfit Doreen used. She told me so last night."

"When the waiters were lined up for their talk with the detectives, there was that one guy that looked like he was about ready to cry."

"The young man with the spiky blond hair?"

"That's the one."

"You think he was involved?" Drayton asked.

"Not exactly. I'm fairly positive the police checked him out and then released him. But what if he saw something and was just too afraid to talk?" Theodosia thought for a few moments. "I've got to stop by the catering company and find out exactly who was working that day."

"You're planning to visit soon? Their storefront's just over on East Bay Street, you know."

"You know what?" Theodosia glanced at her watch. "I'm going to try and duck out in twenty minutes or so and then be back in plenty of time for lunch."

More customers streamed in, and along with them came Delaine Dish. Delaine was a tea aficionado, local busybody, and proprietor of Cotton Duck Boutique.

"Theo," Delaine said in her trademark purr, "I just received a shipment of the most *sublime* silk dresses. There's one, a mint-green fit and flare, that would go spectacularly well with your auburn hair."

Theodosia posed next to Delaine's table. "I'm not sure I'm a dress person." She really preferred tailored slacks paired with fun T-shirts, clothes that let her dash more freely about the tea room.

But Delaine rarely took no for an answer. "You have to at least *try* a few on, dear. I mean, seriously, men really do prefer women in dresses." She took a delicate sip of tea and threw Theodosia an arch look. A look Theodosia knew was aimed at her single status. "Oh, and what did I hear about you attending that *disastrous* tea on Saturday?" Delaine blotted her lips. "Must have been awful."

"It *was* awful," Theodosia said. "Not the tea, but the outcome."

"And poor Doreen Briggs tried to make it so much fun. My friend Yvonne Cataldo was at the tea, and she said the rat waiters were a hoot and the centerpieces were to *die* for."

"She wasn't that far off," Theodosia said. "The centerpiece at the head table caught fire and then poor Beau Briggs collapsed a few minutes later."

"Mmm, but not because of the centerpiece." Delaine pulled out a mirror and checked her lipstick.

"No. It looks as though someone injected him with a fast-acting poison."

Now Delaine was blithely fluffing her hair. Theodosia's revelation about the poison had rocketed right over her head. Pfffft.

"Did you happen to catch the name of the florist?" Delaine asked.

"Afraid not." Theodosia was miffed that Delaine wasn't more upset by Beau's untimely death. "But I'll tell you what. There's a woman by the name of Starla Crane who helped Doreen with all the arrangements. I bet she'd have the florist's name and number tucked away in her hot little Rolodex. She owns a PR firm called the Image Factory."

"I'll give her a call."

Theodosia smiled to herself. "Good luck with that."

"Oh, and be sure to put me down for your Candlelight Tea this Friday night," Delaine said.

"I was under the impression you couldn't make it."

"Of course I'll be there," Delaine said. "And with a date. Honestly, Theo, you know I positively *adore* all your special event teas and want to support you as much as I can." Her mouth pulled into a cagey smile. "I just hope you're coming to *my* next event."

"Excuse me?" Theodosia said. *What event? What am I missing here? Was there an invitation that I totally blocked out?*

"The cat show." Delaine turned in her chair, her green eyes glittering. "Please don't tell me you forgot about the Carolina Cat Show?"

"Delaine . . ." Theodosia was practically speechless. "I don't have a cat, I have a dog. Remember?"

Delaine shook her head. "Doesn't matter. I have two cats, and I'm the chairwoman of the entire event. Which means you *have* to come."

Crispin's Catering was a brand-new catering company located on East Bay Street, close to the Cooper River. After her go-round with Delaine, Theodosia was happy to be outside and breathing sips of fresh air. Honestly, Delaine could be the most high-handed, dictatorial person she'd ever known. Of course, she was also a social powerhouse who, over the years, had raised millions of dollars for charity. So you always had to walk a fine line.

Crispin's Catering was a storefront operation with bouncy red lettering that stretched across their front window (CRISPIN'S CATERING — MACARONS AND OPERA CAKES OUR SPECIALTY) and a cheery yellow awning. As she stepped inside, Theodosia was pleasantly surprised to find that Crispin's was also a full-service bakery. The small shop featured a large glass case that contained croissants, a rainbow of macarons, berry tarts, brioche, and a fabulous assortment of opera cakes.

"May I help you?" said the smiling young woman behind the counter.

"Would it be possible to speak with your owner?" Theodosia touched a hand to her chest. "I'm Theodosia Browning. I own the

Indigo Tea Shop over on Church Street."

Two minutes later, the owner came hustling out, obviously eager to win over a potential customer for his commercial baked goods.

"I'm Bobby Ware," the man said, introducing himself. "If you're looking for a good bakery or a catering company to help with special events at your tea shop, I'd love to sit down and talk. We can handle cakes, scones, muffins, brownie bites, even tea sandwiches."

"I'm on a kind of fact-finding mission right now," Theodosia said.

Ware's smile slipped a bit. "Oh?"

"I was a guest at Doreen Briggs's rat tea this past Saturday."

Now his enthusiasm hit rock bottom. "Oh."

"I've been looking into a few things for Doreen." Before Ware asked her for some bona fides, Theodosia quickly added, "I'm particularly interested in the employees you sent over to work as waiters."

Ware shook his head. "The police were already here asking me about them. And they're not full-time employees, they're basically part-timers. Freelancers." He shrugged. "Though I guess they still have to run a check on them."

"And that's something you do, too, am I right? Run an employment check before you send people out on a catering job?"

"Oh sure," Ware said.

"And did the waiters you sent over to the rat tea check out okay?"

Ware shrugged. "You're always gonna find some minor issues here and there. A DWI or something like that. My waiters didn't have any biggies, though. They were okay guys."

"There was one young man who worked as a server at the rat tea," Theodosia said. "The guy with the spiked blond hair?"

"I know who you mean," Ware said. "Yeah, he's an okay server."

"Just okay?"

"That's right. Some of our guys are wonderful. They really thrive in that kind of white-glove environment. Some of them are just okay."

"Would you be able to give me the names of the servers who worked at the rat tea?"

Ware shook his head. "I can't do that. It's against company policy. Besides, the police asked me to keep quiet." He looked a little unsettled. "I guess because it's still an unsolved murder."

"I completely understand," Theodosia said. "But maybe I could ask you a few questions about the costumes?"

"The costumes don't belong to us. They were rented. In fact, the woman who arranged the catering . . ."

"Doreen Briggs?" Theodosia said.

Ware shook his head again. "No, it was some snippy PR gal."

"Starla Crane?"

Bobby Ware snapped his fingers and pointed at her. "That's it. She was the one who rented the rat costumes and messengered them over here the morning of the tea. So the waiters could get all gussied up in their coats and ties and crazy rat heads."

"Do you know where those costumes came from?"

Ware thought for a minute. "Seems to me I remember seeing a black plastic bag that said something like Big Top Costumes. Or maybe it was Big Time. I'm not entirely sure."

"I'll check it out," Theodosia said. "Thanks for your help."

"No problem."

"Oh, there's one more thing . . ."

"Yeah?"

"Can I get two of those opera cakes? The chocolate ones, please."

Two minutes later, Theodosia was out the door and balancing two white bakery boxes, hoping that a piece of the puzzle might be starting to slip into place.

11

"You have a guest," Drayton said as Theodosia came flying through the front door of the Indigo Tea Shop.

"What?" She gently set her cake boxes down on the counter. "Who?"

Drayton inclined his head. "Detective Blue Eyes. Sitting over there in the corner." He glanced over quickly. "Don't look now, but he's sitting up straight and smiling at you as if you're a tasty little bonbon."

Theodosia did a kind of double take. "Oh my." She hadn't been expecting Detective Riley to show up. Then again, she wasn't averse to his presence, either.

"Tell you what," Drayton said. "You can take him this sencha as a lovely icebreaker. We already gave him a couple of scones." He lowered his voice. "Your detective ripped through the first one without taking a single breath."

If the way to a man's heart is through his

131

stomach, then how do I get inside his head?
Theodosia wondered.

But Theodosia smiled prettily as she set the pot of tea on the table and slipped into the chair opposite Detective Riley.

"I see you found your way here," she said.

"It wasn't difficult. I just followed a trail of scone crumbs." Riley was dressed in a tweedy jacket and blue jeans and looked more like a college English professor than a homicide detective. She also noticed that his brown hair had a few threads of silver at the temples, which gave him a nicely seasoned look.

"Let me pour you some of this tea." Theodosia lifted the red Chinese teapot and poured out a cup of tea for Detective Riley. It was fragrant and sweet, carrying just a hint of herbs.

"Am I supposed to add sugar to this?" Riley asked.

"You do have a sweet tooth, don't you?"

"Mostly I'm just trying to be proper. To do the right thing and not look like a blundering tea-drinking amateur."

"I'd say you're fine as is. This is one of Drayton's favorite Kyoto Estate green teas. I think you'll find it sweet enough." Theodosia paused. "What brings you in today? Besides our tea and scones?"

132

"Business," Riley said. "And I wanted to see you."

"I'm flattered," Theodosia said. "But perhaps we should take care of business first?" She liked this detective who seemed dedicated and sincere, but also had a sense of humor.

Riley reached for a brown envelope and pulled out a half-dozen black-and-white photos. He laid them carefully on the table. "I was wondering if you might recognize any of these people?"

"This is a kind of lineup?"

Riley nodded. "Yes."

"You're wondering if I recall seeing one or another of these people at the rat tea?"

"That's exactly it."

Theodosia studied the photos carefully. They were all men who had the hard-eyed, unyielding look of what she assumed was a dangerous criminal. The kind of guys who were probably wanted by police in five states. Or maybe by the FBI.

"I've never seen any of these men before. I think I might remember if I had."

"It was a long shot," Riley said. He started to gather up the photos.

Theodosia put a hand out to stop him. "Wait a minute. Who are they exactly?"

"A cast of very unsavory characters."

133

"Known criminals?"

Riley tapped one of the photos. "This guy is wanted for extortion." He pointed to another. "This sweetheart is a drug dealer. Do you really want me to go on?"

"And you think one or more of these men might have been involved in Beau Briggs's death? Are they known for being hired killers?"

"No," Riley said. "Let's just say they're morally flexible."

"Why these six?" Theodosia indicated the photos.

"Because they're probably in the area right now."

"Lucky us." Theodosia picked up a butter knife and twiddled it. "Have you gone back to question the rat waiters? To see if one of them remembered seeing something fishy?"

"We're working on that," Riley said. "You know, your scones are absolutely delicious."

"Thank you. I have a question concerning the Whitleys."

Riley gave her a blank stare. "Who are the Whitleys?"

"You should know the name," Theodosia said. "They were guests at the rat tea."

Riley touched a finger to his forehead. "Okay, maybe I do recall that name. Why are you asking about them?"

"Because they've been lobbying hard to buy Doreen's house."

Riley gave a slow reptilian blink. "What?"

"They've been trying . . ."

He held up a hand. "I heard what you said. What I meant was . . . um . . . why on earth didn't I know about this?"

"I have no idea."

"These Whitleys are seriously trying to buy Doreen Briggs's house?"

"So they can turn it into a B and B," Theodosia said. "They want to link it up with the place they own right next door." She paused. "Do you think that could have been a motive for murder?"

"You mean, like, a death in the family could prompt a quick sale?"

"That would be one scenario, yes," Theodosia said. "Doreen doesn't know which way to turn, so the Whitleys sweep in and rescue her."

"I guess it's been known to happen," Riley said.

"Come on," Theodosia chided. "Don't act so cool about this. I can tell by the way your eyes are moving back and forth that you think there's a very real possibility here."

"Okay, maybe I am a bit interested," Riley said. "This is the first I've heard about the Whitleys. It's a lot to digest."

135

"And I'm sure you've had time to question Reggie Huston, the business partner?"

Riley gazed at her. "We've had a conversation, sure."

"Rumor has it he's using Gilded Magnolia Spa as his personal checkbook."

Riley frowned as he took a quick sip of tea. "May I ask exactly where you're getting your information?"

"I . . . hear things," Theodosia said.

"You're investigating," Riley said.

"Noooo," Theodosia said, knowing full well she was telling him a little white lie. Maybe not the best way to start a relationship. Wait a minute, *was* there a relationship? Have to wait and see.

Riley wasn't buying her answer. "You know, Tidwell warned me about you."

Now Theodosia's curiosity was amped. "He did? What did Tidwell say about me?"

Riley leaned forward in his chair and gave her a level gaze. "He told me you were very smart. But to watch out."

"I'm not sure whether I should be flattered or offended." When Riley didn't respond, Theodosia said, "May I offer you some more tea?"

Riley shook his head no.

"Another scone?"

"No, thank you."

Theodosia glanced over at the two bakery boxes that sat on the counter. "How about a slice of chocolate opera cake?"

Riley's staid look slowly morphed into a sheepish grin. "Choc . . . ho boy, you really don't play fair, do you?"

Gotcha, Theodosia thought.

"You certainly had a cozy little confab with Detective Riley," Drayton said. They were in the middle of their lunch rush, Drayton brewing endless small pots of tea, Theodosia taking orders as well as delivering plates from the kitchen.

"He didn't have a clue about the Whitleys," Theodosia said.

"But you very capably steered him in their direction?"

"Of course."

"What if you're wrong?" Drayton asked. "What if they're just an innocent but highly enterprising couple?"

"Then they've got nothing to worry about," Theodosia said. "But until they're cleared, they'll remain on my suspect list."

"I suppose on mine, too," Drayton said. "They did seem awfully solicitous."

"Maybe a little too eager to put in yet another offer on Doreen's home?"

"Agreed," Drayton said, measuring out

two scoops of gunpowder green tea and dumping them into a floral teapot.

Lunch continued at a fairly brisk pace. But by one fifteen, almost every guest had their luncheon order in front of them and was sipping tea and contentedly munching away.

Good thing. Because that's when Doreen and Opal Anne showed up.

Doreen was dressed in a black skirt suit covered in frilly ruffles and wore a jaunty black hat with a floppy veil that hid her eyes. To Theodosia it looked like something you might wear to the Ascot races, should you be invited to sit in the Queen's private box.

"We want to thank you so much for helping out last night" were Opal Anne's first words. She was dressed in tan slacks and a navy blazer. In other words, normal.

"No problem," Theodosia said. "I'm just happy everything worked out the way it did." She led them to a corner table and got them seated. "How about a slice of quiche and a citrus salad?" she asked.

"That would be wonderful," Doreen said. "Planning a funeral is hard work." She looked tired, but didn't seem as discombobulated as she'd been the night before.

"Before we get started," Opal Anne said, "we have a request."

"Surely," Theodosia said.

"We were wondering if you could cater our family funeral luncheon on Thursday?" Opal Anne asked.

"I know it's a little late to ask," Doreen said, jumping in. "But the idea just occurred to us." She made a little mewling sound, like a sick kitten. "I can't seem to keep a single thought in my head these days."

"Of course we can handle the catering," Theodosia said. "Did you have something specific in mind?" She pulled out a pen and paper and sat down at the table with them.

Doreen gazed at Opal Anne.

"Tea and scones?" Opal Anne ventured. "Maybe salad and quiche? Something easy."

"For how many people?" Theodosia asked.

Again Doreen turned to Opal Anne.

"I'm guessing two or three dozen people at most," Opal Anne said.

"Would this be a sit-down luncheon or . . . ?" Theodosia started.

"Nothing fancy," Doreen said. "A luncheon buffet would be fine. You could just set everything out on the dining room table and people could help themselves."

"That sounds fairly easy to manage," Theodosia said. She knew Haley could prep all the food, and she could transport it and maybe even set up by herself. "We'll be

139

happy to handle your luncheon." She thought about the box of sad little tea bags she'd found in Doreen's pantry. The box that had probably been sitting there since disco was king. "And I'll bring along some tins of fresh tea as well."

When Theodosia returned with luncheon plates for them, Drayton was standing at their table, pouring cups of Lung Ching, or Dragon Well, tea. It was a delicate Chinese green tea that he brewed when he wanted to impress someone, and Theodosia figured he still had his heart set on getting a nice big grant from Doreen.

"Thank you, Drayton," Doreen said. "I don't know what we'd do without you. You've been such a comfort."

"Kind of you to say," Drayton said. He backed away from the table, flashed a knowing look at Theodosia, and then returned to the front counter.

"And Theodosia," Doreen said. "I have those lists you requested." She dug in a black purse that was roughly the size of a bread box and pulled out a stack of paper.

"Excellent," Theodosia said. She placed their luncheon plates in front of them, scurried to the front counter to grab a bowl of Devonshire cream for the scones, and then sat down with them. "I hope the lists didn't pose too much of a problem for you."

"It wasn't much fun," Doreen said, drawing a shaky breath. "I brought the guest list, of course, the whole entire thing. Then I drew up a list of possible suspects." She hesitated. "People that I either didn't know all that well, or people who had dealings with my husband."

"In other words," Theodosia said, "people who were Beau's invited guests."

"I guess you could say that."

That was the list Theodosia was particularly interested in. But when she scanned the list, she didn't recognize a single name. "Were any of these *possibles* sitting at your table?" she asked. "Or at nearby tables?"

"Not really," Doreen said. "Oh, I also brought along some financial information." She lowered her voice. "It's what I could find concerning, you know, some of Beau's more recent investments."

"Thank you," Theodosia said. "That information could prove very helpful."

"I felt awful writing people's names down for that hit list you wanted," Doreen continued. "But . . . well, you asked. And Opal Anne said I had to do it. That it was the right thing to do. The smart thing to do."

Theodosia smiled at Doreen. "Opal Anne

is right."

"But I want to tell you," Doreen said. "I don't feel good about any of this."

Theodosia wanted to say, *Imagine how bad Beau feels.* But of course, the man was dead. He couldn't feel anything.

Instead, Theodosia said, "You've told me about the people who were sitting right there at the table with you. But what about your guests at the nearby tables?" She knew that many of them had been clustered around Beau just before he sputtered and died.

"What about them?" Doreen said.

"We're going to need their names," Theodosia said.

"Told you so," Opal Anne said.

Doreen rapped the table with her knuckles. "You want me to write down the names of my dear friends as well as business associates?"

"If you could," Theodosia said. She dug the pen from her pocket and handed it to Doreen.

Doreen wrinkled her nose, clearly upset. "I suppose," she said. While Opal Anne enjoyed her scone and lentil soup, Doreen laboriously printed out eight names. When she was done, she shoved the paper toward Theodosia and said, "There. Happy now?"

Doreen looked decidedly unhappy.

"I'm sorry this is so trying for you," Theodosia said.

Doreen took a sip of tea and turned a fairly hard gaze on Theodosia. "I'm hoping for some answers, you know? Drayton promised me answers. He said that you were exceedingly smart. Scary smart."

"I've been working on this," Theodosia said, suddenly feeling as if she'd been called on the carpet. "I've spoken with the Charleston PD several times, met with the caterer, and will be checking out the waitstaff. I'll also be investigating the costume company that provided the rat costumes." What she *didn't* mention was that she'd turned over a box of rat poison to the Charleston PD. And that Doreen was still on her radar as a possible suspect.

"Well . . . okay," Doreen said, a bit grudgingly. "It sounds as if you have been busy."

"Theodosia was busy last night as well," Opal Anne pointed out. "She didn't have to come to the funeral home and play referee."

"That was . . . generous," Doreen said.

Drayton was suddenly back at their table, pouring refills of tea.

"Everything okay?" he asked.

"Theodosia was just giving us a rundown on her investigation so far," Doreen said.

143

"It sounds like she's been busy."

"She's been nose-to-the-grindstone busy," Drayton said. "Working nonstop."

"That's good," Doreen said. "The more progress we make, the better your chance of getting that grant."

"Of course," Drayton said. But Theodosia could tell from the pinched look on his face that he was biting his tongue.

"One more thing," Doreen said as she dug into her handbag and pulled out a half-dozen small slips of paper. "I brought along some spa passes." She handed them to Theodosia. "Give some to your friends if you want — they'd probably enjoy having a massage or a manicure. Gilded Magnolia Spa does a fabulous job."

"Thank you," Theodosia said. She was suddenly feeling like the hired help. And didn't much like it.

"And of course I expect you'll want to take a complete tour of the spa," Doreen said. "I'll phone Cindy, our client services manager, and make the arrangements." She gazed at Theodosia and blinked rapidly. "When would be good for you? How does your schedule look first thing tomorrow morning?"

Theodosia thought for a moment. They had their Madame Pompadour Tea at noon, but if she dropped by the spa early enough . . . "I think I could manage that," she said.

"Good," Doreen said. "And I'll be sure to inform Reggie Huston that you'll be dropping by for a visit."

"That's right," Opal Anne cut in. "You'll definitely want to talk to Reggie." She threw a meaningful glance at Theodosia.

"Okay," Theodosia said. "I'll do that. Take the tour, I mean. And talk to Reggie." For some reason she felt rattled and under a good deal of pressure. Then again, she was doing this for Drayton, right? And because she *wanted* to? Because she'd been curious?

Or was something else plucking at her? Some misplaced sense of justice?

12

Theodosia was sitting in her office, going over the lists Doreen had given her. They included the guest list, suspect list, and Doreen's hand-printed list of people who'd been sitting at her table as well as the nearby tables.

"I thought you might like some lunch," Drayton said. He was standing in the door-way, holding a small tray. "I know you haven't eaten yet."

"I'm not sure I'm all that hungry."

"Did you lose your appetite because of Doreen?" Drayton asked. "I was wondering how you felt after that meeting."

"Are you kidding? I felt as if Doreen's boot was planted squarely in the middle of my back," Theodosia said. "I didn't realize she could be so pushy and aggressive. Those are not the nicest traits in a woman. Or in anyone, for that matter."

"I had no idea everything would become

so complicated," Drayton said. "First it was just about helping Doreen. And securing a grant for the Heritage Society in return."

"Now it's a lot more tricky," Theodosia agreed. "Doreen's become a suspect, other suspects have emerged from the shadows, and there are a few business deals involved. To top it all off, Doreen seems to take delight in dangling that grant over our heads."

"Let's just hope it's not a bait and switch," Drayton said. He set down his tray and said, "Soup and a scone. Plus some chamomile tea, which is always conducive to relaxation."

"Thank you." Theodosia tapped her pen against the hand-printed list she'd been studying. "The thing is, Doreen hasn't exactly been forthcoming with her information. Her initial suspect list didn't even include the people who'd been seated at her table."

"But she did finally part with those names," Drayton said.

"Still, it was like yanking teeth." Theodosia turned the list around for Drayton to read.

"Reggie Huston," he said, reading aloud. "Robert Steele." He frowned. "Who's Robert Steele?"

"I'll tell you who Robert Steele is," Theodosia said. "I've been going through these financial papers that Doreen gave me, and it turns out Robert Steele is a financial muckety-muck who owns a company called Angel Oak Venture Capital."

"I've never heard of it," Drayton said.

"Well, Beau Briggs did. As a matter of fact, he invested seven hundred thousand dollars in Angel Oak VC."

"Are you serious?" Drayton looked surprised at the huge sum.

"Not only that, according to these papers, Beau was trying to get his money back."

"Did he? Get it back, I mean?"

"It doesn't appear that he did," Theodosia said. She twiddled her pen, thinking. "You know, that's an awful lot of money to have hanging out there."

"Enough to kill for?" Drayton asked.

"That's what worries me."

"What is Angel Oak, anyway? Where did they come from?"

"I'm not exactly sure," Theodosia said. "Let's call Doreen and see if she knows anything about this." She reached for her phone and punched in the number. When Doreen was finally on the line, Theo said, "Doreen, I was just going through those financial papers you gave me."

"You don't waste any time, do you?" Doreen said. "You really are a go-getter, just like Drayton said you were."

Theodosia plunged on ahead. "Doreen, I was wondering if you were familiar with an investment firm by the name of Angel Oak Venture Capital?"

"No, I don't think so," Doreen said slowly. Through the phone, Theodosia could hear the rattle of ice cubes in a glass.

"Okay, then, how about a man by the name of Robert Steele?"

Doreen was quiet for a few moments and then she said, "You must be talking about Bob. Bob Steele."

Theodosia turned toward Drayton and mouthed, "Suddenly she knows him."

"You met Bob, didn't you?" Doreen asked. "He was sitting right there at our table. He was one of Beau's guests."

"Listen, Doreen, are you aware that Beau invested seven hundred thousand dollars in Robert Steele's company? In his Angel Oak Venture Capital fund?" There was dead silence on the line, and for a minute Theodosia thought Doreen might have hung up.

Then Doreen's voice rose in a shrill scream. "Whaaat? What did you say?"

"Are you aware that . . . ?"

"I'm completely stunned!" Doreen gasped

out. "Your question . . . that amount of money . . . it literally punched the wind right out of me. How much did you say again? Seven hundred thousand dollars?"

"That's right."

"No, that can't be right." She did sound breathless. "Please tell me that's not so."

"I've got the confirmation right here in front of me," Theodosia said. "It's in the papers you just gave me."

"Oh no," Doreen moaned. "Seven hundred thousand dollars? That's a lot of money. Isn't that a lot of money?"

"I would say it's a great deal of money." *Is she kidding? That's a huge matzo ball to have hanging out there.*

"Do you . . . do you think there's any way to get it back?"

"I have no idea," Theodosia said. "But it looks as if Beau was trying to do exactly that. Opt out of this investment fund and get the money returned."

"From Robert Steele?"

"Yes, from Steele," Theodosia said. *What is her problem? Does she not get this?* "From his company, Angel Oak."

"Please, can you help me?" Doreen asked. Her voice rose in a pleading mewl. "Can you *please* try and get the money back?"

"Let me think about it," Theodosia said.

An idea had just struck her. If she could somehow recover those funds from Angel Oak, a grateful Doreen might just kick it all over to the Heritage Society. After all, seven hundred grand would goose the Heritage Society along for a good long while.

Theodosia set down her phone and said to Drayton, "You heard most of that?"

"I heard the part where you said Beau invested seven hundred thousand dollars in Angel Oak."

"Yup. And Doreen wants to know if we can get it back."

Drayton looked perplexed. "Can we? Better yet, can you?" He hesitated. "I realize that's asking a lot of you."

Theodosia thumbed through the stack of papers again. "Like I said, from the looks of things, Beau's already tried." She glanced up at Drayton. "But Angel Oak hasn't given up a penny."

"So what are you saying?"

Theodosia leaned back in her chair. She'd just had another thought. "Think about this for a plot twist, Drayton. Maybe Robert Steele killed Beau rather than refund his investment."

Drayton clutched at his throat. "Dear Lord. Do you suppose that's what happened? I mean, if Robert Steele was right *there* at the tea, he certainly could have . . ." Drayton seemed to sag inwardly. Then he worked to compose his thoughts. "Are you going to tell Detective Riley?"

"I don't know. Maybe." Theodosia reached for her teacup and took a sip of tea, trying to gather her thoughts. "You know, there's another way to look at this, too."

"What's that?"

"Maybe Doreen *wanted* us to paw through her papers and discover this information. Maybe she killed her husband and is trying to shift the blame to Robert Steele."

"That would mean she has a very devious mind."

"It would mean Doreen is a sociopath," Theodosia said.

"Is there some way we could investigate Robert Steele and Angel Oak?" Drayton asked. "To see if they're on the up-and-up? Maybe this Angel Oak fund is like buying a CD, you have to commit your money for a certain period of time."

"Maybe so. But I agree that we should take a good hard look at them. Because right now I'm pretty much in the dark. I don't know if Angel Oak is a hedge fund, a mutual fund, or a private equity group."

"How would we find that information

out?" Drayton asked.

Theodosia scanned the papers in front of her. "I suppose we could call Robert Steele and simply ask him." She spotted the company's phone number on a sheet of letterhead and hastily punched it in. When her call was answered, she said, in a very businesslike tone, "I'd like to speak with Robert Steele, please."

"I'm sorry," an efficient-sounding receptionist said back, "Mr. Steele is out of the office right now. Are you by any chance calling about his presentation tonight?"

It took Theodosia about one millisecond to make up her mind. "Yes, I am." She tempered her words to sound friendly. "I know I jotted down the information somewhere, but if you could just run the particulars by me again it would be so helpful."

"Certainly. My pleasure. Mr. Steele will be at the Lady Goodwood Inn in the Swamp Fox Room tonight. His presentation begins at seven o'clock sharp with coffee and cookies to follow afterward."

Theodosia hung up the phone and gave Drayton a cryptic smile. "Guess where we're going tonight?" She'd been planning to drop by the costume rental place, but now this seemed a lot more important.

Drayton looked nervous. "Please don't tell

me we're going on another dreadful errand."

"Nothing as gruesome as last night. We're going to attend a seminar on investing."

Drayton fingered his bow tie. "Considering the flux that Wall Street's been going through lately, that sounds even gloomier than picking out caskets."

The Lady Goodwood Inn was a historic inn located in Charleston's French Quarter. It was charming, very old-world, and a favored spot for local businesses to hold meetings, seminars, and presentations.

Tonight, the floral carpeting whispered underfoot as Theodosia and Drayton crossed the dimly lit lobby. The wooden check-in desk, looking like something out of a fine European hotel, dominated one wall, while overstuffed chairs tucked next to large potted plants made for cozy, intimate spots. In fact, guests had already gathered here in small groups, enjoying the inn's complimentary wine and cheese before they headed out for dinner at local favorites like Poogan's Porch or the Peninsula Grill.

Theodosia wondered if the Whitleys also offered wine and cheese for their guests at the Scarborough Inn. Probably. Didn't everyone these days?

"What are we looking for again?" Drayton asked as they turned left and headed down a long corridor.

"The Swamp Fox Room," Theodosia told him.

"Ah, in honor of our brave Francis Marion." Drayton was a history buff and liked nothing more than to recount tales of Francis Marion, the Swamp Fox, and his derring-do during the Revolutionary War. Especially when it involved outsmarting General Cornwallis and his British troops.

"Maybe this room?" Theodosia said. But no, this meeting room was clearly marked as the Plantation Room.

"Here it is," Drayton said. "And there's even a sign for Angel Oak."

They both peered at the cardboard sign that hung to the left of the door. It said ANGEL OAK VENTURE CAPITAL — AT THE LEADING EDGE OF TECHNOLOGY.

"Technology," Drayton said. "Oh dear. That arena is so foreign to me."

Theodosia patted his arm as they entered the room. "Don't worry, Drayton, I promise not to spill the beans about your being a confirmed Luddite."

They took seats in the back row of chairs in the small meeting room. All in all, Theodosia figured there were about twenty

155

people who'd shown up for the presentation. Not a huge turnout. Then again, maybe there weren't that many potential tech investors out there.

At exactly seven o'clock, Robert Steele bounded to the front of the room. He was a good-looking man. Tall, hair blow-combed just so, a winning smile, elegantly tailored suit. Theodosia thought Steele looked like a cross between a slick salesman and a televangelist.

There was a spatter of applause from the guests and then Steele's commanding voice boomed out. "Welcome, welcome. But please hold your applause. Because this presentation is all about *you*. About how you can *profit* mightily from the coming tech boom."

"We're poised for *another* tech boom?" Drayton whispered to Theodosia.

"News to me," she whispered back.

The lights were dimmed and, from somewhere above and behind them, a computer projected multiple colorful images on the white wall directly behind Steele. He waved at one of the images as it flipped past and launched into his pitch.

"Well-seasoned emerging tech stocks are some of the best investments that are out there today," Steele said. "They offer the perfect mix of overt riskiness as well as hidden strength and potential growth."

Theodosia leaned back in her chair, somewhat impressed by the multimedia presentation on Angel Oak's Equity Crowdfunding program, as well as Robert Steele's slick patois. He was a cajoling cheerleader for what turned out to be a private hedge fund. He doled out just the right amount of technical information and hyped his own tech smarts, dropping his voice to a reverential tone when he talked about return on investment.

Twenty minutes into the presentation, Drayton nudged Theodosia. "What do you think?" he whispered.

"The man is good," Theodosia whispered back. "He could sell ice to Eskimos. I can see why Beau fell for his pitch."

"You don't think Robert Steele has a line on the next hot tech companies?"

Theodosia listened as Steele tried to persuade them to join what he called an elite corps of investors. "Let me put it this way," she said. "I don't think we should stick around long enough to grab a prospectus. Or even one of his store-bought cookies."

13

Gilded Magnolia Spa looked exactly as its name implied. Gilded. The enormous double doors leading into the spa were painted a shimmering gold and covered with raised images of females wearing vaguely Grecian-looking togas. Theodosia figured if the sun struck them just so, the toga ladies would all melt into a friendly tangle.

Inside, the lobby looked like a tropical paradise, with potted magnolias, palm trees, and banana plants circling a sitting area that was composed of gold suede couches and chairs. All this glamour, as if it were the green room for Fort Knox, was sandwiched between a gilded cove ceiling and a plush gold carpet.

Theodosia stepped briskly up to the receptionist desk. "Good morning, I'm Theodosia Browning. Here for a tour?"

"Oh yes," the receptionist said. She was blond and tanned (practically gilded, too) and achingly youthful. "Cindy Spangler, our client manager, is expecting you."

Whether some secret button was pushed or not, precisely thirty seconds later, Cindy came bouncing out to greet Theodosia. Blond haired, tall, and sinewy, Cindy wore a crop top, low-slung yoga pants, and trainers. She also looked like she could run ten miles without breaking a sweat, twist herself into a tantric yoga pretzel, and still walk away with the Miss Universe crown.

"I'm Cindy Spangler," Cindy said, pumping Theodosia's hand enthusiastically and flashing a dazzling smile. "Manager of client services."

"Theodosia Browning. Nice to meet you." At that moment Theodosia made up her mind to dedicate her life to fitness much like this perfect specimen of a woman obviously had. To jog eight miles instead of four, to buy a set of barbells or stretch bands or kettle balls. To give up bread and pasta. To follow whatever magic formula would yield killer abs like Cindy had.

"You're here to take the tour," Cindy said. She dropped her voice. "Mrs. Briggs called me yesterday to tell me you'd be by. You know we're all just heartsick over her husband's death. He was such a kind and lovely man. We've already posted a tribute to him on our website and plan to hold a memorial service tomorrow afternoon. Probably at the Eden Pool."

"I'm sure Doreen will appreciate your show of solidarity," Theodosia said.

But Cindy still seemed distressed. "It's just so weird. I mean, Gilded Magnolia Spa has only been open a little over two months. And Mr. Briggs seemed fairly healthy. He drank blueberry smoothies and worked out and everything."

"I guess a shot of poison trumps fitness any day," Theodosia said.

Cindy made a worried face. "Is that true? That's the rumor going around here, but is it really true?"

"It's what the police are saying."

"Wow. So somebody really . . . um . . ."

"Poisoned him," Theodosia said, filling in the blanks.

"How terrifying," Cindy said. She had a stricken look on her face, as if a maniac might pop out and offer her a chalice filled with hemlock at any moment.

"But you were going to show me around the spa," Theodosia said, bringing the conversation back to the subject at hand.

"Of course," Cindy said. "Right this way." She led Theodosia down a carpeted hallway. "The spa is basically one part fitness and one part beauty treatments." They stopped at a door and looked into a large, well-lit studio where a yoga class was taking place, everyone stretching and breathing and looking very Zen. "So we offer yoga, spin classes, Pilates, that sort of thing."

They continued down the hallway, hooked left, and walked into a small reception area with a fancy French desk and shelves lined with myriad spa products — lotions and potions and candles and creams.

"This is the entrance to our spa treatment area."

"It's lovely," Theodosia said. The walls and carpeting were blush pink with a few pieces of artwork that featured gilded ballerinas.

"We offer hot stone massage, manicures and pedicures, acupuncture, glycolic peels, Botox, and our special twenty-four-karat facials featuring real gold," Cindy said as they walked along, peeking into a few of the individual treatment rooms. She reached out and grabbed a fluffy towel. "Look, even our towels are embroidered with gold thread."

"This is all quite magnificent," Theodosia said. "A girl could spend the entire day here."

"Some ladies do," Cindy said.

"So how's business?" Theodosia asked.

After all, that's what was really on her mind. If the partner, Reggie Huston, was siphoning off money as fast as Opal Anne suspected he was, maybe Cindy had picked up on something.

"Business has been good," Cindy said. "At least I *think* it's good. There was a huge membership flurry when we first opened two months ago, but now it's settled down some. But I don't really deal with marketing and membership fees. And I sure don't have anything to do with accounts payable or receivable. That's all handled by our accountants."

"Who might they be?"

"We use an outside firm called Harrison and Whales. Big Reggie hired them."

Theodosia lifted an eyebrow. "Big Reggie?"

Cindy gave a sheepish smile. "That's what we call our co-owner, Reggie Huston. Although maybe he owns the whole thing now? Now that Mr. Briggs is, um . . . gone."

"Dead," Theodosia said. After all, Briggs hadn't just left the building, he had left the living. "But tell me about Big Reggie. Like, why do you call him Big Reggie?"

"Oh . . ." Cindy's eyes skittered away from her. "It's just something we dreamed up."

"I'm supposed to meet with Reggie in a

few minutes."

"Certainly," Cindy said. "Why don't we go check in with his office and see if he's ready for you? It'll probably be tight, though. Big Reggie's a very busy man."

"I'll just bet he is."

Sally, Reggie Huston's administrative assistant, was in a blind panic. Three phone lines were ringing, her desk was heaped with paper, her eyes carried a haunted look, and her hair looked like she'd just plugged herself into an electric light socket.

"Mr. Huston can only give you a few minutes," Sally told Theodosia in a tight voice. "He's working on the grand opening party so he's extremely busy."

"So I've been told," Theodosia said. She noted that Sally was a walking advertisement for stress. She decided that the poor girl really should slip down to a treatment room, slap a couple of cucumber slices on her eyelids, and try to chill out for a while. Maybe try chanting or meditation.

Sally knocked on Reggie's door. "Mr. Huston? Ms. Browning is here to see you." There was a noncommittal grunt from inside and then Sally, looking even more frightened, backed away from the door and said, "Go right in."

Big Reggie was sitting behind his desk, talking on the phone when Theodosia walked in. He was wearing white Bermuda shorts, a navy-and-white-striped shirt with the cuffs rolled up, and had his feet up on his credenza. His eyes slid lazily over to Theodosia and then slid back to where they'd been focused on his Tod's loafers.

"Yeah, I know," Reggie said. "I hear you." He chuckled softly. "I don't necessarily sympathize with you, but I know where you're coming from." He yawned, opening his mouth wide and impolitely, and then said, "Gotta go. Yeah, business. Talk to you later." He hung up the phone, swiveled his chair around, and let his feet crash to the floor.

"Hiya," he said to Theodosia, giving her a lazy smile.

Theodosia, who'd had time to study the framed photos on his desk, as well as the mosaic of photos plastered all over the walls of Reggie's office, said, "I love your photo display." She didn't really, of course. Big Reggie probably had an ego the size of a Russian czar, because he'd hung framed color photos of *himself* all over the place. Big Reggie standing next to his Porsche 911, on the golf course at Hilton Head, with his arm around a pretty dark-haired woman, playing polo, and posing with the governor of South Carolina.

"My wall of fame," Big Reggie said.

Wall of shame, Theodosia thought to herself. She noted that none of his photos had anything to do with Gilded Magnolia Spa; they were all vanity shots of Big Reggie. To Theodosia's eyes, Reggie Huston looked like an all-American hustler with a hint of playboy thrown in for good measure. But what she really wondered about was how Big Reggie got his all-American financing. Did he have family money or was he living off Beau Briggs's family money?

Big Reggie pushed up the sleeves of his shirt and eyed his Rolex Submariner watch. "I have a squash game in fifteen minutes. I'm sorry I can't give you any more time."

"This won't take long," Theodosia said. She sat down in the chair facing Big Reggie's desk and smiled. "As you may or may not know, Doreen Briggs has asked me to look into things for the family. That includes taking a look at Gilded Magnolia Spa."

Big Reggie frowned. "What are you? Some kind of auditor?"

"Something like that, yes," Theodosia said. Better to keep him guessing. "Doreen has concerns about the spa's financial stability."

"Who are you again?"

"Theodosia Browning."

"You're an attorney? Or . . . what? With the state board of health?"

"No. Like I said, I'm looking into things privately."

Reggie narrowed his eyes. "Wait a minute, I know you. I'm good with faces and I'm pretty sure I've seen you before."

Theodosia lifted an eyebrow. "Perhaps at the rat tea party?"

"That's it," Reggie said, pleased with himself. "I knew I'd figure it out eventually."

Actually, you didn't, Theodosia thought.

"So exactly what is it you want?" Reggie asked. He was starting to look bored.

Theodosia pitched her voice lower. "The murder of Beau Briggs . . ."

"Tragic," Reggie said. "A terrible loss."

"Still, I'm sure everyone here will soldier on."

"Of course we will. Heck yes." Reggie eyed her carefully. "You know, the initial report was that Beau choked to death."

"I guess after toxicology tests the medical examiner saw it differently," Theodosia said.

Reggie pretended to look interested. "Poison . . . yeah. I heard. Do they know, was it from the tea or something?"

"Not the tea. Apparently there was another method of delivery."

"So do they know how it got inside him?"

"No," Theodosia said. "Do you?"

Reggie seemed to uncoil himself like a big cat. He leaned across his desk and said, "Say, what is this? Some kind of setup?"

"Not at all. Like I told you, I'm helping Doreen out."

Doreen's name seemed to settle him down. "Doreen. Poor woman. What she must be going through."

"Concerning Beau's murder," Theodosia continued. "I've been looking into several different angles."

Reggie lifted a hand. "Such as?"

"Beau's financial dealings, for one thing. He didn't always make smart investments."

Reggie kept his poker face. "Is that so?"

"Then there's the matter of the guests who were sitting the closest to Beau just before he died."

Reggie didn't say a word.

"And then," Theodosia said, "there are the servers who worked at the rat tea."

Reggie looked interested. "You think one of those rat guys could have killed him?"

"It's certainly possible."

"I thought they were awfully strange," Reggie said. "Buzzing around our table all the time, wearing those crazy rat heads." He looked thoughtful. "They were kind of unnerving." His eyes locked on to hers. "A perfect disguise, yes?"

"Maybe," Theodosia said.

"Maybe the police didn't question them as carefully as they should have." Reggie stood up and kicked his chair back hard. "Maybe it's good you're asking questions. Maybe it's good that somebody from the outside *is* looking into this."

"Now you know why we call him Big Reggie," Cindy said as she led Theodosia back through the spa. "It's not just his size, it's his grandiose manner and zero-to-sixty temper!"

"He did seem a bit on edge," Theodosia said.

Cindy lowered her voice. "I heard that Reggie was kicked out of the Peninsula Grill once. And that he was, like, disbarred from the Greenvale Polo Club."

On their way out, Theodosia noticed the gift shop. "What a lovely-looking shop."

"You want to go in and take a look around?" Cindy asked.

"If it's part of the fifty-cent tour, why not?"

"If you see something you like," Cindy

said, "we'd be more than happy to give you a member discount."

"Thank you." Theodosia looked around at the spa robes, yoga pants, sport bras, special soaps and oils, and workout DVDs. Everything looked upscale and very well curated. She wondered if maybe some healthy, antioxidant teas would go well in here, too. "Who does your buying?" she asked.

"Mr. Briggs was in charge of merchandising," Cindy said.

"He had very good taste." A fancy display on the glass counter in front caught Theodosia's attention. Glam Baby Cosmetics. "This makeup line looks interesting."

"Oh." Cindy rolled her eyes. "That display just went in today. First we *weren't* going to carry the Glam Baby line and now it looks like we are. I don't know what changed, but . . . well, I just work here. I've got my marching orders and that's to be super accommodating to all our guests. Which, most of the time, is a genuine pleasure. I don't deal with vendors and I certainly don't have the power to say what products are carried in our gift shop."

"Who does have that power?"

"Well . . . I suppose now it's Big Reggie," Cindy said.

"Big Reggie," Theodosia said. "Who suddenly carries a very big vote."

Outside in the parking lot, Theodosia ran smack-dab into Bill Glass.

"What are you doing here?" Glass asked in his trademark blunt manner. He not only looked rumpled, he looked like he was lurking.

"It's a women's spa," Theodosia said. "What do you *think* I'm doing here?"

"Oh . . . yeah. Whatever."

"The question is, what are you doing here?"

"Taking a few photos for my article," Glass said. "The one on the Briggs murder."

"I really wish you'd drop that."

"No way," Glass sneered. "Beau Briggs was the mover and shaker behind this fancy spa, so I gotta have a little art on it." He patted one of the cameras slung around his neck and leaned against a red car.

"You there!" a loud voice boomed. "Get away from my car."

Theodosia turned to see Big Reggie thundering toward them like an enraged bull. His eyes were focused exclusively on Bill Glass.

"Stop leaning against my Porsche!" Reggie hollered. "If you so much as put a scratch on that factory finish I'll sue your sorry butt for everything it's worth. Don't you know that Amaranth Red Metallic costs a small fortune?"

Bill Glass put a fake, apologetic grin on his face. "Sorry, Mr. Huston. No harm intended."

"You," Reggie said, pointing a finger at him. "The photographer?"

Glass held up his camera in one hand and nodded pleasantly. "How about posing for a photo for *Shooting Star*?"

The idea of being in a photo appealed to Reggie. "Okay," he relented. "Maybe just a couple of shots. But make me look good, huh? Last time you caught me, I was eating a cracker at some stupid charity event and ended up looking like a blowfish."

"No problem, Mr. Huston," Glass said. He threw a surreptitious wink at Theodosia. "I'll make sure this shot's a winner." He raised his camera. "That's it, move over to the left a little bit so the spa's directly behind you. That's right. Perfect."

Snap.

14

It was midmorning when Theodosia knocked on Doreen's door. She'd gotten a weird vibe off Reggie Huston and wanted to see if Doreen felt the same way.

"Theodosia," Doreen exclaimed when she opened the door, dressed in a peppermint-green top and slacks. "What a surprise."

Is it really, Doreen?

"I just took a tour of Gilded Magnolia Spa," Theodosia said. "As you suggested. And then had a short meeting with Reggie Huston."

"Isn't Reggie a sweetheart?" Doreen asked. Without waiting for a reply, she said, "Come," and led Theodosia down a long hallway and into a bright and airy sunroom. Interestingly enough, Honey Whitley, her next-door neighbor, was there. "You remember Honey, don't you?"

"Of course," Theodosia said. "Nice to see you again."

"Hello, dear," Honey said as she stretched languorously on a chaise longue. Honey wore white distressed jeans, a pink designer T-shirt, and sandals. Her toenails were painted the same color pink as her shirt. Maybe she got perks at Gilded Magnolia Spa?

"Can I get you something?" Doreen asked. "Lemonade? Tea?"

Theodosia thought about the dusty box of tea in the pantry and said, "No thanks. I just have a couple of quick questions for you."

"Don't mind me, dear," Honey said, waving a hand.

I don't mind you right now, Theodosia thought. *But I will if you continue to be overly solicitous by calling me* dear.

Theodosia took a seat in a wicker chair; Doreen sat down across from her.

"So how was your visit to the spa?" Doreen asked.

"Gilded Magnolia Spa was lovely," Theodosia said. "But I'd like to ask you a few questions about Reggie Huston."

"Yes?"

"Will he be taking over the day-to-day running of the spa?"

Doreen's face crumpled. "That's . . . I don't know . . . completely up in the air for now. I don't think I can make any critical decisions until after the funeral."

"That's smart," Honey said.

Theodosia continued. "Opal Anne mentioned to me that you might want to step in and run the spa."

"I don't know about that," Doreen said, looking a little panicked.

"You'd never be able to juggle that many things," Honey said. "How on earth would you keep up this great big house, attend to your social obligations, and run a spa?"

"I . . . I don't know," Doreen said, looking overwhelmed. "It all sounds baffling. Enough to give me a case of the whim-whams." She leaned closer to Theodosia. "Did you get any further in your inquiry with Robert Steele about the, uh, money?"

"Drayton and I attended Steele's presentation last night," Theodosia said.

"Did you ask him for the money?"

"We didn't quite get around to that. The venue was a little too public."

Doreen frowned. "But you *will* get around to it, won't you?"

"I'm going to try," Theodosia said. She wondered exactly when "functioning as a collection agency" had been tacked on to her job description.

"Because seven hundred thousand dollars

is a princely sum of money," Doreen said.

"*Seven hundred thousand?*" Honey exclaimed. "My Lord, that's a small fortune!"

Before Theodosia was able to figure out if Doreen had spilled the beans to Honey about Beau's bad investments, she heard a hubbub of voices just outside the sunroom. Seconds later, Opal Anne and Charles appeared.

Once everyone had exchanged polite hellos, a tearful Doreen grabbed Opal Anne's hand and said, "Well? Tell me."

"All the arrangements have been finalized," Opal Anne said. "We went to Gruenwald Brothers and confirmed the details."

"And then we stopped by the church," Charles added.

"The music?" Doreen asked in a whisper.

"That's all been taken care of," Opal Anne said.

"Oh, thank goodness," Doreen blubbered, gazing at Theodosia and then at Honey. "You see how it's simply too traumatic for me to handle Beau's final arrangements? Thank heavens that Opal Anne and Charles are doing it for me."

"So kind," Honey murmured.

"Now I just have to stumble through the funeral," Doreen said, sniffling. She shook her head as if to clear it, pulled a Kleenex from her pocket. "But we'll cross that bridge when we come to it."

"You'll do fine," Opal Anne said. She threw a hopeful gaze at Theodosia. "You have news for us?"

"Mostly she just had questions," Doreen said. "Although Theodosia's made some decent progress, I must say."

"I didn't realize you were a private investigator," Honey said in a tone that sounded almost hostile.

"I'm not," Theodosia said. "I'm just looking into a few things for Doreen."

"And the police aren't?" Honey said.

"Theodosia's practically working *with* them," Opal Anne said, rushing to her defense. "And she's been doing a wonderful job."

"After you talk to Robert Steele," Doreen said, "what's next on your agenda?"

"For one thing," Theodosia said, "I want to look into the rat costumes."

"Rat costumes?" Honey said with a touch of scorn. "I can't imagine they'd lead anywhere."

"I'm actually trying to get a bead on one of the servers," Theodosia said.

Doreen blinked at her. "Which one? And why?"

"There's one particular young man I'd

176

like to speak with again," Theodosia said. "I exchanged a few words with him last Saturday but . . ."

Opal Anne jumped in again. "But back then Theodosia hadn't been enlisted to play detective yet. Had you, Theo?"

Theodosia smiled as she rose to her feet. "Not yet. But now things have changed."

"And thank goodness you're here to help," Opal Anne said.

Honey waved a hand dismissively at Theodosia. "Good luck with your rats," she said with a barely suppressed giggle.

Theodosia rushed in the back door of the Indigo Tea Shop, dropped her bag on her desk, snatched up an apron, and sprinted for the front of the shop.

"Honey, I'm home," she called out in a joking manner.

But she was also worried that Drayton might be overwhelmed with handling their morning's tea service and getting ready for their Madame Pompadour Tea luncheon.

Haley leaned out of the kitchen and caught her as she ran by. "Hey, Theo. Do you want to know what we're serving for lunch today?"

Theodosia skidded to a stop. "Absolutely, I do."

"I tried to come up with a French-inspired menu. In honor of . . . you know . . ."

"Madame de Pompadour."

"Anyway," Haley said, "we'll start with rose petal scones . . ."

"Wait a minute. With real rose petals?"

"Duh." Haley put her hands on her hips. "Of course."

"Wow."

"Then we'll move on to a small plate that includes three mini sandwiches. Brie cheese and fig spread on brioche, duck mousse pâté on French bread, and ham with Dijon mustard on a mini croissant."

"My kind of grazer's lunch," Theodosia said. "What's for dessert?"

"What else?" Haley said. "Macarons and *pain au chocolat*."

"This is all very fabulous and French. Have you shared this menu with Drayton?"

"Oh, totally. I printed out mini menus on fancy purple-and-gold paper for all our guests. And I gave one to him."

"Always a step ahead, aren't you, Haley?"

"Better than a step behind."

"And we're all set for the funeral luncheon tomorrow?" Theodosia asked. "No problems?"

Haley nodded. "The menu suggestions you gave me are easy peasy. And I already called Miss Dimple to see if she can come in tomorrow and help serve."

"Drayton and I shouldn't be gone more than a couple of hours. I'm sure the two of you can handle things just fine."

"I know we can."

"Theodosia," came Drayton's voice. "Is that you?"

"Oh my, it's the master's voice," Haley said. "Tea master, anyway."

"Scuse me," Theodosia said as he darted into the tea room. "Yes, I'm back," she said to Drayton. "Sorry to be so late."

"Thank goodness you're finally here," Drayton said with a sigh. "I've been working like a one-armed paperhanger all morning."

Theodosia looked around the tea room. Half the tables were occupied and everyone seemed content. The fragrant aromas of Assam, Nilgiri, and jasmine hung in the air, along with the quiet hum of conversation. The tea room looked perfectly copacetic. "You've been busy?"

"Frantic," Drayton said.

"It doesn't look frantic."

"Looks can be deceiving, Theo. Suffice it to say I *missed* you. But enough about my woes. How was your visit to Gilded Magnolia Spa? Did you learn anything new?"

179

"For one thing, I met Big Reggie."

Drayton threw her a quizzical look. "*Big Reggie?*"

"That's what everyone who works there calls Reggie Huston," Theodosia said. "Mostly because of his big personality and big, bad temper."

"That doesn't sound particularly encouraging."

"In meeting Reggie, he struck me as someone who loves having a fancy title, but doesn't really want to do any of the work."

"In other words, he's living off Beau Briggs's good graces," Drayton said.

"More likely Doreen Briggs's good money."

"Ouch."

"It's not a good situation at all," Theodosia said. "I'm guessing that if Big Reggie continues to run the spa, he'll fleece Doreen like a prize sheep. Until she eventually goes broke."

Drayton looked downcast. "That's terrible. So . . . where do we go from here? What do we do next? How do we put a stop to Big Reggie's reign of terror?"

Theodosia tapped a toe nervously and looked around. "I'm not sure. It's an awful lot to think about. Maybe we should worry about our Madame Pompadour Tea first?

We've got almost twenty reservations and I'm sure a few more people will wander in looking for lunch."

Drayton nodded. "I suppose you're right. But please, Theo, keep working on this."

"I will. You know I will."

Wednesday might have been their Madame Pompadour Tea, but it was also let's-stop-in-for-lunch-at-the-Indigo-Tea-Shop Day for Theodosia and Drayton. Their reservations streamed in, as well as customers who just popped in for the fun of it. Two B and Bs (not the Scarborough Inn) sent groups of guests their way, and a horse-drawn jitney stopped outside and all the passengers jumped off and came tumbling in. Except, of course, for the chestnut horse, who was given a feed bag as he waited patiently outside.

"This is crazy," Drayton said as teakettles burbled and teapots steeped, enveloping them in a fragrant cloud of steam. "We're absolutely jammed."

"Just keep those pots of tea coming," Theodosia told him. She was taking orders, rushing them into the kitchen, then picking up finished orders to deliver to tables. Drayton had brewed Adagio Tea's Madame de Pompadour, a lavender tea imbued with fresh fruit flavors and a hint of smokiness, and that had proven to be a huge favorite. That and the rose petal scones.

"We can't keep up this pace," Drayton said as Theodosia grabbed two just-filled floral teapots.

"Can you say 'profitable'?" she asked. "Remember how I talked about making a profit versus just making a living?"

"We're making a profit?" Drayton asked.

Theodosia nodded.

"Then I shall work harder. My two-week vacation to the tea shops and manor homes of the Cotswolds still looms on the horizon. Along with my need for plane tickets and hotel reservations."

"And by the way, you're supposed to be out there front and center to give a little speech."

"Do I have to?" Drayton asked.

"People will expect it," Theodosia said. "I'm sure you don't want to disappoint."

"No," he said, "you're right. The Indigo Tea Shop never disappoints."

So Drayton traded his apron for a tweed jacket, gave his bow tie a final tug, and stepped around the corner.

"Ladies and gentlemen," he said. "Welcome to our Madame Pompadour Tea." Necks craned, chairs swiveled, and all eyes were suddenly on Drayton. He held up one of the menus. "You've all received souvenir menus, so you're quite familiar with the delicious food we'll be serving today. But I thought I'd give you a short primer on Madame Pompadour herself." He gave a quick smile and continued. "The marquise de Pompadour, also known as Madame Pompadour, was a member of the French court and a close friend and confidant to King Louis XV. At an early age, she played the clavichord, danced, sang, and painted. It was this artistic beginning that laid the groundwork for her prestigious position at court. She became a major patron of architecture and the arts and was a patron of the philosophers of the Enlightenment, including Voltaire. As a champion of French pride, we salute Madame Pompadour's accomplishments today with our special tea, French cheeses, pâtés, macarons, and *pain au chocolat.*"

"C'est magnifique," someone called out as Drayton finished.

Another woman shouted, *"Très bien!"*

"Do you think they liked it?" Drayton asked as he joined Theodosia back at the counter.

"No," she said. "I think they loved it."

■ ■ ■ ■

By one thirty, the luncheon was pretty much concluded and Theodosia found a little time to breathe. Good thing, because Delaine came strutting in like an entitled grand duchess. Looking like one, too, in a plum-colored tweed skirt suit, matching cap set with a jaunty feather, and an enormous jewel-encrusted pin on her jacket lapel.

"You just missed our Madame Pompadour Tea," Theodosia told her.

Delaine waved a hand. "No time."

"You want to grab a quick bite?" Theodosia asked. She looked around. "Maybe sit by the window?"

Delaine's feather bobbed in agreement as Theodosia led her to a table.

"I'm still holding several dresses for you," Delaine said as she plopped down and made herself comfortable. "I wish you'd find time to drop by Cotton Duck."

"I'll for sure try," Theodosia said. "But I've been awfully busy."

"Haven't we all," Delaine said. She pulled a compact from her purse and hastily checked her lipstick.

Something about the small bronze disk looked familiar to Theodosia. "Your compact . . ."

"Glam Baby Cosmetics," Delaine said, smiling at herself in the tiny mirror and then snapping it shut.

"Now isn't that interesting. I was just looking at some of their products this morning. Over at Gilded Magnolia Spa."

Delaine raised her thinly penciled brows. "The spa is carrying Glam Baby in their gift shop?"

"Yes, they are. How do you know about those products?"

"Glam Baby is a brand-new line that was just being introduced when I attended the Makeup Show in Orlando," Delaine said. "Who knows, if it gets popular enough I might start carrying it at Cotton Duck." She gave Theodosia a thin smile. "The woman who developed that makeup line lives right here in Charleston. In fact, she stopped by my shop earlier this week to deliver her sales pitch along with a few nice samples."

"Who's that?" Theodosia asked. "Do I know her?"

"I don't think so. Her name is Jemma Lee and . . . well, you can read about her right here . . ." Delaine snapped open her bright red Chanel bag and pulled out a colorful brochure. She handed it to Theodosia. "It tells all about Miss Lee and her products.

You're welcome to keep that brochure if you want."

Theodosia skimmed the brochure, which pictured a number of Glam Baby products, all encased in cool, bronze-hued compacts and tubes. "This is a pretty comprehensive line," she said.

"Isn't it?" Delaine said.

Theodosia turned to the brochure's back page. A color photo showed Jemma Lee, the makeup line's founder, smiling brightly. The woman had dark hair, wide-set, slightly canted eyes, and wore lots of bright red lipstick on her pouty lips.

With a start, Theodosia recognized her.

Wait a minute. Isn't this the woman Big Reggie had his arm around in the photo that was sitting on his desk? Sure it is. It has to be the same girl. Now I know how she managed to get her products into the spa's gift shop so easily.

"Excuse me," Delaine said. "About how many carbs are there in one of your scones?"

Theodosia looked up from the brochure. "I don't know, maybe twenty?"

Delaine made a face. "That sounds a little low to me."

"Okay, then, thirty-six carbs. Does that make you happy?"

"No!" Delaine shrieked. "Absolutely not.

Perhaps I'd better order a poached chicken breast instead."

"We've got chicken mousse pâté."

Delaine shook her head.

"Suit yourself then."

Delaine stared at Theodosia through half-lidded eyes. "You know, Theo, man — and particularly woman — does not live by bread alone. You have to incorporate a little Paleo in your diet as well."

"Got it," Theodosia said. She pulled out her order pad. "One low-carb, no sauce, no salt, poached chicken breast coming right up."

"Thank you."

As fresh as if I'd just grabbed the bird and wrung its little neck. Or yours.

As soon as Theodosia put in Delaine's order, she told Drayton about Glam Baby Cosmetics.

"The thing is, they weren't going to carry the makeup line at all, and now they are."

"You think Big Reggie killed Beau just so his girlfriend could have her makeup line in the gift shop?" Drayton asked. "I find that awfully far-fetched."

"Are you kidding?" Theodosia said. "These days perfect strangers are murdered for twenty bucks and a carton of Marlboros.

Or a slightly dented laptop computer."

Drayton shook his head. "It's a different world. You see why I try to resist change?"

"And a fine job you do," Haley said as she swung by to drop off a plate of scones. "No cell phone or laptop computer for Drayton, and he only plays vinyl records on . . . wait, what was that called again? A phonograph?" She chuckled. "Your life is like a perfect time capsule from 1972."

"You weren't even born then," Drayton said.

Haley cocked her head and grinned. "That doesn't mean I don't know about the olden days."

"Kindly don't upset the tea sommelier," Drayton said. "He might just spill something on you."

Haley raised both hands in a sign of surrender. "Okay. I'm going, I'm going."

Drayton turned to Theodosia. "About your boy, Fat Reggie . . ."

"Big Reggie," Theodosia said.

"Whatever," Drayton said. "I don't think he'd kill his business partner just to get his girlfriend's line into the gift shop. It's not that big a deal. But he certainly could be embezzling the spa's money."

"Or he might have designs on running the place all by himself," Theodosia said.

"Do you think Gilded Magnolia is profitable?"

"Run correctly, I think the spa could be extremely profitable," Theodosia said. "They're high-end, don't have a lot of competition, and offer a very desirable product."

Drayton looked curious. "That being . . . ?"

"Pampering."

By two thirty, Theodosia was sitting in her office, noshing on a scone, and sipping a cup of oolong tea.

"What do you think of that Simpson & Vail oolong?" Drayton asked. He was suddenly lounging in the doorway, looking very dapper in his gray herringbone jacket and primrose-pink bow tie.

"It's delicious. Very fresh and bright, with a fragrance like honeysuckle."

"What is it you're doing on that computer of yours?" he asked.

"Exactly what you asked me to do. I'm running a search on Angel Oak Venture Capital." Theodosia's expression turned to one of concern. "From what I've found so far, they don't exactly have a stellar track record."

"Does that surprise you?"

"I guess not. Not considering the way Robert Steele was pitching last night anyway. With his slick huckster salesman's patois."

"Maybe because he really is a slick huckster?" Drayton asked.

"According to an article I found that ran in the *Post and Courier*'s business section, the state attorney general has looked into his company a couple of times."

"That's never good," Drayton said. "Do you think Steele completely conned Beau Briggs out of his money?"

"I don't know. And I'm not exactly sure how to find out, short of dangling a pile of money in front of Mr. Steele."

"To see if he lunges at it like a hungry crocodile?"

Theodosia smiled as she glanced back at her screen. "Something like that."

"I spoke with Timothy Neville earlier today."

Theodosia looked up from her work again. "About Doreen's grant? Or possible grant?"

"Obviously that's preying on Timothy's mind. But he has something else that he's bouncing around, too. He wondered if we could drop by the Heritage Society later this afternoon. Would you have time?"

"I think so," Theodosia said. "Why? What's

up?" She picked up a copy of *The Tea House Times* and began thumbing through it, her eyes falling upon a short review of a new tea shop that had just opened in Savannah.

"Timothy is interested in harnessing our brain power."

That caught Theodosia's attention even more. "Brainstorming? About what?"

"I don't know. I suppose we'll have to wander over there and find out."

15

In Drayton's eyes, the Heritage Society wasn't just a nonprofit organization. To him it was a temple of knowledge, a place where like-minded history buffs gathered to exchange ideas, and a repository of fine art and cultural treasures.

To Theodosia, the Heritage Society represented a grand old building with stone turrets, creaking staircases, lead-paned windows, and enormous fireplaces. Add in the Oriental rugs, velvet draperies, leather furniture, fine art, and private library, and you had a place you could practically call home, should your taste run to medieval castles or eighteenth-century manor homes. It was baronial splendor at its best. In her wildest fantasies, she could almost imagine living there.

"Let me check in at the reception desk first," Drayton said as they entered the marble-tiled foyer. "I probably have a few memos and a stack of mail waiting for . . ." He stopped abruptly as a woman in a black leather jacket came barreling out of nowhere. "Whoa!" His tin of tea was almost knocked out of his hands.

The woman skidded to a wild stop in front of him and flashed an angry, confrontational glance, as if Drayton had no business blocking her way.

Theodosia instantly recognized Starla Crane.

"Starla?" she said.

Starla, who also recognized Theodosia and Drayton at the exact same moment, planted herself stolidly in front of them and said, "What on earth are you two doing here?"

Theodosia wanted to ask her the same thing, but deferred to Drayton for an explanation.

"If you must know," Drayton said, "I serve on the Heritage Society's board of directors."

"Oh really," Starla said in a condescending tone.

"Let's go," Theodosia said. They didn't have to stand there and put up with Starla's nonsense.

"If you'll excuse us," Drayton said, "we have a rather important meeting to attend." They brushed past her, with Starla barely yielding an inch.

"Well, la-di-da," Starla called out, throwing them another hostile glance.

"I wonder what *she* was doing here?" Theodosia said, once they were halfway down the hallway and out of earshot.

"No idea," Drayton said. "But I detest the idea of her setting foot in this place. I love the Heritage Society, and I don't want it touched by her bad temperament."

"I hear you," Theodosia said. Starla had invaded Drayton's turf and it had unsettled him to no end.

Drayton stopped in front of the arched doorway that led into the Great Hall. "But I refuse to let that woman bother me." They both gazed into the Great Hall, where curators and their assistants were scurrying around, setting up a new installation. "You see what's going in?" he said. "A rare weapons show featuring pieces used in the military, as well as for hunting and dueling."

"That sounds like it could prove very popular," Theodosia said.

"Which is exactly what we need right now. An exhibit that will bring more people in."

"Bring more money in," Theodosia said. "That seems to be the major concern."

They continued down the hallway and

then veered left into the administrative wing, where most of the offices were housed. Stopping outside a large door, Drayton knocked softly. "Timothy?"

"Come in," Timothy Neville called out. "It's open."

"It's us," Drayton said as they both filed into Timothy's slightly darkened office.

Timothy gave a faint smile. "About time."

Timothy Neville was an octogenarian with the mental faculties and spryness of someone forty years younger. His skin stretched tightly over his compact skull, his dark eyes were pools of intensity, and he was lean and angular. He sat (in a special chair raised to make him appear taller) behind an enormous rosewood desk littered with antique magazines and anchored by a fine old Cartier pen set in a solid gold holder. A bronze dog made by the French artist Emmanuel Frémiet held a large stack of papers in place.

Timothy himself was impeccably dressed in a gray pinstripe suit. His pocket square was red Chinese silk and his Church brogues were buffed to a high-gloss shine. His office looked just as buffed. High, varnished shelves held all manner of antiquities that included rare coins, Greek statues, American pottery, and even a jeweled crown that had once belonged to some long-exiled Russian prince.

"We just ran into a PR person out in your lobby," Theodosia began. "Starla Crane of . . ."

"The Image Factory," Timothy said. "Yes, Miss Crane was just here, making a pitch to our marketing people. I sat in for a short while."

"Please tell me you're not going to hire her," Theodosia said.

Timothy's expression remained benign. "The young woman's not your cup of tea?"

"She's rude and abrasive," Theodosia said. "Other than that, she may be very good at what she does."

"Forewarned is forearmed," Timothy said. "A sandpaper personality would definitely not play well with our rather genteel members and donors."

Theodosia was about to say more when she suddenly realized that Starla could have been sent here covertly on a fact-finding mission. Could Doreen be relying on Starla's advice to help her allocate grant money? Had Starla been doing due diligence on the Heritage Society? She fervently hoped not. Should she say something to Timothy? She decided that she almost had to.

"You know," Theodosia said, "Starla Crane has been doing a good deal of PR work for Doreen Briggs."

Timothy looked at her sharply. "Is that right?"

"Which means," Theodosia continued, "that Starla could have been sent here as a kind of scout."

Timothy's brows pinched together. "You mean Starla Crane might possibly hold sway over Doreen Briggs's decision to award us a grant?"

"It's possible," Theodosia said. She felt kind of sick telling Timothy all this. But there was more to reveal. A lot more.

"As you know, Drayton and I have been counting on receiving a rather large grant from Doreen Briggs," Timothy said. "If that doesn't come through, our goose could be cooked."

"There's a problem," Drayton said. He set his tin of tea down on Timothy's desk.

"I can see that," Timothy said.

"No," Drayton said. "I mean there's an even *bigger* problem. Tell him, Theo."

Theodosia drew a deep breath. "The Charleston police are looking at Doreen as a possible suspect in her husband's death." There. It was out in the open now. Spit out like a hunk of bad-tasting meat.

197

Timothy registered shock all the way down to his silk socks. "What!" He hunched forward in his chair. "Doreen Briggs is a suspect? How is that even possible?"

"It just *is* possible," Theodosia said. "Doreen was right there when her husband was poisoned. She could have even been the one who slipped it to him."

"It's possible, but not probable," Drayton said.

Theodosia shook her head. "We don't know that, Drayton. We haven't gotten that far yet."

"Gotten that far," Timothy repeated. "You two are looking into her husband's death?"

"Somewhat," Drayton hedged.

"Yes, we are," Theodosia said. "And I hate to say this, but Doreen has been making us jump through hoops every step of the way. In fact, she's been dangling your grant over our heads. If we find the killer, you get the grant."

"Oh no," Timothy said slowly. "She's using our grant as a carrot."

"But we only get our carrot if Doreen isn't the killer," Drayton said.

Timothy shook his head and pulled his lips into an icy smile. "Because Doreen would find it rather difficult to write a check sitting in a cozy little cell at Leath Correctional."

Drayton lifted a hand. "When you put it that way . . ."

"We've got to put her on the back burner, then, and consider other sources of funding," Timothy said. "Some sort of stopgap until I can either rally our donors or our numbers people can fumble their way through this up-and-down stock market."

"Things are that bad?" Drayton asked.

"We're going to need an act of God to keep this place open," Timothy said.

"Is the Heritage Society running at a deficit?" Theodosia asked.

"Not right now we're not," Timothy said. "But we will be shortly. The problem is, and I know Drayton has gone over some of this with you, our investments are flat as a pancake. So are our donations." Timothy rapped a knuckle against his desk and cocked his head at Theodosia and Drayton. "So I'm wondering what we can do."

"Perhaps another fund-raiser?" Drayton said.

Timothy shifted uncomfortably in his chair. "We've done innumerable fund-raisers and we've done them to death. Orchid Lights, Crystal Ball, seasonal galas, garden parties ad nauseam." Now he focused his gaze directly on Theodosia. "What we need is some fresh thinking. Something that's outside the box, perhaps even outside our comfort zone." He bent his head forward and massaged the sides of his head with the tips of his fingers. "I've been thinking about this — *worrying* about this non-stop — and I haven't come up with a single idea."

Theodosia was silent for a few moments, thinking about Timothy's predicament. Then she said, "I can think of only one thing at the moment. But it might be a bit unorthodox . . ."

Timothy lifted his head. "Try me. I'm open to any and all suggestions at this point."

Theodosia took a deep breath. "Have you ever thought about deacquisitioning some of your art and antiquities?"

Timothy looked at her sharply. "Excuse me?"

"I don't believe we're *that* open to suggestion," Drayton said hastily. "Selling off pieces is definitely outside our comfort zone."

"Hear me out," Theodosia said. "There are a lot of top museums that deacquisition pieces on a fairly regular basis. I mean, if the Met in New York or the de Young in San Francisco can sell off a couple dozen pieces a year, why can't the Heritage Society?"

"Selling off some of our inventory never occurred to me," Timothy said.

But Drayton still looked upset. "I hate to think of all our valuable pieces marching out the door."

"Then don't sell the really valuable pieces," Theodosia reasoned. "You must have duplicates of some things. I know you have paintings and antique furniture that have been in storage so long the donors have long since forgotten about them. In some cases the donors are even deceased."

"That's true," Timothy said. "Many of our donated pieces date back to the middle eighteen hundreds."

"There you go," Theodosia said. "Get your curators to go through the collection with a fine-tooth comb. Keep the good stuff, weed out the pieces that aren't all that relevant to your mission today, or are second rate, or just don't fit with your collection anymore."

"And sell it where?" Drayton asked in an arch tone. "On eBay?"

"Send it to Sotheby's in New York," Theodosia said. "Or Bonhams or 1stdibs or wherever. But, for goodness' sake, don't apologize for the fact that you're deacquisitioning. Make a big deal of it, like it's the smart, forward-thinking thing to do."

"That's a very skillful PR attitude," Timothy said. "And certainly not a bad idea at all." He leaned back in his chair and steepled his fingers together, furrowing his brow as if in deep thought. "In fact, it's a very *interesting* idea."

Theodosia smiled. When Timothy said something was interesting, that was high praise indeed. It meant he was probably in.

One of Timothy's gnarled hands reached out and tapped the top of the tea tin. "What is this you brought me?"

"It's Keemun Hao Ya," Drayton said. "Very rich and full-bodied."

"Excellent," Timothy said. "Yes, this should all work quite nicely."

Theodosia smiled. She knew he wasn't talking about the tea.

"Are you up for one more errand?" Theodosia asked as they climbed into her Jeep.

Drayton glanced at his watch. "I suppose. What did you have in mind?"

"I think we should visit that costume supply company," she said as they pulled away from the curb.

"Did you ever find the name for it?" He pulled the seat belt across and fastened it.

Theodosia nodded. "I sure did. It's Big

Top Costumes over on Fulton Street."

"Do you really think this will prove worth-while?" Drayton asked as they drove along.

"It's a long shot. But you never know. Mostly I'm trying to get a bead on that one particular server."

"And you think the costume shop can help? I thought you said the costumes were just sent over to Crispin's Catering."

"They were," Theodosia said. "So this really is a long shot."

It was a long shot in more ways than one. Because Mort Ruskin, the owner of Big Top Costumes, was reluctant to offer much in the way of assistance.

"If you could just answer a couple of questions about the rat costumes," Theodosia said.

Mort rolled his eyes. "Those darned things." Mort had a hangdog face, rounded shoulders, and slumped so badly he resembled a truculent teenager. He wore a rumpled white shirt and brown slacks; his shirt hung open at the neck and his too-wide necktie hung down practically to his knees.

"I'm guessing you already know what took place at Doreen Briggs's rat tea," Drayton said.

"Heard about it, yeah," Mort said. "Read

about it in the newspaper, too. Terrible thing. Don't blame it on the costumes, though. Or my company. Not my fault, not my fault." He shook his head vigorously and threw up both arms in a manner that was reminiscent of Richard Nixon giving his "I'm not a crook!" speech.

"So the white rat costumes are here?" Theodosia said.

"They're not really costumes per se," Mort said. "The jackets and pants are from our Napoleonic collection. Lots of call for that, lots of folks here with Frenchie ancestors."

"And the rat heads?" Theodosia asked.

"The rat heads come from our Nutcracker collection," Mort said. "You know, those ballet-dancing rats?" He gave a dry chuckle that turned into a wheeze. "Anyway, we just put the two elements together for that so-called rat tea. Hah! Look where it got us."

"Look where it got Beau Briggs," Drayton said.

"We're interested in . . ." Theodosia began.

But before the words had escaped her mouth, Mort shook his head and said, "No, no, no. I'm not gonna let that stuff go out of here again."

"Why not?" Drayton asked.

Mort seemed to fish around for a reasonable answer. "Uh . . . for one thing, those costumes need to be dry-cleaned."

"Listen," Theodosia said hurriedly, "we just need one quick favor. We only want to check the costumes, okay? Not wear them. Something might have been left in one of the . . . um . . . pockets."

Mort scrunched up his face. "Who are you people with again?"

With an absolute straight face, Drayton said, "Crispin's Catering."

Mort seemed to relax some. "Why didn't you say so in the first place? Okay, yeah. I guess you could *look* at them. But that's all." Seemingly relieved to be done with them, he waved an arm. "Go through that door, it's the rack on your left. Eight costumes. And don't think I haven't counted them."

The back room of Big Top Costumes was a melting pot of Halloween, circus, animal, World War II, and princess party costumes, along with every opera or Broadway play that had ever been cast, staged, and produced. Costumes were flung on tables, hung on racks, and even suspended from rods in the ceiling. The scent of mustiness, mothballs, and dry cleaning fluid permeated the air.

"This is awful," Drayton said. "Like a way station for old costumes. A purgatory of sorts."

"Don't think about it, Drayton," Theodosia said, quickly locating the rack they were looking for. "Here are the rat costumes right here. The jackets and stuff." She wasted no time in sifting through them. "And look at this, there *are* pockets."

"Find anything?"

"Not yet." Theodosia started digging through the jacket pockets like mad.

Drayton stared at the rat heads that were lined up on a shelf directly above the costume rack. "Does this look strange to you? All these heads, I mean?"

"This whole thing has been one strange litany," Theodosia said. She was on her fourth costume, patting the jacket, digging in the pockets of the pants, trying not to sneeze as the aroma of mothballs tickled her nose. "Come on, Drayton, give me a hand. Before that guy Mort comes back and kicks us out of here."

Drayton got busy then, working shoulder to shoulder with Theodosia. "This dry cleaning fluid is killing my sinuses."

"I hear you — it's awful," she said.

"I'm . . ." Drayton sneezed so abruptly it sounded like an explosion. "Excuse me."

He pulled out a hankie and swiped at his eyes and nose.

"Hey there," Theodosia said, excitement tingeing her voice. "I think I might have found something."

"What is it?"

"Not sure." Theodosia pulled a crumpled slip of paper from one of the pockets. "Let's take a look."

"What is it? Looks like a fortune cookie message."

"No, I think it's something else." She unfolded the paper and studied it.

"Let me see," Drayton said. "Wait, you'd better read it to me, my eyes are watering."

"It says 'Port City Bistro.' And there's a time stamp on it."

"Port City is a fairly tony restaurant over on Market Street," Drayton said.

Theodosia rubbed the paper between her fingers. "I think this is a parking receipt."

"Maybe one of the rats works there?"

"Let's go find out," Theodosia said. "Let's pay him a visit."

16

By the time they pulled up in front of the restaurant it was full-on dark. A trendy neon sign with chase lights spelled out PORT CITY BISTRO; more lights glowed in the windows. Two young men in matching red jackets with gold trim looked bored out of their minds as they stood in front of a stand that said VALET PARKING $5.

Inside Port City Bistro, the dining room was elegant and dimly lit. It wasn't exactly a fig and fern bar, more like the next generation's iteration of upscale orchids and candles. White linen tablecloths covered the tables, nautical photos and paraphernalia hung on whitewashed walls, a central fireplace, low and square in its modernity, flames dancing, lent a cheery air. A few early bird couples occupied tables while most of the real action seemed concentrated in the bar just off to their left.

It was still a little early for dinner, Theodosia decided. And it would seem that most of Port City's customers were assembled in the bar — folks who'd fled their work cubicles for the day and dropped in for a quick cocktail. Or maybe not so quick.

"You see anyone you recognize?" Drayton asked. "From the rat tea?"

"Not yet," Theodosia said. "But I've only seen one of the waitstaff so far and it's a woman."

"I'll go check the bar."

"Good thinking," Theodosia said.

Just as Drayton headed off to the bar, a waiter emerged from a swinging door at the rear of the restaurant.

"Excuse me," Theodosia said, holding up a hand. Then her heart began to beat a little faster. This wasn't the young man they were looking for, but she was pretty sure she recognized this waiter. He was the pink rat who'd escorted them to their table. He was in his late thirties or early forties with a long face, bushy eyebrows, and a pompadour hairdo that hearkened back to the fifties.

"The hostess will be right with you, ma'am," the waiter called to her.

Theodosia crooked a finger at him. "Actually, it's you I need a word with."

"Who, me?" The waiter came closer, clearly puzzled. The name tag on his black

209

jacket said PERRY.

"You were one of the waiters who worked at the rat tea last Saturday, weren't you?" Theodosia asked

A look of worry seeped across Perry's face. "If you're with the cops, I already told you I'm not your guy. I'm no killer, okay? Go bother somebody else."

"I'm not with the cops. I'm a friend of Doreen's."

"Who's Doreen?" Perry asked.

"She's the woman who hosted the rat tea. The one whose husband was poisoned." Theodosia had seen this man Perry before. And not just at the rat tea. Maybe working in another restaurant?

"Listen, you're still barking up the wrong tree," Perry said. "I already talked to the cops. I'm sorry but I don't know anything about poison. I've worked in the hospitality industry for over fifteen years and I've never even seen a case of *food* poisoning."

"Wait a minute," Theodosia said. "I know you. You used to work at Solstice, right?"

"That's right," Perry said. "And now I'm working here and I really like it." He leaned toward her and lowered his voice. "I want to keep this job, okay? Please don't make trouble for me."

"I only have a quick question," Theodosia said.

"About . . . ?"

"The young guy who was working the rat tea along with you. The blond guy with the spiky hair. When the police had all you guys lined up on Saturday, he looked like he knew something but was holding back."

"You're talking about Marcus?"

"Marcus?" Theodosia said, pouncing on his words. "That's his name?"

"Yeah," Perry said. "Marcus Covey. I've worked with him a couple times through Crispin's Catering. He always seemed like an okay kid. But now that you mention it, he did seem a little shaky last Saturday." Perry looked around to make sure the hostess or his boss wasn't about to holler at him. "But you could chalk it up to that poor guy dropping dead. You don't see nasty stuff like that every day."

"Do you know where Marcus lives?" Theodosia asked as she noticed Drayton heading right toward her. She held up a finger to stop him.

Perry shook his head. "I don't have Marcus's home address per se, but I can give you directions to his place. He asked me to pick him up once when we were both working a freelance gig at the Campbell Club."

"Good," Theodosia said. "Appreciate it."

"The kid's name is Marcus Covey," Theodosia said as she drove. "And he lives over near the College of Charleston. Here." She handed the hastily scribbled directions to Drayton. "You can navigate."

"You think talking to this Marcus guy is going to help?" Drayton asked.

"I have no idea. All I know is, it couldn't hurt. And looking back, it just feels like this kid might have been holding back. Or been worried about something."

"Hopefully he didn't see Doreen administer the fatal dose."

"You know," Theodosia said, "more and more I'm thinking that she's a little too schizo to kill her own husband in cold blood." She moved around a slow car and into the left lane. "Then again, you never know."

They cruised down Meeting, past a number of small retail shops, and turned left on Wentworth.

"We're getting close," Theodosia said. "Just be on the lookout for Pitt."

"There it is!" Drayton yelped. "Turn. Right here. This block."

Theodosia cranked the wheel hard and skidded into a turn.

Drayton's feet practically lifted up from the floor. "Whoa!"

"You okay?" she asked.

"Fine, just fine," Drayton said as they coasted to a stop. "Give me a minute to get my adrenaline under control and my systolic pressure back to normal." He put a hand to his chest. "There. Better. But this errand won't take long, will it? I have to get home and feed Honey Bee."

"Five minutes," Theodosia said, holding up five fingers. "And then we're out of here. I promise."

They walked up to Covey's house, a classic Charleston single house, long and narrow, made of modest clapboard. But it was completely dark, not a single light burning inside.

"Maybe less than five minutes," Theodosia said. "Because it doesn't look like anybody's home."

"Good. I didn't think this side trip was going to pan out."

"Well, let's at least go knock on the door."

They both stepped up onto a sagging porch and Theodosia knocked on the front door. Then they waited. Ten seconds went by, then a full minute.

"Nobody home," Drayton said. "Let's go."

"You still owe me three more minutes,"

Theodosia said.

"To do what?"

"Look around?"

"No. Oh no."

"Maybe Marcus went in the back door and he's . . . I don't know, flaked out on the couch in the dark, eating Doritos and watching *TMZ* or something." Theodosia stepped off the front porch, spotted an overgrown path spelled out in cracked flagstones, and started around the back.

"Seriously?" Drayton called after her.

"Come on, where's your sense of play?"

"Uh . . . back home with my chess set?" But Drayton followed her anyway. Reluctantly.

A car — a ten-year-old Saab, dusty black, with a dented right-front fender — sat on a patch of hardpan in the backyard.

"His car's here," Theodosia said.

"*A* car is here," Drayton said.

"Like I said, maybe he's watching the tube? Or snoozing?" Theodosia climbed two low steps and pulled open a rickety screen door. She was about to knock on the inside door when she saw that it was open a few inches. "Uh-oh."

"What's wrong?"

"Door's open," Theodosia said.

"Your boy probably came home, then

ducked out again. Dashed over to the neighbor's house or something."

"Or something," Theodosia murmured. But it didn't feel right to her. She nudged the back door open another few inches with her foot. "Marcus?" she called out. "Are you in there?"

"He's not home," Drayton said.

"But what if he is? What if something's wrong?" Theodosia couldn't shake the feeling that this scenario seemed a little bit off. Was she just projecting her own fear — or could something have happened to Marcus Covey? She didn't know. But she was reluctant to just spin on her heels and leave. She took a deep breath. "I'm going in."

"Don't," Drayton hissed. But it was too late. Theodosia had already slipped through the door and stepped inside. Worried now for her safety, Drayton doggedly followed her in, the screen door banging loudly behind him. "This is a terrible idea," he fumed, finally catching up to where she was standing in the middle of a dark kitchen.

"I know it is," she said. The house felt warm and oppressive. As if the stove had been turned on for a while. Small orange lights and a green digital readout glowed from a toaster on the counter.

215

Drayton touched her arm gently. "Let's go."

"One more minute." There were two wineglasses turned upside down in the sink. From last night or . . . ? Theodosia stuck out a finger and touched one of the glasses. Still damp, as if it had just been washed.

"Theodosia, you are courting danger . . ."

"Thirty seconds," she said, ducking through a doorway and easing her way down a long hallway. "And then we'll . . ." Her words suddenly died on her lips.

Drayton frowned as he nervously fingered his bow tie. "Theo?" he called out. He was pretty sure he could hear her soft breathing, just fifteen feet away from him in the dark. "It's time to . . ."

"Drayton," came Theodosia's anguished voice.

Terrified now, Drayton tiptoed out of the kitchen and slid down the hallway, his back against a wall. "You're scaring me," he said. "I don't like this one bit." His voice was cross and accusing and he could barely make her out in the darkness. She was a slight figure just standing there, looking up at something.

"You're certainly not thinking of . . ." Drayton's brain suddenly shut down. As if the batteries had suddenly been pulled or

216

the master switch had been thrown to OFF. He couldn't remember what he'd been about to say. Instead, he stood there and, ever so slowly, tilted his gaze upward in the same direction Theodosia was staring. Or, rather, where she was being held spellbound.

It was a body, of course. Hanging down from the second-floor landing. Suspended from a thin rope. Or maybe from a wire. It was hard to tell in the dark. The only thing that was for sure was that the body was twirling slowly, rotating, almost like an oversized ham hung up to dry.

Theodosia was the first to recover. She pulled out her phone, took two giant steps toward Drayton, and gave him a hard shove. "Outside!" she yelped. She was dialing 911 even as they scrambled back through the kitchen — it didn't matter how much noise they made now — and into the backyard. And then the dispatcher came on the line and she was babbling for help.

It felt like they'd been waiting forever, but it was really only a few minutes before they heard the first siren. It rose up, high-pitched and sharp, like a mechanical coyote. Then a second and third *whoop* joined in the cacophony.

217

The first two officers who arrived ran into the house, guns drawn. And came out a few minutes later with grim faces.

They immediately separated Theodosia and Drayton and demanded to hear their stories. When both stories seemed to jibe, and Theodosia and Drayton explained about the rat tea, things calmed down a bit.

"Did you call Detective Pete Riley?" Theodosia asked the officer who'd questioned her. His name tag read GROVER. "He's going to want to see this for himself. And hear our stories, too."

"Called him and he's on his way," Grover said as two more patrol cars pulled up. "Crime scene unit's coming, too."

"Thank you."

There were six officers milling around now, two inside the house and four outside. When the four outside officers decided to go in, Theodosia followed them. Then Drayton worked up the gumption to go in, too.

The police had turned on the lights and were studying the hanging body.

"Suicide," one of the cops spat out, shaking his head. "Crazy, stupid kid."

"Drugs," another one said. "See it all the time."

Theodosia made a low noise in the back of her throat.

Drayton looked sideways at her. "You don't think it was suicide, do you?" he asked in a quiet voice.

Theodosia shook her head. "No, I don't. I think somebody killed him."

"But who? And why?"

"Maybe because this poor kid knew something. Or because someone *thought* he knew something."

"You think Marcus Covey might have figured out who the killer was?"

"Maybe he didn't know for sure," Theodosia said. "But he could have suspected someone."

"Who knew that we were looking for Covey?" Drayton asked.

"Pretty much everybody," Theodosia said. She felt sick to her stomach over what had just happened. "We pretty much broadcast it to everyone we talked to that we were trying to get in touch with him. That we wanted to question him." Her voice cracked. "We should have just painted a big red arrow to his door."

"You're being too hard on yourself."

Theodosia shook her head, holding back tears. "No, I'm not."

Detective Pete Riley showed up at the same moment the shiny black crime scene van pulled in.

"Grand Central," Drayton observed. They were back outside, standing next to Covey's Saab. The police had set up three floodlights that cast an eerie, icy glow over everything. Two next-door neighbors peered out of their second-story window, silhouetted in a rectangle of light, as they watched the hub-bub in the yard.

"Now we've got a crowd," Theodosia said. "Where was all this manpower when Marcus Covey was being murdered?"

"Maybe the poor boy really did commit suicide."

"No, he didn't." Theodosia's face was a dark mask of despair.

Detective Riley was hurrying toward them. "You were the one who found him?" he asked, looking directly at Theodosia.

"We both did," Theodosia said.

Riley posed with his hands on his hips. "And what exactly were you *doing* here?"

Theodosia swallowed hard, trying to push her emotions down. She couldn't afford to cry now or act upset, otherwise Riley wouldn't take her seriously.

"We wanted to talk to him," Theodosia said.

" 'Him' being Marcus Covey," Riley said. "What did you want to talk to him about?"

"Drayton and I wanted to get Covey's general impression of what happened last Saturday," Theodosia said.

"Because you're investigating?" Riley asked.

"Not really," Theodosia said, but she could tell from the look on Riley's face that he wasn't buying it.

Riley gazed off in the distance for a moment, as if lost in thought, and then glanced back at her. "Did you think Marcus Covey was the killer? Did you think you could apprehend him by yourselves?"

"Not exactly," Drayton said.

"Of course not," Theodosia said. "Like I told you, we only wanted to *talk* to him."

"Wait right here," Riley said. "And by that I mean *Do not move.*" He turned and headed for the back door.

"Are we in the glue?" Drayton asked once Riley had gone inside.

Theodosia shook her head. "I don't think so." Then she reconsidered. "Well, maybe a little."

"He didn't look happy."

"It's a murder scene," Theodosia said.

"No," Drayton said. "I meant he didn't look happy to see you."

"Oh."

Five minutes later, Detective Riley was back outside to question them again.

"Two of the officers inside are calling it a suicide," he said. "Their theory is that Covey might have killed Briggs, couldn't handle it, and then hung himself because of a guilty conscience."

"Wait a minute," Drayton said. "If that's what really happened, then the case is solved."

Riley lifted a shoulder. "Maybe."

"It's not solved," Theodosia said. "Not even close. In fact, now it's even more confusing." She fixed her gaze on Riley. "What's your take on Covey's death?"

"If it looks like a duck, quacks like a duck," Riley said.

"It could still be a guinea hen with a loud, squeaky voice," Theodosia said.

Riley took a step backward and put a hand to his mouth. Theodosia was pretty sure he was trying to cover his laughter. "I'm . . . not convinced either way," he said finally.

"Then let me try to convince you," Theodosia said. She paused as one of the crime scene guys humped a metal gurney up the two back steps and into the kitchen. "This guy Marcus Covey, I can't imagine that he fits the profile of a homicidal maniac or even as a suicide. I sincerely doubt that he nursed a grudge against Beau Briggs, schemed to murder him, and then experienced terrible, soul-searching remorse. Fact is, Covey's only apparent contact with Briggs was at Saturday's rat tea where he was a server."

"Do we know that for sure?" Drayton asked

Theodosia gazed at Riley. "You interviewed Covey that day. Did you think he came across as a potential killer or even a suicide risk?"

Riley shrugged. "Not really, he seemed like a typical guy. Fact is, we talked to *all* the rat tea servers, quizzed them pretty good. Every one of them seemed fairly normal and their backgrounds were relatively clean."

"So why is Marcus Covey hanging inside, dead as a doornail?" Theodosia asked.

"Good question," Riley said. "But I have to say . . ." He looked around, surveying the high level of activity that was unfolding in the backyard. "It would be easier if this guy Covey was the killer."

"Easier for who?" Theodosia asked. "For you? For Beau Briggs? Look, I just don't think there should be a rush to judgment

223

here. There are a number of perfectly good suspects that still need to be checked out."

"And we're going to do exactly that," Riley said. "I'm not going to drop this investigation," he assured her. "One way or another, this case *will* be solved."

"Promise?" Theodosia asked.

"Yes," Riley said. "I promise."

"Okay, then," Theodosia said. "Thank you." It wasn't the definitive answer she was looking for — that would come when this case was finally solved — but it would have to do for now.

17

After the death of Marcus Covey last night, this morning's funeral for Beau Briggs seemed anticlimactic. Theodosia and Drayton arrived at St. Stephen's Church some fifteen minutes before the service was scheduled to begin, both feeling a little out of sorts. Neither of them had slept very well and they were uneasy over this second murder.

As they walked up the steps to the church's double doors, cameras snapped, TV lights popped on, and video cameras whirred softly.

"Media," Drayton said, a derogatory note coloring his voice. "What are *they* doing here?"

"You can thank your good pal Starla Crane for drumming up this media circus," Theodosia said. "She's the one who wanted to make Beau's funeral a public spectacle."

"Lovely," Drayton said as he pulled open

the heavy door and they stepped inside.

The interior of St. Stephen's Church was cool and dark. Soft organ music filled the air, while up on the altar, at the front of the church, a dozen candles burned. Just to the left of where they'd come in, over near a white marble baptismal font, Beau Briggs's open casket sat on a wooden dais surrounded by a bed of flowers.

Drayton wrinkled his nose. "I suppose we have to subject ourselves to the so-called viewing?"

"We don't have to," Theodosia said. "But it might be nice."

"Nice for whom?"

"For Doreen and Opal Anne and Charles."

Drayton's shoulders slumped visibly. "I suppose. Although looking at a dead person in a casket always reminds me of going to one of those dreadful all-you-can-eat buffet restaurants."

"What a bizarre thing to say."

"But it's true."

"Because of all those pink heat lamps shining down?"

Drayton nodded. "That's right."

Squished into the rear of the church, the casket arrangement did look a little like a bad buffet. Or maybe an overgrown salad bar. Salmon-pink lights shone down upon Beau Briggs's embalmed body, bathing his chubby little countenance in a halo of luminosity, making his expensive Brioni suit look like a warehouse special. Doreen was firmly positioned next to her dead husband, sobbing loudly into a lace hankie.

Surrounding his hotly contested Exeter casket was a jungle of orchids, roses, and lilies. An enormous wreath of magnolia blossoms sat to the right of his casket on a metal three-pronged stand. Curling across the wreath was a gold ribbon that said REST IN PEACE FROM YOUR FRIENDS AT GILDED MAGNOLIA SPA.

"That floral arrangement is tasteless and gaudy," Drayton said, gesturing at the wreath. "It looks more appropriate for the winner of the Kentucky Derby."

"Shh," Theodosia said. "The wreath is awful, but please don't let Doreen hear you."

They stood in the line of mourners and edged their way toward Doreen. When they were finally standing in front of her and able to express their condolences, Doreen grabbed Drayton's arm and blubbered, "Beau looks so peaceful lying there. Doesn't he look peaceful?"

"As if he's fast asleep," Drayton said, trying not to look at the casket as he attempted to pull away from her.

"Detective Riley told me what happened to that poor waiter last night," Doreen said in a harsh, gurgling voice. Then her face pulled into a feral snarl. "There's a madman on the loose." Her eyes practically rolled back in her head. "Not one of us is safe!" Sniffling loudly, she pinched Drayton's arm harder as she clung to him.

Theodosia grabbed Drayton's other arm. Engaging in a sort of tug-of-war, she finally emerged victorious, pulling him free of Doreen's grasp.

"I need to speak to both of you later," Doreen rasped as they backed away.

"Bull hockey," Theodosia said as she and Drayton slid into one of the church pews. "Beau Briggs didn't look one bit peaceful. If anything he looked angry."

"Because he was murdered?" Drayton said. "Do you think somewhere at the cellular level he knew that someone did him in?"

"That sounds awfully metaphysical. Or maybe supernatural. But still, wouldn't you be angry if someone poisoned you?"

"I'd be positively livid."

Theodosia leaned closer to Drayton. "You know, Drayton, Doreen seems to have gone off the deep end."

"You think?"

"That business about none of us being safe. That's just not true."

"What about Marcus Covey?" Drayton asked. "You still think somebody murdered him, don't you?"

"Well . . . yes. But that's different."

"How so?"

Theodosia thought for a minute. "I don't know yet. But I'm going to figure it out."

The organ began to play again. Soft notes wafted above them and resonated off the church's stone walls. Theodosia and Drayton watched carefully as more people came in and sat down. Then, interestingly enough, Big Reggie marched up the center aisle and took a seat right near the front. He was dressed in khaki slacks and a casual light-blue sports jacket, looking like he might be anxious to get out of there as soon as possible and maybe squeeze in a round of golf.

Then, as even more people hurried in to be seated, Robert Steele and Honey and Michael Whitley pushed their way up the aisle.

"The gang's all here," Theodosia whispered.

The organist was getting serious. "You'll Never Walk Alone" rang out, thundering mightily like it was the end of days. Something was about to happen.

Theodosia turned in her seat and saw Frank Gruenwald nudging the casket up the center aisle on some kind of metal conveyance. Behind him walked Doreen Briggs, Opal Anne, and Charles, heads bowed, all of them dressed in black and carrying a single white rose. Starla Crane followed in their wake, wearing a tight black dress and a large black hat, glancing to and fro at the mourners who were seated. When the whole cortege reached the front of the church, Doreen, Opal Anne, and Charles took their places in the very front pew. Starla continued to buzz around, whispering in Gruenwald's ear, making sure he seesawed the casket just right, so that it rested horizontally to the altar. When that arrangement was finally to her liking, she waved her hand impatiently, and Gruenwald scurried to grab several large sprays of flowers and place them atop the casket.

Drayton watched Starla for a few minutes and then frowned. "Why is she here?"

Theodosia glanced sideways at him. "Billable hours?"

"Seriously?"

"She could be racking up a small fortune. A hotshot PR firm probably bills out at a good two hundred dollars an hour."

"Is Starla Crane a hotshot?"

"I doubt it. But I think she'd like everyone to believe she is."

"So she's taking advantage of Doreen."

"Almost certainly."

"And maybe trying to drum up some more business in the process?"

"Maybe," Theodosia said. "Or maybe Starla's been keeping up a constant stream of chatter and activity so nobody takes a careful look at her."

Drayton drew back, his eyes going wide. "You think Starla could have poisoned Beau?"

"I don't know. Somebody did." Theodosia picked up a hymnal and flipped through a few pages, then set it down again. She glanced around the church and noticed that Detective Pete Riley was sitting in a pew some ten rows behind them. He looked tired, like he'd been up all night. And maybe he had.

"The thing is," Theodosia said, resuming her train of thought, "Starla seems to have Doreen's ear. I mean, just look around. Starla not only art-directed this funeral, she convinced the media to show up. If she can do that, what else is she capable of?"

"If Starla's a suspect in Beau's death, if she's a potential poisoner, then how do you explain Marcus Covey's death?" Drayton asked.

"I don't know. Maybe Starla thought Covey knew something. I sure thought he did. So I suppose she could have . . . lured him."

"Lured him to his death?"

"If Starla pointed a loaded gun at Covey, she could have gotten a noose around his neck and engineered his hanging."

"That would be cold-blooded murder at its absolute worst," Drayton said. He touched a hand to his polka-dot bow tie, as if to reassure himself. "Do you think Starla owns a gun?"

"I don't know, but I certainly wouldn't want to find out the hard way."

Just as Drayton was about to respond, the minister came flying out to take his place at a small podium. He looked a little breathless, as if he were late to the party. But he delivered what seemed to be a heartfelt welcoming tribute. And, after a few minutes, it all settled down into a fairly routine funeral.

Prayers were offered, music rang out, Doreen sobbed right on cue.

There were two testimonials, one by Opal Anne that was quiet and moving. Another by Doreen's neighbor Michael Whitley that felt a little disjointed and closed with him quoting a few verses of poetry.

"They had a *neighbor* give a testimonial?" Drayton whispered.

"Better than having Big Reggie do it," Theodosia whispered back.

There was one final song — the organist belted out a sedate version of "Amazing Grace" — and then Beau's funeral was over. The procession reversed itself and Beau Briggs's casket was pushed down the aisle, with Doreen, Starla, Opal Anne, Reggie Huston, Robert Steele, and Honey and Michael Whitley trailing right behind it.

Outside, standing on the steps of the church, Theodosia looked around for Detective Riley, but couldn't find him anywhere. Instead, she saw Bill Glass elbowing his way through the mourners, poking his camera in people's faces and snapping pictures every few seconds.

"Glass," she muttered. Still, if he could manage to shake something loose that would be good, wouldn't it?

Starla Crane seemed to be everywhere, buzzing around like a queen bee, talking to the media, offering solace to Doreen. When she caught sight of Theodosia and Drayton, she turned her head away quickly.

Doreen was a different story.

When Doreen spotted Theodosia and Drayton she made her way over to them and said, without preamble, "The police aren't any closer to catching this crazed killer. If you two come up with anything, and I mean *any* useful information at all, I'll double the size of that grant!"

"My heavens," Drayton said, looking surprised.

"I mean it," Doreen said. She put a hankie to her mouth and gave a muffled sob.

"Please don't get so upset, Momma," Charles said. He was standing beside Doreen, trying to calm her.

"I'll get as upset as I *want*," Doreen cried.

"Come on, people," Opal Anne said, sounding a little tired. "We've got to keep moving. We still have to attend the short service at the cemetery and then get back home for our luncheon."

"Come on, Momma," Charles said. "Please?"

"And for goodness' sake," Opal Anne whispered to both of them, "let's try not to make a scene in front of the cameras."

"Whatever," Doreen said as she toddled away, clinging tightly to Charles's arm.

Theodosia and Drayton stood in the middle of the crowd of mourners, watching them climb into a long black limousine.

"Well," Drayton said finally, "Doreen's offer was fairly shocking. But with double the amount of money on the line, we dare not poop out now."

"I agree," Theodosia said. "Unfortunately, we're not making that much forward progress."

"You've been on the right track . . ."

"But always a step behind," Theodosia said. "Now it's time to try and get a jump on this thing."

Drayton glanced at his watch. "Let's discuss this later. For now we have to swing by the Indigo Tea Shop and pick up the food for the buffet. Then we need to head over to Doreen's house and get everything set up."

But as they were hurrying to her Jeep, Theodosia recognized a familiar face. "Just a minute, Drayton." She stepped across the street, holding up a hand to give a wave. "Excuse me, excuse me . . ."

The woman Theodosia was waving to stopped and turned. She was dressed to the nines in a bright-yellow sundress and matching floppy hat. Her sandals were raffia and she carried an oversized straw bag.

"You're Jemma Lee, am I right?" Theodosia asked as she hurried to greet the young woman. "Of Glam Baby Cosmetics?"

Jemma Lee smiled broadly. "That's right." Though she was jumping the gun on the season, she looked like the perfect Southern belle. Until she opened her mouth. Then she sounded as if she'd just emigrated from Ukraine. Or hopped off a freighter from Minsk.

"I'm Theodosia. I'm a friend of Doreen Briggs."

Jemma pulled her face into a sad smile. "Wasn't it awful about her husband?"

"Terrible," Theodosia said. "But I'm guessing you're fairly familiar with the circumstances. You're Reggie Huston's friend, am I right?"

"That's right," Jemma said.

"I saw your photo in Reggie's office."

"My sweet boyfriend," Jemma said with a smile.

"I'm guessing by your accent that your given name probably isn't really Jemma?" Theodosia asked, smiling.

Jemma dimpled prettily. "My name is Svetlana Radovitch," she said in heavily accented Russian, "but nobody here can pronounce. Besides . . ." She shrugged. "Name must fit in with . . ." This time she gestured with both hands, indicating all the Charleston folks who were still clustered around, talking in honeyed tones. "Fit with

236

South," she finally spit out. "And work with new makeup product."

Theodosia was sizing Jemma up and decided to take a chance. "Reggie is quite a character, isn't he?"

"Oh yes," Jemma said. "Big Reggie is a very important man." She pronounced it *beeg,* sounding a little bit gangster, a little bit Russian. "He give me my big chance."

"Let me guess," Theodosia said. "Reggie helped finance your makeup line?"

"Yes. Of course."

"And then Reggie paved the way for your line to be featured in Gilded Magnolia Spa's gift shop?"

Jemma clapped a hand to her chest. "My big break."

Theodosia smiled. "Reggie really is quite the charmer." *He's quite the manipulator, too.*

Jemma leaned forward as if to share a secret. "Generous, too. Pays for my apartment."

"Of course he does," Theodosia cooed. "That doesn't surprise me in the least."

"Theodosia!" Drayton called to her from across the street. He tapped a finger against the face of his watch. "We have to get going."

"One minute," Theodosia called back. She was wondering how she could question this girl some more when her brain suddenly spit out a crazy impromptu idea. "You know, Jemma, I'd love it if you came to my Candlelight Tea tomorrow night. At my tea shop."

"You own tea shop?"

"It's the Indigo Tea Shop over on Church Street."

"You're a lady bigshot," Jemma said with admiration.

Theodosia smiled. "Not quite."

"I'd like very much to come."

"And be sure to bring your boyfriend, too. Bring Big Reggie."

"You call him Big Reggie, too?"

"Sure. Everybody at Gilded Magnolia Spa does."

"And you really want us to come?"

"By all means," Theodosia said. "The more the merrier."

Theodosia was quiet as she drove to the Indigo Tea Shop to pick up the food. While Drayton chattered away about the funeral, all she could think about was Detective Riley telling her about the poison. What she thought of now as scratch 'n' sniff poison. And about how it was sometimes employed as a Russian mob technique. She wondered if Jemma, née Svetlana, was somehow connected to the Russian mob.

Or was Jemma just a hopeful immigrant who'd escaped the nasty Putin regime and was trying hard to build a better life with Reggie Huston?

Good question.

18

"Do you know what that snake Big Reggie was doing all the while poor Beau Briggs was in the back room of Gruenwald Brothers Funeral Home being cosmetically enhanced for his big moment?" Theodosia asked heatedly.

"No," Drayton said. "But from the tone of your voice it must have been something ghastly."

They were fussing about in Doreen's kitchen, unpacking the scones and tea sandwiches, heating up the quiche, getting ready to set out a buffet luncheon on the dining room table.

"Big Reggie was out canoodling," Theodosia said. "With his Russian tootsie."

Drayton's brows angled up. "A tootsie?"

"You know what I mean, his girlfriend." She whipped the plastic wrap off a bowl of fruit salad and crumpled the plastic into a ball. "The one I was telling you about on the way over here."

"I get that, yes," Drayton said. "It's not like I exist under a rock. You were grumbling plenty about Big Reggie's girlfriend. The Russian lady. But what's the big deal? The man is single, isn't he? He's allowed." Drayton filled three copper teakettles with water and set them on the stove to heat.

"I didn't tell you the whole story," Theodosia said. "Besides introducing his girlfriend's cosmetic line into Gilded Magnolia Spa, it turns out that Reggie also *financed* the whole project. Manufacturing, marketing, the whole enchilada."

"Using his own money?"

"If he's embezzling from Gilded Magnolia Spa, I would imagine it would be more like using Doreen Briggs's money."

"I suppose so," Drayton said slowly.

"There's more," Theodosia said. "Big Reggie is paying the freight on the girlfriend's apartment."

"Holy butter beans," Drayton said. "Is it possible that Big Reggie *did* kill Beau? That he was broke and desperately needed the money?"

"Reggie certainly had every opportunity during the rat tea. He was right there, seated at the head table the whole time."

"You didn't answer my question."

241

"That's because I don't have a definitive answer," Theodosia said. "I don't *know* if Reggie killed him."

"You sound pretty angry," Drayton said. "So I'm guessing you have some kind of hunch about Reggie."

"I do and I don't." Theodosia grabbed a basket of scones. "Reggie might have been feeling desperate, worried that Beau was about to tumble to his conniving ways. So Reggie *could* have plotted and carried out the whole sordid murder."

"Do you think Reggie also killed Marcus Covey?"

"That's the tricky part. It feels like Beau Briggs's death and Covey's death are related. That the same guy killed them both. But I don't know how to put it all together. All I can surmise is that somebody out there, maybe even a person we've been rubbing elbows with, is a double murderer."

"Just maybe not Reggie?"

"Like I said, I don't know."

"Still, there's something rotten in the state of Denmark," Drayton said.

"But *rotten* doesn't necessarily mean *dead,*" Theodosia said.

Drayton jacked up the heat on the burners. "Only that it's beginning to smell."

They got busy then, setting out plates,

silverware, and napkins. Making sure the food they'd brought along was arranged just so. Scones in baskets, tea sandwiches set out on three-tiered trays, quiche cut in easy-to-grab wedges. Drayton hunted around, found some tall pink tapers and brass candle-sticks, and placed them on the table. By the time Doreen's guests began arriving for lunch, the dining room glowed with warmth and the buffet luncheon looked like a carefully styled photograph from a fancy tea magazine.

"Everything looks beautiful," Doreen said to Theodosia as they watched guests file through the buffet line. "Not just the food, but the table setting, too. Are those my candles or did you bring them along?"

"Drayton pulled them out of the cupboard. I hope you don't mind."

"I don't believe we've used them in ages."

"You seem to be feeling somewhat better," Theodosia said. It was true, Doreen had pulled herself together and was a lot less weepy. She'd also tossed on a shiny black bugle bead jacket over her dress. Now, instead of sad Doreen, she was glitzy Doreen.

Doreen waved a hand. "Oh, you know . . . I'm trying." She blinked several times, wiped at her eyes, and said, "Didn't Starla do a wonderful job this morning?"

"She certainly demonstrated her ability at pulling in the press."

"Yes, I was very pleased."

Theodosia glanced around. "I'm surprised Starla's not here." *Since the two of you have been joined at the hip lately.*

"Oh, she had some pressing business over at the spa." Doreen pushed an errant curl out of her face. "You know our big grand opening party happens this Saturday night."

"That's right." Theodosia was surprised that Doreen hadn't canceled or at least delayed the party. Then again, it wasn't her call to make. Maybe there were too many plans in place, too many vendors to notify. Maybe . . . the show must go on?

"In fact," Doreen said slowly, "would you mind stopping at the spa later today? Like . . . maybe on your way home? I have an envelope that needs to go to Starla." She pulled an envelope out of her pocket and gave a helpless shrug.

Theodosia recognized Doreen's shrug as a gesture she used a lot. Whenever she didn't want to do something herself.

"I mean," Doreen continued, "if it's not too much out of your way."

"I'd be happy to help," Theodosia said,

taking the envelope. But not feeling one bit happy about it.

"What was that all about?" Drayton asked. He'd just refilled the basket of scones and put out a fresh pan of quiche.

"Doreen wants me to drop off an envelope at Gilded Magnolia Spa."

"Now? I'd say we're a little busy for her to be asking you to run errands."

"No, I can do it later. What do you need from me? How can I help?"

"Well, we're in the final countdown, probably not that many more guests will be coming through the buffet line, so we'll need to clear and pack up pretty soon."

"What if I started packing up in the kitchen?" Theodosia asked.

"Bless you," Drayton said.

Back in the kitchen, Theodosia began stacking empty plastic containers into one of her baskets. Then, just as she was about to carry the basket outside, where she was parked in the back alley, she heard a faint tapping at the kitchen window.

What?

She peered out, only to find Bill Glass's face peering in at her.

Theodosia eased open the back door. "What are you doing out there?" she hissed.

"Trying to talk to you," Glass said. "I saw you at the funeral and then you suddenly disappeared down the rabbit hole."

"And you followed me here?"

"Yeah. Why not? What's wrong with that?"

"Get out of here, Glass. There's a cop at the front door who'll run you out of town if I give the word."

"You wouldn't do that."

"Try me."

Glass edged toward her. "Tell me about the murder last night."

Theodosia was taken aback. "What!" Then, "How would you know about that?"

"It's my business to know the sordid things that go on in Charleston. That's how my little magazine stays in business."

"Little scummy magazine, you mean." Theodosia turned to duck back inside, but Glass caught her by the arm.

"I have a police scanner in my car."

"Aren't those illegal?"

Glass smirked. "I won't tell if you don't."

Theodosia sighed. "What is it you want to know?" She figured he'd get all the details sooner or later. It may as well be sooner. "Marcus Covey, one of the waiters at Doreen's rat tea, was found hanged inside his home."

Glass stared at her intently. "Yeah, I know

all that. What do the police think?"

"At first they said suicide, now they're not so sure."

"Do you think old lady Briggs offed her own husband? Do you think she could have hanged that Covey kid?"

"I think there are a number of people who could have wanted Briggs and then Covey out of the way."

"Yeah," Glass said. "Obviously. But what's your personal theory?"

"I'm not going to tell you."

"If you ask me," Glass said, "I'd put my money squarely on the business partner. Reggie Huston."

"You know," Theodosia said, "I might be persuaded to put some coin on him, too."

"You're back," Haley said when Theodosia and Drayton trooped in the back door of the Indigo Tea Shop. "How was the funeral?"

"Sad," said Theodosia, handing Haley a basket piled with empty plastic containers.

"Silly question," Haley said. "Funerals are always depressing. So let me rephrase that. How was the luncheon?"

"Top-notch," Drayton said, dropping two more wicker baskets on the floor. "Your tea sandwiches and quiche were a huge hit.

247

Doreen was delighted with the food, and her guests pretty much picked everything clean. There wasn't a single crust left over."

"Probably because I cut off all the crusts?" Haley said.

Drayton shrugged. "I think you know what I mean."

"How were things here at the tea shop?" Theodosia asked. Truth be told, she'd been a little anxious about leaving Haley and Miss Dimple in charge, even though they only had to handle an abbreviated menu.

"Morning tea service and lunch couldn't have gone smoother," Haley said. "Since I made everything ahead of time, all we had to do was throw a couple of sandwiches on a plate and add a bowl of soup." She grinned as she pushed a hank of blond hair out of her eyes. "You guys were hardly even missed."

Drayton raised an eyebrow. "Hardly?"

Miss Dimple saw them all talking and came toddling over on her tiny size-five feet. She was a plump little lady, an octogenarian who still worked as their twice-a-month bookkeeper. With her halo of silver-white hair and rounded features, she bore more than a slight resemblance to a Cabbage Patch doll.

"Haley and I had so much fun," Miss

Dimple enthused. "It's always a thrill to work here." She gave a delighted little shiver. "Kind of like playing tea party."

"We're happy to have you," Theodosia said, giving her a hug. "It's always good luck for us when you're able to fill in."

"You didn't encounter any problems in brewing the tea?" Drayton asked Miss Dimple. He sounded almost hopeful.

"Nary a one," Miss Dimple said. "You had everything laid out so nicely. And with your precise notes for measuring and steeping times, it was practically child's play. I didn't even have trouble with that Fujian white tea that you said was so tricky."

Drayton tucked his chin down. "Indeed. But of course we still have afternoon tea to worry about, and those guests can sometimes be a bit more picky. So I'd better make sure we're properly prepared." He took off, still mumbling to himself.

"I think his nose is out of joint because everything went so well," Haley said.

"Drayton's just being fastidious," Miss Dimple said. In her eyes, he could do no wrong.

"Can you work for a few more hours?" Theodosia asked. "You know we'd love to have you."

Miss Dimple's eyes sparkled. "I was hoping you'd ask."

19

Theodosia spent the next twenty minutes stowing away baskets and teakettles and grabbing a quick bite of lunch herself. Then, just as the clock was ticking toward two thirty and the tea shop was practically full, Honey and Michael Whitley sauntered in.

"Helloooo," Honey called out in a high-pitched singsong voice. "Are you folks still serving tea?"

Theodosia turned, frowned when she saw who it was, then quickly put a pleasant smile on her face. The Whitleys weren't exactly her dream team, but they'd shown up for afternoon tea so what could she do? Basically nothing.

"Come in," Theodosia said. "And, yes, we're still serving tea."

The Whitleys crowded in eagerly.

"We missed the luncheon at Doreen's," Michael Whitley explained. "So we thought we'd stop by your tea shop and have ourselves a bite."

"I'm not sure we have any tea sandwiches left," Theodosia said.

"Oh, that's okay, dear," Honey said. "Just a pot of tea and some scones would be fine."

Theodosia led them to a table, where they plopped down happily.

"We were invited to Doreen's for lunch," Honey said, "but we had some pressing business to take care of." She was dressed casually now, in a white blouse and flouncy navy skirt.

"Of course we attended the funeral this morning," Michael said. He had a mint-green sweater draped around his neck in a fey-preppie-Southern manner. Theodosia snuck a look at his socks. Mint green also.

"You saw that Michael gave one of the homilies," Honey gushed. "And what a lovely service it was. I've never seen more gorgeous flowers. And the music . . ."

"Quite a *coup* to have the *media* covering it," Michael said, rolling his eyes. "That's big-time."

"That PR lady that Doreen employs is really a whiz, isn't she?" Honey said. She frowned slightly. "What's her name again?"

"Starla Crane," Theodosia said, finally managing to get a word in edgewise. "So. What kind of tea may I bring you? Maybe a

fragrant Darjeeling? Or a full-bodied Assam? Or perhaps you'd like a flavored black
tea — with black currants or passion fruit?"

"Do you have anything with a little spice
to it?" Honey asked.

"We have a lovely Indian spice tea. Assam
with cardamom, orange peel, and cloves."

"Perfect," Honey said. Theodosia was
taken aback at how friendly Honey was acting. Every time she'd encountered her thus
far, Honey had been condescending, bordering on rude. Was she suddenly up to something?

"And scones," Michael said. "We have to
have scones."

"Those we have," Theodosia said. "Poppy
seed scones, I think."

She put in an order for spiced tea with
Drayton, then strolled into the kitchen and
grabbed four scones. She placed them on a
floral plate and then plopped a couple of
puffs of Devonshire cream into a small glass
bowl. Everything went onto a silver tray
along with napkins, teacups, silverware, and
a small container of fruit jam. She picked
up a pot of spice tea from Drayton on the
way to the Whitleys' table.

"This looks spectacular," Honey said as
Theodosia set cups and saucers and plated
scones in front of them.

253

"Really delish," Michael echoed.

"Enjoy," Theodosia told them, then went off to check on her other guests. Of course, Miss Dimple was three steps ahead of her, ferrying out refills and treating everyone like royalty. Which was just fine with Theodosia since she wanted to check in with Haley about tomorrow's event tea.

Twenty minutes later, when Theodosia circled back through the tea room, Michael Whitley was standing at the counter, chatting with Drayton, while Honey was sipping her second, or maybe even third, cup of tea.

"We had some of your B and B customers in here the other day," Theodosia said to her, just to be friendly. Or was she testing the waters? Whatever.

"I'll bet you did," Honey said. "We've been full up with guests lately and have tons of reservations pending. In fact, that relates directly to the business we had to take care of over lunch. We were meeting with our Realtor to discuss buying a second property."

"Do you still have your eye on Doreen's home?" Theodosia asked.

"Oh my, yes," Honey said. "Do we ever. Her place is my absolute first choice. If and when she's willing to sell, we'd go ahead and physically connect the two properties.

Build a breezeway between them. That way we could carve out another six to eight suites in the Scarborough Inn and then have another eight suites in the Calhoun Mansion. Then we could use Doreen's much larger kitchen, dining room, and two parlors for all our guest events. Not just breakfast, but mini concerts, wine and cheese parties, bridal showers, that sort of thing. And Doreen's place even has a three-car garage and nice cement apron for additional parking!"

"It sounds like you've got it all planned out," Theodosia said. There was something unsettling about the bullheaded assumptions Honey Whitley was making.

"Oh, we have a definite plan," Honey said. "There's just one teensy little problem."

"The fact that Doreen doesn't want to sell?" Theodosia said.

Honey's brows puckered together. "She doesn't right now. But we'll keep chipping away at her. I'm positive she'll eventually see the light."

"Are you ready?" Michael Whitley asked. He was back at their table, a tin of tea clutched in his right hand. "Bought this from Drayton." He held it up. "A tin of strawberry sencha."

"You'll enjoy that tea," Theodosia said.

"Say," Michael said. "I saw a poster for a Candlelight Tea you're having here tomorrow night?"

"That's right," Theodosia said.

"Honey," he said, "would you like to attend?"

Honey stared at Theodosia. "Do you have room for two more?"

"I'm sure we could squeeze you in," Theodosia said. She knew for a fact they had four places open yet.

"Good," Michael said. "Count us in."

"You don't mind if I scoot out of here a little early, do you?" Theodosia asked.

Drayton glanced up from his tea magazine. "Of course not. You're the boss, aren't you?" He'd just hung a CLOSED sign on the front door and was sitting at a table, sipping a cup of Irish breakfast tea and reading an article on the tea salons of Quebec.

"I'm not the boss, I'm one of a triumvirate," Theodosia said.

"Mighty big word for our small shop," Drayton replied.

"Okay, then, what if I said we're the Three Musketeers?"

"Much better. It sounds quite . . . traditional."

■ ■ ■ ■

Standing at the reception desk at Gilded Magnolia Spa, Theodosia said, "I have an envelope for Starla Crane and I was told she'd be here this afternoon?"

"Oh yes," the receptionist said. "They're all set up in the Cypress Room. Do you know where that is or should I ring for someone to take you back?"

"I think I can find it."

Ambling through the spa, Theodosia worked her way past the juice bar, where blenders whirled fruit and yogurt into frothy concoctions, and past a workout room where a bunch of women were dancing about and waving colorful ribbons in the air. Or maybe they were flexible rubber tubes. Whatever. To Theodosia it looked like a Chinese video she'd seen where kids waved brightly colored ribbons in front of Chairman Mao's portrait.

Theodosia heard Starla, her voice raised raw and hectoring, before she saw her.

"Is anyone *listening* to me?" Starla screamed.

Theodosia hesitated in the doorway of the Cypress Room and peeked inside. There appeared to be a fashion shoot going on. A cameraman held a large video camera, while lighting and sound guys clustered around him. Three attractive-looking young women — models, presumably — were dressed in colorful yoga pants and crop tops. And then there was Starla, waving her arms and shrieking, her face gone bright pink.

"Didn't I tell you to dial back the fog machine?" she screamed at one of the crew

"I did," the man said. "I have."

"Then pull it back some more. We're trying to shoot a *spa* video here, in case you haven't noticed. Not recreate the misty London back alleys of Jack the Ripper."

"Yes, ma'am," said the man, making another quick adjustment to the fog machine.

Starla turned and glared at the models, who were whispering among themselves and tittering at some shared joke.

"You there," Starla said. She walked over and grabbed the arm of a long-limbed blond model. "Try to look like you're having fun, will you? Try to show some enthusiasm." She turned to the dark-haired model. "And you, suck in your stomach, for goodness' sakes. Do I have to remind you people for the hundredth time that this video is for a *spa*? Can't you at least try to project an air of health and fitness?"

Starla moved on to the lighting guy. "Why didn't you put a pink filter on that overhead key light like I asked?"

"We tried that," the lighting guy said, with all sincerity. "But it looked weird. Interfered with the flesh tones. If you look through the lens you can see what . . ."

"I don't want to hear your opinion," Starla screamed, cutting him off. "Just *do* it. And do it *now,* not next Tuesday." She backed away and shook her head angrily. "Don't you people understand that time is money?"

"Starla," Theodosia called out, but in a normal tone of voice.

Starla whirled around. "What!"

"I have something for you," Theodosia said.

Starla seemed to make a slight attitude adjustment as she moved toward Theodosia. "Okay," she said. "Thank you." She reached out a hand and accepted the envelope. "Doreen told me you were going to bring this by."

"I hope I didn't interrupt anything," Theodosia said, partly in jest.

"No, no, we're just in the middle of trying to tighten up our production values. Actually the shoot is going rather well."

"You're shooting a TV spot?"

"More like a corporate video. A fast-paced

259

introduction to Gilded Magnolia Spa that we'll show at the grand opening Saturday night." She bobbled her head back and forth. "I realize it's all very last-minute, but what can you do? The situation has changed dramatically."

"I suppose it has," Theodosia said, unsure as to what Starla was referring. Beau's death? Doreen's craziness? Starla stepping in to take over? Or something else entirely?

Starla turned and cast a dour look at the cast and crew. "Anyway, it is what it is."

"Right," Theodosia said. "Well, I'd better let you get back to your shoot." She took a step backward, wondering how to extricate herself from what looked like a messy situation. Then she smiled and gave a thumbs-up. "By the way, great funeral this morning."

"Thank you," Starla said. "I'm thrilled we had such a great turnout. From the media, I mean."

20

Theodosia stared at the large sheet of paper that sat on her dining room table. She'd come home, fixed a quick pasta dinner for herself and a bowl of kibble for Earl Grey, and was hard at work on . . . well, she wasn't quite sure what it was.

She'd started out with a kind of Venn diagram — scribbling Beau Briggs's name in the center of the page and then adding the names of possible suspects around him like spokes in a wheel. Doreen, Reggie Huston, Starla Crane, Honey and Michael Whitley. As a kind of outer rim, she'd added the names of the various characters that had played a walk-on role in last Saturday's drama.

A murder chart. I'm making a murder chart.

The notion both tickled and unnerved her.

She picked up her marker again and added Marcus Covey's name. Drawing a circle around it, she connected it with an arrow to Beau's name. As an afterthought she added the name of Robert Steele, the guy who headed Angel Oak Venture Capital, to the outer ring.

"Rrowr?"

Theodosia looked up to find Earl Grey staring intently at her. "What?" she said.

"Oowr?"

"Yes, of course we're still going out. You didn't think we were going to miss our evening run, did you?"

She pushed back from the table and stood up.

"Besides, I'm fresh out of theories."

Walking into the living room, she pulled a purple fleece hoodie over her head. She bent forward and did a quick toe touch, looked around, and smiled.

Theodosia loved her home, loved everything about it. From the living room with its brick fireplace set into a wall of beveled cypress panels, to the oil paintings she'd handpicked at Gilbert's Antiques. The place was hands down gorgeous and homey, and it was all hers. No, it didn't come close to the grandeur of Doreen Brigg's mansion, but owning an expensive showpiece didn't matter to her as long as she was happy and comfortable. And when she was tucked beneath a blanket on her chintz sofa, her dog sprawled out on the Oriental carpet, and a fire crackling away, it felt like heaven. Like all was right with the world.

"Rrowr?"

"Yes, now," Theodosia said, pulling herself out of her reverie. "Sorry to keep you waiting."

The route Theodosia took tonight bordered on being slightly illegal. In other words, as she and Earl Grey dashed down East Bay Street, she veered down a private driveway and then ducked into Stoll's Alley. Just seventeen bricks wide at its entrance, the alley was a relic, a time traveler's leap into Charleston's historic past. Stately homes were basically jammed up one against the other, sheltered by a curtain of overhanging trees, hidden by tall brick walls that dated back to the Revolutionary War. Stoll's Alley was also kind of a Peeping Tom's delight. Many of the window shades weren't always drawn as carefully as they should be, so you could catch slivers of life inside the magnificent old homes. Here was an elegant masculine-looking library filled with leather-bound volumes. A few yards on was a window that offered a peek into a cozy kitchen complete with repurposed wooden planks for counters and shelves holding a to-die-for collection of sterling silver tankards.

Theodosia and Earl Grey popped out at Church Street, waited for a sleek-looking car to go by, and then ran across the street. Seconds later, they were once again cloaked in darkness, save for a few old-fashioned lamps that cast dribbles of light against the cobblestones. Pounding down another back alley, they zipped along a narrow lane that snaked between two enormous mansions, both with spectacular walled gardens complete with white marble statuary and pattering fountains. They turned down Meeting Street to Price's Alley where more town houses — expensive town houses — were clustered in a tight row with an eight-foot-high brick wall snugged up on the right.

Theodosia was always amazed at the high density of the area. Yet each cottage, townhome, and mansion felt like its own fiercely independent principality, surrounded as they were by green gardens, statuary, small reflecting pools, and wrought-iron gates. Shut off from the world, yet still very much *there.*

Feeling like she'd blown off the dust of the day, Theodosia tugged gently at Earl Grey's leash and turned for home.

And that's when it all went a little bit crazy.

Just as they were crossing Tradd, a car came hurtling out of nowhere. Engine roaring full bore, headlights blazing, the car headed straight for them. Caught in the middle of the street, Theodosia froze for a split second, uncertain of which way to jump.

Surely he's going to swerve! That driver has to see us!

But no, the driver stayed his course. Crouched over his steering wheel, this shadowy ghost driver put the pedal to the metal and roared at them like an Indy car screaming down the straightaway.

With not much time to think, Theodosia gave Earl Grey a hard shove that sent him flying, and then she lurched after him. There was a sudden high-pitched squeal of brakes as the car swerved, made a slight course correction, and kept coming at them!

Theodosia screamed as she made a second awkward, panicked leap out of the way. She felt the hot, swift slipstream of air and rush of metal as the car shot by, missing her by mere inches.

Flying through the air, she and Earl Grey were a tumbling mass of legs, arms, paws, and tail. Shocked grunts and *oof*s escaped their lips. Then they hit the ground in a crazy humpty-bumpty sprawl, rolling and bouncing up and over a low curb, finally coming to rest in a patch of French hydrangeas.

Alive? was Theodosia's first dazed thought. *Are we still alive?*

Earl Grey was the first to recover. He pulled himself up, shook himself vigorously from his nose to his tail, and gazed around in surprise. The startled look on his face clearly said, *Good heavens, how did we end up here?*

When Theodosia saw her dog standing upright, panting, but not in any obvious distress, her heart relaxed.

Thank goodness my boy is okay!

She rolled over slowly and lifted a fist. "Who would do that?" she shouted, loud and angry, railing at the night sky. She felt bumped and bruised and battered. "Who would try to intentionally hit us with their car?"

Her own words suddenly registered inside her brain and brought her up short.

Intentionally? Somebody tried to hit me intentionally? Who?

But deep in her brain's frontal lobe, the rational, problem-solving part of her brain, she was slowly spinning out an answer.

"The murderer," Theodosia said, her voice dropping to a low whisper. "He thinks I know more than I do. Or else this person, this cold-blooded killer, thinks I'm getting way too close to finding out the truth."

She was kneeling in the flower bed on mud-streaked hands and knees, dumbfounded by her own revelation.

Until Earl Grey nudged her gently with his nose. *Time to go.*

Gingerly, Theodosia pulled herself to her feet and stared down the street at . . . darkness. The car that had menaced them was long gone.

Theodosia's trip home was slow and thoughtful. She and Earl Grey, still shaking out the kinks and quieting their pounding hearts, ambled down Tradd Street. Earl Grey seemed okay, none the worse for wear, but Theodosia's left knee was sore and achy. She'd pay for this tomorrow.

As she walked past Doreen Briggs's home, she gazed across the gardens toward the tall, arched windows that defined the front of the house. The velvet drapes were pulled tight, but slivers of light seeped out at the sides.

Was Doreen in there? Had she just come ghosting in her back door with a smirk on her face? Was she hanging up her keys in the hallway thinking about a job well done? Was her car's engine slowly ticking down in her garage out back?

Maybe. Possibly.

Theodosia limped along, finally turning down her own block, thankfully, mercifully, almost home now. And was startled to see lights blazing from every window of the enormous mansion that sat next to her little cottage.

The Granville Mansion had sat empty for almost two years now, ever since its owner had been murdered. She wondered who might be looking at the old place now? People with money, no doubt. The last she'd heard, the home was on the market for something like two-point-nine million dollars. She'd have to sell scones and tea from here to eternity to garner a fortune like that. And then, if she owned the place, she probably wouldn't be able to afford drapes.

A sour note rose up in Theodosia's mind. What if Honey and Michael Whitley were the people who were inspecting the place? With a keen eye to extending their reach and opening another B and B?

Theodosia knew that if the Whitleys bought the old mansion, there would be only one thing for her to do. Move.

She pulled back gently on Earl Grey's leash and they both hesitated at the mansion's front gate. She was tired and couldn't wait to take a hot shower and crawl into bed, but she was profoundly curious, too. And she could see shadows flitting back and forth inside the foyer. Maybe the potential buyers had finished their inspection and were just about ready to leave?

Yes, they were. At least somebody was. A small figure was making its way slowly down the front walk. Then that small figure suddenly materialized into a woman that Theodosia had more than a nodding acquaintance with.

"Maggie?" Theodosia said. She thought her voice sounded rusty and hoarse. Maybe from screaming at that horrible driver?

Maggie Twining gave a sort of start and then peered at Theodosia through the darkness.

"Theodosia?" Maggie said. She'd been startled but recovered quickly. "How are you?" she asked, her voice immediately warming. Maggie Twining was an agent with Sutter Realty. In fact, she was the one who'd helped Theodosia find and purchase her cottage.

"Not too bad," Theodosia said. She didn't feel like explaining her hit-and-run experience of fifteen minutes ago.

"It's nice to see you," Maggie said. "And Earl Grey, too." She stretched a hand out and patted Earl Grey on the head. "You're such a fine-looking gent."

"You just showed the Granville house?" Theodosia asked.

"Not just showed. Sold." Maggie looked pleased. "In fact . . ." She hesitated as a tall man in an expensive-looking charcoal suit hurried down the front walk. He was talking on his cell phone, sounding upbeat and jocular. Then he signed off, stuck his phone in his jacket pocket, and joined them.

"Hello," he said to Theodosia. He turned his attention to Earl Grey. "Hey, nice dog."

Earl Grey wagged his tail.

"There's no time like the present to meet your new neighbor," Maggie said. "Theodosia, meet . . ."

"I know who you are," Theodosia said, staring at the man who stood in front of her, offering a friendly smile. "You're Robert Steele. I was at your presentation this past Tuesday night."

Steele focused on Theodosia and immediately clicked into his salesman's patter. "Glad to hear it," he enthused. "I hope you enjoyed it."

"I was also a guest at the rat tea this past

270

Saturday. And the funeral this morning," she added.

Steele never missed a beat. He shook his head and looked sorrowful. "Heck of a thing, wasn't it? Beau was such a great guy. Have you heard anything new? Are the police any closer to catching who did it?"

"I think they're very close," Theodosia said, not because they actually were, but because she was curious to see Steele's reaction.

"Let's hope so," Steele said. "Better times ahead, huh?"

"Maybe," Theodosia said.

Steele made a motion to leave. "Thank you," he said to Maggie. And to Theodosia, "I hope we were able to convince you to invest with Angel Oak."

"I'm certainly considering it," Theodosia lied. "But I might have a few more questions."

"Contact me anytime," Steele said. "Ask away."

"I might just do that," Theodosia said. "Contact you, that is."

"Well, now you know where to find me," Steele said. He flapped a hand to indicate the house he'd just committed to purchase and flashed a megawatt grin at Maggie. "As long as all the paperwork sails through."

"I can't imagine why it wouldn't," Maggie said.

I can think of a few reasons, Theodosia thought to herself.

21

"You'll never guess who's buying the property next door to me," Theodosia said. It was Friday morning and she and Drayton were scurrying around the tea shop, setting up tables, lighting candles, and getting the place shipshape for their morning rush.

"Who might that be?" Drayton asked. He paused, giving a thoughtful look as he considered whether to set out the Royal Albert Old Country Roses or the Coalport Pink Flamingo plates and teacups.

"It's that Angel Oak VC guy we saw the other night. Robert Steele."

"My goodness," Drayton said. "The same Robert Steele who sat across from Doreen at the rat tea?"

"That's the one."

"What a strange coincidence. And I have to say, business must be booming for Angel Oak. That mansion is enormous, which means the mortgage must be astronomical."

"Business might be good because Robert Steele is probably a crook," Theodosia said.

Drayton looked startled. "Theodosia, you don't know that for sure."

"I did some more research on Angel Oak last night. Right after Maggie Twining told me that Steele wanted to buy that place."

Drayton pulled a tin of Lady London Ceylon tea off the shelf. "What did you find out?"

"Besides the state attorney general, the SEC has had a watchful eye on Robert Steele."

"Because of his venture capital fund?"

"Yes, but it's complicated," Theodosia said. "An article I found online in *Charleston Business Daily* hinted that the SEC was looking at Steele's personal investments. Apparently they want to know if he has a financial interest in the companies that are included in his venture capital portfolio."

Drayton put up a hand and zoomed it across the top of his head. "You just lost me."

"Here's the thing," Theodosia said. "If Steele owns stock in the companies he's recommending to buyers, then he would stand to profit personally. And that would be a no-no."

"Ah, now I understand. That does sound

like double-dealing."

Bang bang bang. A cascade of loud knocks sounded at the front door.

"Now what?" Theodosia said. She was right in the middle of explaining her theory on Robert Steele to Drayton and the tea shop didn't open for another fifteen minutes.

Drayton eased his way toward the door. "I'll see who our overanxious guest is. Tell them to hold their horses."

"Be nice about it," Theodosia said.

"I'm always nice."

But when Drayton pushed the curtain aside and looked out the window, he let out a disdainful snort.

"Obviously it's not a women's tea club come to call," Theodosia observed dryly. "Or your reaction wouldn't be quite so snide."

Drayton's mouth pulled tight. "It's that awful Bill Glass again. Should I shoo him away or do you want me to let him in?"

"Let him in," Theodosia said, sounding resigned. "If we don't he'll just stand there banging away and drive us all bonkers."

Drayton pulled open the door. "Theodosia says you can come in, but you have to be nice."

"I'm always nice," Glass said as he strode

briskly into the tea shop. He made a big show of sliding to a stop, then flashed a grin at Theodosia and said, "Howdy."

"What?" Theodosia asked. "What do you want?"

"A cup of tea would be great for openers," Glass said.

Theodosia wasn't buying it. "What else is on your evil little mind?"

"I have some information to share with you," Glass said.

"Oh?"

"Concerning a certain rat who is no longer among the living."

"You know something more about that?" Theodosia asked. Glass was obviously referring to Marcus Covey.

"In case you haven't guessed, I have friends in high places. As in the Charleston Police Department."

"They're probably paid informants," Drayton said from behind the counter.

"What if they are?" Glass said. "Who cares *how* I get the poop as long as I *get* the poop?"

"You mean get the gossip," Drayton said.

"What exactly is this new information?" Theodosia asked. She was curious but repulsed by Glass. Kind of like dealing with a snake you'd found slithering through your

276

garden. That snake might keep the rodent population in check, but you still had yourself a snake.

Glass tapped the counter and curled a finger at a steaming pot of tea. "Do you think . . . ?"

"Yes. Whatever." Theodosia poured a splash of black currant tea into an indigo-blue paper cup and handed it to him.

"How about a scone, too?" Glass asked. He patted his stomach. "Gotta keep the old tank filled."

"They're still baking in the oven," Theodosia said.

Glass pointed to a lone scone sitting in a glass cake saver. "What about that one?"

"It's from yesterday," Drayton said.

"No problem," Glass said.

So Theodosia placed the day-old scone on a plate and shoved it toward him.

There were a few moments of noisy slurping and chewing, and then Glass said, "The police discovered something very interesting in the trunk of Covey's car."

"What was it?" Theodosia asked. She narrowed her eyes, recalling the banged-up black Saab that had been parked in Covey's backyard.

Glass was chewing loudly. "A twist of guy wire. You know, the kind of metal cord you

277

use for pegging tents to the ground? It's what was used to hang Covey with."

"A kind of wire? And some of it was actually in the trunk of his car?" Theodosia asked.

Glass held up a finger as though he had more hot news. "And . . . lying next to the wire was a crumpled-up business card that belonged to that PR lady."

"What!" Theodosia said. "You mean Starla Crane?"

"No!" Drayton said, suddenly coming alive.

Theodosia was completely dumbfounded by Glass's revelation. Was that the answer right there? Was Starla Crane the killer? Had Starla poisoned Beau Briggs and then hanged Marcus Covey?

"You mean the police actually *found* Starla's business card along with the wire used to hang Covey?" Theodosia finally gasped out.

Glass aimed a finger at her. "You catch on fast, tea lady."

"Wha . . ." Theodosia was stumbling over her own words. "So what's going on? What are the police . . . ?"

"What are the police doing about it?" Drayton asked, jumping in.

"Unfortunately, the cops didn't get around

to examining the car trunk until last night," Glass said. He rolled his eyes. "Stellar police work, huh? Anyway, I understand the police will be hauling Miss Crane in today to ask her some very tough questions."

Theodosia cocked her head at Drayton and said, "Starla? Could it have been her all along?"

Drayton shrugged. "It sounds like . . . maybe."

"But why?" Theodosia asked. "What was her motivation?"

"She was trying to play Svengali?" Drayton said. "Get Doreen under her control so she could . . . I don't know . . . influence how all her money was spent? Or maybe even con Doreen out of her money?"

"Or take over the spa?" Theodosia said. Fresh in her mind was Starla Crane screaming at the models and videographers yesterday afternoon, trying to get some sort of corporate video rushed through for tomorrow's big event. A video that might have showcased her skills? Or her leadership ability?

"This is big-time, huh?" Glass said, grinning at Theodosia like a demented Cheshire cat.

Theodosia gave an absent nod. "This is truly . . . puzzling."

■ ■ ■ ■

Theodosia was still ruminating over the Starla factor a few hours later as she rushed about the tea shop. When she stopped at the front counter to grab a pot of chocolate mint tea, she said, "Is it possible Starla could have murdered both Beau and Marcus Covey?"

"It doesn't feel exactly right," Drayton said as he measured out scoops of Madoorie Estate tea into a floral teapot. "But, yes, I suppose it's possible."

"You're right," Theodosia said.

Drayton stopped measuring. "Wait a minute. I'm right about what?"

"You're right that it doesn't *feel* right. If that makes any sense."

"Theo, your logic has always made perfect sense to me."

"Just not to me," Theodosia said.

Lunchtime came and customers rolled in like crazy. A couple of neighborhood shopkeepers, six ladies from the Broad Street Garden Club who were in the throes of planning a garden tour, a few art students who had found their way in after spending the morning sketching at the Gibbes Museum of Art.

Haley had whipped up some fabulous offerings: mini chicken potpies, avocado tea sandwiches, shrimp salad, and popovers.

Of course, she was saving the best for tonight's Candlelight Tea. She'd shared a bare-bones menu with Theodosia and Drayton, but promised that she had a couple of big surprises up her sleeve. One being a tipsy cake for dessert. Which in Southern parlance meant a fruit and pudding trifle.

After the last few days, Theodosia wasn't sure she was ready for any more surprises.

At two o'clock, with the luncheon crowd departed and a small-to-middling afternoon tea crowd, Theodosia said, "I'm going to run over to the Cabbage Patch and grab our candles."

Drayton looked up from behind the counter. "We need candles? I thought we had an entire stash of candles."

"We do. But those are mostly tea lights and a handful of tapers. If we're going to hold a Candlelight Tea, we have to do it right."

"What about the box of red candles that's under the counter?" Drayton asked.

"If you want this place to look like Benito's Pizza Parlor, that's fine with me. But if we want to impart an elegant, old-world atmosphere, if we want this tea shop to shimmer and glow, we're going to need better candles."

Drayton touched a hand to his tortoise-shell half-glasses and pushed them up his nose. "You've convinced me. I surrender to your judgment and good taste."

The Cabbage Patch Gift Shop was only two doors down from the Indigo Tea Shop, and Leigh Carroll, its owner, was ready for her.

"I've got your candles," Leigh said as Theodosia stepped through the door and into her eclectic little gift shop. Leigh was a pretty African American woman, midthirties, with almond eyes, sepia-toned hair, and beautifully burnished skin.

"And I've got a cup of rose hips tea for you," Theodosia said. "Along with a couple of maraschino cherry scones."

Leigh put a hand to her heart. "Be still my heart." She was a raving tea fanatic. Favored everything from Japanese Gyokuro to Russian country blends. "I love this tea." She grabbed the cup, snapped off the lid, and took a sip. "Delicious."

"We still have room tonight if you want to come."

"I want to but I can't," Leigh said. "Not tonight, but next time you have a big event."

"I'm going to hold you to that," Theodosia said. She glanced around the shop at Leigh's spectacular inventory. She saw beaded purses, antique linens, elegant pottery, silk kimonos, tea towels, and French perfume. And candles. Theodosia pointed at a candle arrangement. "Are those the kind of candles you ordered for us?"

Leigh shook her head. She grabbed a white cardboard box that sat at her feet and hoisted it onto the counter. "I've got your candles right here. Take a look."

Theodosia peered into the box. "Wow. These are great." She lifted out a tall cream-colored pillar candle. "Are they all the same?"

"Oh no. I made sure to get you a nice assortment. There are pillar candles in three different sizes, some candles in small square tins, a few twisted tapers, and candles in apothecary jars. They're all different kinds, too. Some are beeswax candles, a few are honey candles, and some are even soy candles."

Theodosia touched the candle to her nose. "But unscented."

"That's right. I made sure they're all unscented so they won't compete with your wonderful tea aromas. And the good thing, the really cool thing, is that they're all the exact same creamy color. So when you light them and douse your overhead spotlights, you'll get a nice, warm, even glow." She waved a hand. "Imagine an elegant little chapel just outside of Paris. No incandescent lights, just flickering candles to illuminate that most contemplative of places where you can say your prayers and offer up a blessing."

"Wow," Theodosia said. "I wish you could come tonight and weave that little story to our guests. I think they'd be mesmerized."

"Abracadabra," Theodosia exclaimed as she stepped into the Indigo Tea Shop. "It looks as if you two have worked quite a bit of magic in here."

Drayton and Haley glanced up from where they were laying out plates and teacups. In Theodosia's short absence they'd covered the tables with cream-colored French linens, added Belleek Basketweave plates and teacups, and set out Waterford crystal water glasses.

"All our customers took off so we decided to close the tea shop and get cracking," Drayton said.

"Be honest, Drayton," Haley said. "You did exert a subtle amount of pressure."

Drayton straightened up and favored

Haley with a mousy grin. "Don't you know by now that I'm the master of subtle?"

"Oh," Haley said. "We had a couple of deliveries. The flowers arrived from Floradora. Roses, very pale and creamy, exactly as you requested. They're in your office, Theo, sitting in big buckets just waiting to be arranged in glass vases."

"Which I shall attend to as soon as we place these candles on the tables," Theodosia said. "And what else came?"

"Something that's all wrapped up and looks like it might be a painting," Haley said.

"Just one?"

"Were there supposed to be more?"

"I asked for three oil paintings on approval from the Dolce Gallery down the street. Oh bother, I suppose I'll have to run down there later and see what the problem is."

"Have fun, kiddies," Haley said, giving a wave as she twirled away from them. "Because I've got to duck back in the kitchen and tend to my cookin'."

"These are lovely candles," Drayton said. He'd pulled one of the pillar candles out of the box to admire it. "Mmm, beeswax. The very best kind." He placed it carefully in the center of a table. "How many candles did you get all told?"

"There should be two dozen," Theodosia said. "But all different kinds."

They worked the rest of the afternoon, polishing and primping. Theodosia arranged the roses and then stocked all the shelves of her highboy. As they worked, the aromas drifting out from Haley's kitchen just kept getting better and better.

Finally, when everything seemed just about perfect, Theodosia pulled three grapevine wreaths off the wall and replaced them with the large oil painting. The painting was of two women from the late eighteen hundreds sitting at an outdoor French café. The lighting was very soft and moody, the surface of the painting covered with tiny cracks.

"That painting looks very elegant in here," Drayton said. "And you say there were supposed to be a couple more?"

Theodosia adjusted the painting so it hung straight. "They promised me two more. If you don't mind, I'm going to run down to the Dolce Gallery and see what the holdup is."

"I don't mind at all," Drayton said. "Seeing as how that painting adds a very sophisticated note to our tea shop."

22

"Mr. Ritter," Theodosia sang out as she pushed through the front door of the Dolce Gallery. "It's Theodosia. From the tea shop?"

She dodged around an enormous easel that held an oil painting of Charleston Harbor and gazed around the small shop. The walls were a mosaic of paintings, classic as well as contemporary. Smaller paintings were displayed everywhere. On table easels and hung on half walls that made the small shop look like a Chinese puzzle. Dozens more paintings leaned against each other in antique wooden crates.

"Just the one painting got delivered today and you said that . . ."

Theodosia pulled up short. She'd almost run smack-dab into the back of a tall, well-dressed gentleman who was standing in the tiny gallery, holding a painting at arm's length and studying it intently.

"Oops, sorry. I'm afraid I didn't see you," Theodosia said. "I was looking for . . ."

The man turned around to stare at her. Then a flash of recognition lit his face and his jaw muscles tightened.

Theodosia experienced that same electric flash. "Oh jeez," she said, a little too loudly. "It's you. Again." Robert Steele, CEO of Angel Oak Venture Capital was standing right there in front of her. Then, before she could catch herself, she blurted out, "What are you doing here?"

Steele favored her with a slow, quizzical smile. "I'm considering whether I should buy this painting. But a better question might be, what are you doing here?"

"This is my block. Well, what I mean is, my tea shop is just a couple of doors down."

Steele studied her. "Your tea shop."

"That's right, the Indigo Tea Shop." She glanced around, saw Mr. Ritter, the owner of the gallery, standing in the back room, talking on his phone.

A slow smile had spread across Steele's face. "You run a tea shop and you're an investor?"

"Sure," Theodosia said. "Why not?" She had the feeling Steele wanted to put her on the defensive. Well, good luck with that, bub. She wasn't afraid to stand up to him and dish it right back.

"Did you qualify for your mortgage yet?" Theodosia asked.

Steele's brows pinched together, indicating that she'd scored a direct hit.

"Now, why would my mortgage be any of *your* business?" he asked.

Theodosia took a deep breath and decided to go for the jugular. After all, how many chances would she get to confront him?

"Curiously, it *is* my business," she said. "I've been asked by Doreen Briggs . . . you remember Doreen, don't you? As I mentioned last night, you were sitting at her head table when her husband, Beau, dropped dead after being poisoned."

"*Excuse* me?"

Theodosia waved a hand in the air, as if to casually erase her somewhat inflammatory statement. "But that's not my point."

Steele's face had become a thundercloud. "Then what is?"

"Doreen Briggs would like to have her husband's investment returned. I'm referring to the seven hundred thousand dollars that Beau handed over to your company, Angel Oak."

"Wait. What?"

"I think you heard me," Theodosia said. "Because my request is really quite simple.

Doreen would like you to refund her husband's money." She bobbled her head from side to side, as if sorting through her words. "Actually, it was *Doreen's* money . . . the money that Beau handed over to you. Now she'd like it back."

"Why are *you* inquiring about Doreen Briggs's personal finances?"

"Because Doreen asked me to. As a personal favor. And because Doreen is completely overwhelmed right now. You were at the funeral yesterday morning, Mr. Steele. You saw how she was holding up. About as well as a two-legged stool."

"And that's my problem?" Steele asked.

"It is if you don't refund her investment. Yes, it most certainly would be your problem."

Steele set down the painting. "That sounds decidedly like a threat."

"Please try to think of it as a friendly request."

"Not so friendly," Steele said.

"I'm afraid that's your perception." Goodness, Theodosia thought to herself, this man does like to verbally joust. Was she getting anywhere at all with him? She certainly hoped so.

"I can understand that Doreen might want her investment back," Steele said. "But

290

papers have been signed."

"Perhaps they could be unsigned," Theodosia said.

Steele shook his head slowly. "That would present certain difficulties."

"I'm sure it would. But I'm positive the right attorney could help us overcome those difficulties."

"Please don't . . ."

But Theodosia kept right on talking. "For openers, we could start with the state attorney general." She shook her hair back and smiled. "Although that might be a bit heavy-handed."

"I don't threaten easily," Steele said.

"It wasn't intended as a threat," Theodosia said. "Merely a way to help extricate all parties from what may or may not be a legally binding contract."

"What's your game, exactly?" Steele asked. "You say tea shop, but you sound more like a lawyer."

"Funny you should mention that," Theodosia said. "Perhaps you've heard of the law firm Browning and Alston?"

Steele gave an almost imperceptible nod.

"My late father and his brother were the founding partners. My father, God rest his soul, has passed, but my uncle is still very much alive and kicking. I'm sure if I put a bug in his ear he'd be willing to take this case on."

"Jeremy Alston?" For the first time, Steele looked nervous.

Theodosia smiled sweetly. "That's right. You might recall that he served as lieutenant governor a decade or so ago? Well, he's back once again with the law firm. And still very well connected, I might add."

"I told you, Miss Browning," Steele said through gritted teeth, "I don't respond well to threats."

"And I'm generally not a name-dropper," she shot back at him. "But if I need to pull out the big guns, I will."

Steele fixed her with a cold stare.

"Perhaps you could give Doreen a quick call?" Theodosia said. "I'm sure she'd be thrilled to hear from you." She turned on her heel. "And thank you, Mr. Steele, for your cooperation. Thank you very much."

"Where are the paintings?" Drayton asked when Theodosia slipped through the front door.

"Oh, those?" Theodosia said. "I decided we didn't need them after all."

Drayton shrugged. "Very well. Oh, Haley and I decided to put out those decorated sugar cubes."

"The ones by the lady in Savannah? With the tiny flowers and ladybugs?"

"That's right. And I thought it might be fun to use the silver water pitchers we bought when the Hotel Continental went defunct."

"Sounds right to me," Theodosia said.

"You're in a good mood," Drayton said.

"I guess I'm just looking forward to tonight."

"Mmm."

Theodosia glanced around the tea shop. "Before we change into our evening duds, do you think we should try a test run?"

"Why not?" Drayton said.

They turned off all the lamps, as well as the small overhead chandelier, and then lit the candles. The result was transformative. The Indigo Tea Shop shimmered and glowed like a cottage from the magical village of Brigadoon, come back after a hundred-year respite.

"This is spectacular," Drayton declared.

Theodosia nodded. "The candles, dinnerware, the linens and things, they really set the mood. I think our guests will be favorably impressed."

Even Haley came out to see the special effects they'd wrought. She let out a low whistle. "Wow. It's like a really cool dance club or something."

"But without the annoying music," Drayton said. He paused for a minute. "No. What this is . . . the lighting and the fact that our table settings resemble a still life . . . is reminiscent of a Rembrandt painting. Or possibly a Vermeer." His hands carved shapes in the air. "Some parts highlighted, others left in the dark. You know, that lovely chiaroscuro, the subtle interplay of shadow and light."

Theodosia smiled. "How very poetic and apropos."

23

Theodosia and Drayton were dressed to the nines in honor of their Candlelight Tea. Theodosia had changed into a pale-peach silk blouse tucked into a long silver satin skirt. She'd added a peach lipstick, a sweep of black mascara, and swept her abundance of auburn hair up into a fun, messy do. Drayton had exchanged his tweed jacket for a severely tailored dark-blue cashmere jacket.

"Do you think I should switch out my bow tie as well?" he asked.

"The polka-dot tie for what?" Theodosia asked.

"I was thinking my burgundy silk."

"Go for it."

"You guys look so elegant," Haley said. "And here I am with a big old white mushroom perched on top of my head."

"A chef's hat," Theodosia said. "And a well-deserved, hard-earned professional white jacket. Because you're an honest-to-goodness chef."

Haley scrunched up her face and looked at her. "You think so? It's not like I've earned enough credits yet for a culinary school degree."

"Doesn't matter." Theodosia nodded. "You've proved your skills time and again to us. You've won major baking contests and you've certainly won the hearts and minds of our tea shop customers. Why, you've even had several of your recipes featured in the *Post and Courier*."

"Well . . . yeah. And some of my granny's, too."

"That's your pedigree. And it's a fine one," Theodosia said. "So please don't ever think that you're not as good as anyone else. And please don't be nervous tonight when we bring you out for an introduction and a round of applause."

"You'd do that? Really?"

"Our guests would expect nothing less. They'll want to thank the chef who cooked their delicious dinners."

At six o'clock on the button their guests began to arrive. They shuffled in excitedly, not sure what to expect. But eager smiles changed to absolute wonderment as soon as

296

they saw the tea tables bathed in soft candlelight, the sparkling dishware and crystal, and the dreamy rose bouquets. The mood was further set with the lovely painting that hung on the wall and Drayton's beloved classical music playing over the sound system.

"This is spectacular," Honey Whitley exclaimed as she hustled into the tea shop on the arm of her husband, Michael. "It's like your tea shop underwent a complete metamorphosis."

"That's because it did," Theodosia said. "From cute and cozy to four-star elegance."

"I wish our dining room looked this good," Michael lamented as Honey just patted his arm.

More guests arrived. Some of Drayton's friends from the Heritage Society, Angie Congdon from the Featherbed House B and B with her new boyfriend, Brooke Carter Crockett from Heart's Desire, and at least two dozen other tea shop regulars.

Delaine showed up looking anxious and frazzled because her date had canceled at the last minute. That problem was immediately smoothed over when Jemma Lee showed up without Big Reggie, and Drayton seated the two women together at a small table by the window. They immediately put their heads together and began buzzing excitedly about fashion, makeup, and local celebs.

And, surprise, surprise, Doreen and Opal Anne showed up.

"We weren't expecting you," Theodosia said. She'd been checking names off her reservation list and their names were definitely not there.

Doreen immediately confronted Opal Anne. "Didn't you make reservations? I *told* you to make reservations."

"You told me *you* were going to make reservations," Opal Anne said patiently.

"It's not a problem, ladies," Theodosia said. "We've got room." *Thank goodness for those last two available seats!*

Doreen put a hand on Theodosia's arm and said in her I'm-telling-you-a-special-secret voice, "Did you know that Starla was taken in for questioning today?"

"I did hear that," Theodosia said.

"It's shocking," Doreen said, her eyes going buggy, her curls jiggling nervously. "Apparently, the police found one of Starla's business cards crumpled in the car trunk of that man who got hanged." She was practically drooling with excitement, hopped up like she was high on crystal meth. "And the wire cord that was used to hang him — it

298

was the same kind that was used to an-chor . . ."

Opal Anne cut in suddenly to cap off the story. "The cord was the exact same kind used for anchoring *tents.* And Starla had just honchoed a charity fun run in Hampton Park last week."

"Where they had tents set up!" Doreen crowed.

"Do you know . . . was it the exact same kind of wire cord?" Theodosia asked.

"We're still waiting to hear," Opal Anne said.

"This could change everything," Doreen said, looking grim.

Or it could change nothing, Theodosia thought.

"Still," Opal Anne said, "Starla's innocent until proven guilty."

"I guess," Doreen said. "Anyway, we thought we'd share that bit of news with you. It threw our day off quite a bit and is part of the reason why we're in need of a calm, relaxing evening."

Opal Anne nudged Doreen. "Tell her the good news."

Doreen's eyes bugged out. "Oh, I almost forgot. I got a call from Robert Steele just as we were leaving tonight. He said that, under the present circumstances, he was

perfectly fine with refunding Beau's investment. Really *my* investment." She clapped
her hands together. "And of course I said
yes."

"Of course you did." Theodosia smiled.

"Theodosia," Opal Anne said. "Do I
detect your fine hand behind Robert Steele's
change of heart?"

"Let's just say Steele and I had a little
chat," Theodosia said.

"You are a wonder," Doreen said, goggling
at her. "How can I ever thank you?"

*Maybe by taking your seats so I can tend to
my other guests?*

Taking the bull by the horns and Doreen
by the arm, Theodosia led her to one of the
tables. "Are you still planning to hold your
grand opening party tomorrow night?"
Theodosia asked politely. Doreen was
clearly down to the wire on her spa's big
party.

"Yes, we're doing it," Doreen said. "Although we'd been counting on Starla to take
charge." She sighed. "Too late to cancel.
Now I suppose it's all up to Reggie Huston."

"If there's anything I can do," Theodosia
said.

"We'd love it if you brought over some
tea," Doreen said as she settled into her
chair. "We were thinking that, besides serv-

ing champagne and fruit juices, a spot of tea would be nice for our guests. It just seems very healthy."

"I'll run some tea over to Gilded Magnolia Spa tomorrow afternoon," Theodosia said.

"Thank you," Doreen said. She patted Opal Anne's hand. "But tonight we're going to enjoy a well-deserved respite from our problems."

"I'm still surprised you're out and about," Theodosia said. "After all, Beau's funeral was only yesterday."

"I'm feeling somewhat better," Doreen said. "Opal Anne tells me I have to be social and try to get my life back to normal, no matter where this investigation goes. So that's what I'm doing. Besides," Doreen confided, "Opal Anne's been having boyfriend problems, so this Candlelight Tea is a nice cozy respite for us both."

Opal Anne squirmed in her chair. "You don't have to blab to everybody."

"It's okay, dear, we're all friends here," Doreen said.

Theodosia looked out over the crowd and thought, *Are we really?*

"Welcome," Theodosia said as she stood facing her guests. "Welcome to the Indigo Tea Shop and our Candlelight Tea." There

301

was a smatter of applause and then she continued. "We're thrilled you could join us tonight and excited to be serving you a very special four-course dinner. As you might expect, our tea master, Drayton, has carefully matched each individual course with the perfect complementary tea."

"The first tea we'll be serving tonight," Drayton said, stepping in, "will be a Darjeeling from the Longview Tea Estate. Located in the southwest region of India's Darjeeling region, Longview tea is a complex black tea that should make a fine pairing with our first course of dilled crawfish."

That was Theodosia's cue to grab the teapots that Drayton had placed on the counter and begin pouring tea. Drayton grabbed two more teapots of his freshly brewed Darjeeling, and they both set to work. Then they rushed into the kitchen, grabbed the small plates of crawfish that Haley had set out, and rushed them back to their guests.

The second course was a salmon and asparagus tart served with Cheddar cheese scones. That was accompanied with Earl Grey tea.

"This is spectacular," Honey Whitley said. "I'd really love to steal your chef and put her to work at the Scarborough Inn."

"Not a chance of that," Theodosia told her.

As plates were being scraped down to the last morsel and compliments practically shouted out, Theodosia brought Haley out for a well-deserved round of applause. Haley grinned, bowed, turned beet red, and then dashed back into the kitchen.

"What Haley didn't have time to tell you," Theodosia said to her guests, "is that our third course, our main entrée, consists of beef bourguignonne."

"And we're pairing it with a Tippy Yunnan black tea," Drayton said.

"Goodness," Doreen said. "This is as exciting as a food and wine pairing at a four-star restaurant."

"Isn't this imaginative?" Michael Whitley said.

To serve their more complex entrée, Theodosia and Drayton were assisted by Haley. In a carefully choreographed move, they all three brought out the beef bourguignonne entrées and served them with a flourish.

"Now we can relax," Theodosia whispered to Drayton. "Now that everyone has been served, the complicated part is pretty much over."

"You're right," Drayton said. "Dessert will be a snap. Those small bowls of trifle can practically be brought out on two trays."

"We're coming down the home stretch."

"And everyone seems to be enjoying themselves."

"Drayton," one of the guests called out, "can you tell us a little more about this divine tea?"

Drayton put on his game face and strode to the center of the room. "Certainly. A Tippy Yunnan is from China's Yunnan province. The leaves of this big-leafed black tea have golden flecks and when brewed yield a pleasant peppery flavor that —"

Crash! Bam!

The front door banged open hard, ushering in a whoosh of cool air. Then, like a scary clown popping out of a jack-in-the-box, Starla Crane came flying in. Her face was pulled into a grim, determined mask, her dark hair kinked around her head like an angry Medusa, and her eyes blazed with fury.

Flustered, Drayton turned to face her and said, "Excuse me, we're in the middle of . . ."

Starla blew him off completely. She thundered past Drayton, clipping his shoulder and practically spinning him around in a circle. Then she launched herself directly at

Theodosia like some kind of rabid wolverine.

"You!" Starla shrieked at the top of her lungs. "You did this! You put the police on me!"

24

"Now, just one minute," Theodosia said in a controlled, chilly-as-ice voice. No way was she going to let this crazy lady come charging into her tea shop and try to hijack her event. She grabbed Starla by the shoulders, spun her around, and gave her a hard shove.

Whoom.

Starla was propelled through the velvet curtain that separated the back office and kitchen from the front of the shop.

"What do you think you're doing?" Theodosia hissed as she caught up to a breathless, stumbling Starla.

"This is all your fault," Starla cried.

"You are so out of line," Theodosia said, trying to keep her voice low. "I had nothing to do with your being questioned by the police."

"I don't believe you!"

A second later, Opal Anne hurriedly brushed past the velvet curtain and came to

Theodosia's defense. "Believe her," Opal Anne said. "Theodosia had nothing to do with your being questioned. Didn't the police give you the full story? Didn't they tell you what happened?"

"No," Starla said, her eyes still blazing. "They just asked me the same horrible questions over and over again." She took a step backward and found herself halfway into the kitchen.

"Hey, watch it, lady," Haley called out. "You're getting a little too close to my tipsy cake!"

"Come into my office," Theodosia said. "Let's try to sort this out calmly and rationally."

Reluctantly, Starla followed her back, with Opal Anne trailing them.

"Please believe me," Theodosia said. "I had nothing to do with your being interrogated by the police." *Well, kind of nothing.*

"But you know Detective Riley," Starla spat out. "He told me so."

"Yes, I know him," Theodosia said. "But I'm not assisting him." *Not exactly.*

"Starla," Opal Anne said. "Theodosia would never try to throw you under the bus like that."

Oh yes, I would, Theodosia thought.

"Theodosia's on our side," Opal Anne

continued, trying to reason with Starla. "She's on all of our sides."

"Do you have any idea how humiliated I was?" Starla asked. Now her lower lip began to quiver and tears rolled down her cheeks. "I was yanked out of a business meeting and taken down to a *police* station. They made me sit on a wooden chair in the same dirty, crappy room where they interrogate criminals!"

"I'm sure it wasn't nearly as humiliating as the scene you just created in front of my guests," Theodosia said.

"They questioned me for hours!" Starla cried. "Hours."

"And what came of it?" Theodosia asked. Then she hastened to answer her own question. "They let you go. Obviously, they don't view you as a viable suspect."

"It was just my *business* card," Starla blubbered. "I have no idea how it even got inside that car trunk. I pass out so many cards, it could have come from anywhere. I'm proud of my company, for gosh sakes."

"We understand," Opal Anne said.

Starla wiped at her eyes as she gazed at Opal Anne. "You're not going to hold this against me?"

"Of course not," Opal Anne said.

"What about Doreen?" Starla asked.

"She's one of my most important clients. What does she think?"

"That's something you're going to have to deal with yourself," Opal Anne hedged. "All I can say is she's not very happy."

"But this is not the time nor place to sort out any hard feelings," Theodosia said to Starla. "Right now, the best thing, the smartest thing, is for you to go home."

"I . . . I suppose." Starla sniffled. She wiped at her eyes again and looked around Theodosia's office. Her red-rimmed eyes landed on the door leading out to the alley. "This way again, huh?"

Theodosia nodded. "I think that would be best."

An hour and a half later, the Candlelight Tea was pretty much just a memory. Haley's delicious tipsy cake and Drayton's cinnamon spice tea for dessert had helped gloss over Starla's bizarre interruption. And the guests, sated with good food and fine conversation, had pretty much finished their dinner without giving Starla a second mention. Eventually, they stood up and stretched, shook hands with one another, exchanged a few air kisses, and even did a little shopping.

Delaine and Jemma left arm in arm, dashing off to some other event, while the rest of the guests slowly trickled out the door and into the cool night air.

Finally, just the three of them were left — Theodosia, Drayton, and Haley — to do their tea shop ballet. They stacked dishes, cleared tables, and swished out teapots. It didn't take them long; they were a well-rehearsed troupe who'd done this many times before.

"I almost hate to blow out the candles," Drayton said. "The dancing flames are so gorgeous. But most have only burned down halfway so we can certainly use them again."

"And it doesn't hurt to leave a few of them burning," Theodosia said. "Makes the old place look nice and moody."

"Whew," Haley said, twining her hair up into a topknot and then pulling on a leather baseball jacket. "What an evening. And could you believe that Starla person? I mean, what a squirrel to come storming in like that and try to ruin our tea?"

"Starla didn't ruin it," Theodosia said. "She just added a little excitement."

"She's certainly a few berries short of a trifle," Drayton said.

"Maybe I should burn some sage to help get rid of her lingering evil presence," Haley said.

"I believe Theodosia dispatched with Starla's lingering rather handily," Drayton said. "She punted her out the back door."

Haley grinned. "Twinkle, twinkle, little Starla. How I wonder where you arla." She stuck a baseball cap on her head and then twisted it around backward. "Okay, I'm taking off. I've got the kitchen pretty much packed up and the dishwasher running, so I'll see you guys tomorrow."

"Good night," Theodosia called as Haley quickly disappeared out the back door.

"She's not going home?" Drayton asked. Haley lived upstairs, in what had been Theodosia's old apartment.

"It's Friday night, Drayton. Still early for her. She's going to hang with her friends."

"Youth," Drayton said, a faraway look in his eyes.

"Would you like a ride home?" Theodosia asked.

Drayton took a final sip of tea and set his teacup down. "No, no, it's a lovely evening. Fairly mild, so I think I'll walk home. Stretch these old legs a bit. Besides . . . I could use the fresh air. It'll help to clear my head."

"I hope Starla's theatrics didn't upset you."

"Well, they didn't make me happy, that's

311

for sure. The woman not only interrupted my presentation, she acted completely unhinged. I couldn't believe how you were able to deal with her and not lose your cool."

"I didn't have a choice," Theodosia said. "Starla was making an awful scene and I just wanted to get her as far away from our guests as possible."

"Do you think she's over her snit fit? Now that the police have released her?"

"No idea. I don't know if Starla's still considered a suspect or not. For all I know she may come boomeranging back at us tomorrow."

"Hopefully not." Drayton sighed as he pulled on his herringbone driving cap.

"Okay, Drayton, take care. I'll see you tomorrow."

Drayton put two fingers to his forehead in a jaunty salute. "You can count on it."

Candles guttered in their pewter and brass holders as Theodosia puttered about the tea shop by herself. She straightened chairs, found a couple of errant teacups that had been stuck on a shelf along with her depleted stash of scone mixes and T-Bath products.

Thank goodness tonight's guests had also been eager shoppers. She must have sold a dozen tins of tea, several tubes of Chamo-mile Cream, a couple of jars of honey, and, oh yes, one of her grapevine wreaths (the only one she'd left on the wall!) had found a new home as well.

Theodosia glanced around at the tea shop and smiled. This was the time she liked best. The day drawing to a close, the blessed solitude of being by herself in her tidy little shop. It was a time for contemplation, for feeling a glow of pride in the small business that she'd created.

She would never forget what a wreck the place had been when she'd first set eyes on it. But she'd seen the potential, worked up her courage, and signed the lease.

Then she'd set about building shelves and counters and whitewashing the walls. A tea stain had been applied to the pegged wooden floors, a retail area established, and then . . . then she'd added her own brand of love. Because wasn't that what dreams were all about? Taking chances? Embracing your passion in life? Living that passion?

The phone on the front counter began to ring, interrupting her mood.

Theodosia sighed. Should she answer it or let the answering machine pick it up? Oh well, she supposed it might be something important. Might be. But probably wasn't.

Reluctantly, she snatched up the phone on the fifth ring. "Indigo Tea Shop," she said in what she hoped was a moderately pleasant voice. "How may I help you?"

"Is this Theodosia?" a woman asked in a tentative voice.

"Yes." Theodosia didn't recognize the caller at all.

"My name is Lucille Hart," the woman said. "You don't know me, but I'm calling for your friend Mr. Conneley."

"Drayton? Yes?" Theodosia gripped the phone a little tighter. Drayton had asked someone to call her? But why? What was going on?

"There's been a problem," Lucille said. "Mr. Conneley has been . . . well, there's no easy way to say this. Your friend was involved in a hit-and-run accident."

"What!"

"He's . . ."

Theodosia cut her off. "How . . . how badly is he hurt?" she stammered. This was unbelievable. Drayton had just left here barely twenty minutes ago.

"Well . . . there was blood. I think he hit his head pretty hard. And his knee . . ."

"Where are you?" Theodosia barked out. "I'll come right away. Wait. Did you phone for an ambulance?"

"Yes," Lucille said. "In fact, they just arrived a couple of minutes ago. But Mr. Conneley was insistent that I call you, too." She took a deep breath. "We're at the corner of King Street and Tradd."

"I'll be right there as soon as I can. I'll leave immediately. And thank you!"

25

By the time Theodosia arrived, Drayton was lying on a gurney and about to be loaded into the back of a red-and-white ambulance. Lights flashed, the truck engine idled loudly, and Drayton was putting up one heck of a protest.

"I'm fine, I'm fine," Drayton told the two young EMTs who were trying to care for him. Then, when he saw Theodosia jump out of her Jeep and race toward him, her face rigid with fear, he lifted a hand and gave a feeble wave. "Theo, you didn't have to come," he called out in a croaky voice. "I'm fine. No need to worry about me."

"Drayton!" Theodosia cried. Was he serious? He'd been bodily assaulted. He was being carted off to the hospital, for goodness' sake!

Drayton looked pale and a little frail beneath a fluttering white blanket. But he continued to fuss as one of the EMTs, a young woman with frizzy red hair, kept trying to fit an oxygen mask over his mouth and nose.

"Sir, just suck on a few O's, okay?" the lady EMT asked. "It'll make you feel better."

"I told you I'm fine," Drayton protested.

"Please, Drayton," Theodosia implored as she stood at his side. "Let this nice lady put an oxygen mask on you. It'll make you feel better."

"I feel absolutely fine as it is," Drayton said. "But if it will make *you* happy, then all right. I'll wear the silly mask."

"Thank you," the lady EMT said to Theodosia.

She placed the mask on Drayton's face and then she and her male partner finished loading Drayton into the back of the ambulance. Then the partner jumped in, squatted down next to Drayton, and pulled the back door of the ambulance shut.

"We're taking him to the ER at Mercy Medical," the lady EMT said, turning to face Theodosia. "So if you want to follow along, you're welcome to do so."

"Thank you," Theodosia said. "I will. But first I . . ." She gestured toward a middle-aged lady in a khaki raincoat who was standing off to the side with her dog. "I need to talk . . ."

"Are you Theodosia?" the woman called, coming over to join her as the ambulance pulled away with a loud bleat.

Theodosia turned to greet her. "Yes, I am. Are you Lucille?"

The woman nodded. "That's right. Lucille Hart."

Theodosia put her arms around Lucille and hugged her. "Thank you for your call. Thank you for finding him." She was flustered and scared and wasn't exactly sure what to say.

"I just stumbled upon your friend by accident," Lucille said. "I was out walking Madison . . ." She gestured at her fawn-colored shar-pei, who was snuffling around at the end of a leash. "And we saw something lying on the sidewalk. It was so dark that at first I thought it was a pile of leaves or an old coat. And then the coat rolled over and moaned." She put a hand to her chest as if to still her fluttering heart. "Scared me half to death. You don't see something like *that* every day."

"Thank you for your quick response," Theodosia said. "For calling an ambulance right away."

"You know," Lucille said, "Mr. Conneley wanted me to call you first."

Hot tears prickled in Theodosia's eyes. "Oh no, he didn't really."

"Mr. Conneley was quite insistent," Lucille said. "But I figured I should call for help first and notify friends second."

"You figured right. Thank you so much."

"It's very strange," Lucille said. "Madison and I take a walk almost every night and we've never encountered any problems before."

"You said that Drayton was just lying there, so obviously he'd just been attacked. Hit or mugged or whatever. Did you, by any chance, see anyone in the vicinity?"

Lucille shook her head. "I'm afraid not. Like I said, it was dark and pretty quiet. And the fog had just started to roll in from the harbor, so that kind of deadened sounds and obscured visibility." She paused. "Well, there *was* a car maybe half a block away."

"A car?" Theodosia's heart suddenly lurched inside her chest. *A car? Maybe like the one that tried to hit me last night?*

"Yes, but it was just pulling away from the curb, so I can't imagine it was involved."

"Did you happen to get the license plate?"

"I'm sorry, no," Lucille said. "As you can see, it was much too dark."

"Any chance you could tell what kind of car it was?"

"I don't really know much about automobile makes and models," Lucille said. "But I'd say it was a smaller type of car."

"You mean like a Honda or a Buick?"

"Maybe smaller." Lucille put a hand to her mouth and thought for a few seconds. "Oh."

"What?"

"I just remembered something."

"What's that?" Theodosia asked.

"The car that pulled away . . . it was kind of low and rounded." Lucille's eyes fluttered closed and then opened again, as if she was trying to recall a specific image. "For some reason it reminded me of a bug."

"You mean like a VW Beetle?"

"I think maybe bigger than that. Wider. And nicer . . . more like an expensive sports car."

Theodosia was suddenly searching her memory, trying to think of anyone who drove a sports car. And then it came to her. Big Reggie owned a Porsche 911. Big Reggie, who hadn't made it to the Candlelight Tea tonight.

When Theodosia located Drayton in the ER he seemed to be resting comfortably. He was propped up on a bed that had white curtains drawn on either side of it, and a nurse had just finished taking his blood pressure.

"You scared the crap out of me," Theodosia said.

"That's a fine greeting," Drayton said. He still sounded croaky, but his color was better. The oxygen had helped.

Theodosia sat down on the edge of his bed. "How are you feeling?"

"The ER doctor says I'm doing just fine. Nothing broken, just a few bumps and bruises. He mumbled something about a head CT, but I told him I've always been known for my hard head."

"But you got knocked down by a car, is that right?"

Drayton put a hand behind his head and looked thoughtful. "I *think* that's what happened. I mean, everything happened so fast. It was like some bizarre art film with too many jump cuts. One minute I was striding along, playing a snatch of Vivaldi in my head, and the next thing I know I was flying tail over teakettle and going kersplat on the sidewalk."

Theodosia practically ground her teeth together. "So it was a *car* that hit you? You didn't just get dizzy and pass out?"

"I think it was a car. But it mostly grazed me."

"Did you see the car? Can you remember anything about it?"

Drayton closed his eyes for a few moments. "I did not see the actual car. But as I was lying there, viewing an entire constellation of stars and trying to figure out exactly what happened, I heard a crash. I think that after the car swerved, or lost control, or whatever happened when it came at me, that it also clipped a nearby lamppost."

"You're sure about that?"

"Yes, I distinctly remember hearing a sort of *clunk* and then a loud scraping sound. You know, metal rending against metal."

"We need to file a police report," Theodosia said.

"Yes, the nurse said there was an officer that would stop by."

"Forget that," Theodosia said. "I'm calling Detective Riley."

Drayton looked nervous. "Are you sure? Do you really think you should bother him with this?"

Theodosia gave a harsh smile. "It's going to be my pleasure."

"Somebody hit *him!*" Theodosia yelled into her cell phone. "They tried to mow him down like roadkill!" She was standing in the hallway, several hundred yards from the emergency room so Drayton wouldn't hear her screaming. It had taken her a while to get patched through to Detective Pete Riley, but now that she had him on the line she was venting like crazy.

"Whoa, wait a minute," Riley said. "You're telling me it was a hit-and-run?"

"That's exactly what it was. Which is why I'm making a police report directly to you."

"Okay." He sounded just this side of obliging.

"And the cherry on top of the cake is that someone tried to do the exact same thing to me *last* night!"

"Theodosia, are you serious?" Now Riley sounded alarmed. Now she definitely had his attention. "Do you have an idea who the driver was?"

"No, but I think it could have been Reggie Huston. The woman who found Drayton and phoned for an ambulance, Lucille Hart, said she saw a sports car pulling away from the curb." Theodosia was so wound up she was forgetting to breathe. She had to pause and force herself to take a big gulp of air. "And you know who drives a sports car, don't you? It's Reggie Huston. He's got a Porsche 911."

"Theodosia," Riley said. "Think for a moment. Why would Huston do something like that? What would he gain by injuring or even killing Drayton?"

"Are you serious? If he's the guy who murdered Beau Briggs and Marcus Covey, then he probably thinks we're hot on his trail."

"Are you hot on his trail?" Riley asked. "Or someone's trail?"

Theodosia thought for a moment. "I thought we were. Anyway, I think Huston might be trying to scare us off."

"Both of you?"

"Yes, both of us. But it's not going to work. I'm not going to sit idly by and let him come after us like that!"

"Theodosia," Riley said. "Please calm down."

"I'm not going to calm down until we find the maniac who did this and put him behind bars!"

"You mean until *I* find him," Riley said.

"That's the other thing," Theodosia said. She knew she had to shift gears and bring up Starla as well. "It might not be a him. Is Starla Crane still a suspect?"

"Why do you ask?"

"Because she came flying into my tea shop tonight like the Wicked Witch of the West on a nuclear-powered broomstick. She was all upset because you guys brought her in for questioning."

"It was only questioning."

"I realize that, but Starla is one unhappy, hyped-up cupcake right now. She's so angry that . . . well, I suppose *she* could have been the crazed driver tonight. I don't know. Does Starla even own a sports car?"

There was silence on the other end of the line.

"Oh no," Theodosia cried. "She does, doesn't she? Tell the truth!"

"Starla drives an older model Jaguar XJ," Riley said. "But so do a lot of people. Mmm . . . you say she stopped by your tea shop tonight?"

"She came bursting in and started screaming at me. She thought I was the reason she'd been hauled in for questioning."

"Holy cow."

"Yes, holy cow. Holy crap, if you really want to know the truth."

"Okay, okay," Riley said. "I'll jump right on this. It's late, but I'll start rattling some cages."

"Good," Theodosia said. "And while you're at it you should probably take another look at Doreen Briggs as well as the Whitleys. I don't think you should leave any stone unturned."

"Are you still at the hospital? Can I reach you at this number?"

"I'll be here all night if I have to."

Drayton was sitting on the edge of his bed, lacing his shoes when Theodosia came back into the ER.

"Where do you think you're going?" Theodosia asked.

"Home." Drayton gave her a perfunctory smile.

"Do you think that's wise?"

"I've been cleared by the ER doctor."

"Seriously? You're not just making this up because you don't want to stay overnight, get fussed over, and be forced to eat boring hospital food? I know how much you detest gelatin with little bits of fruit."

"Do you want to see the release form?" Drayton asked.

"Okay, I believe you."

"So you'll drive me home?"

"No, Drayton. I'm going to let you hitch a ride with some other banged-up refugee from the ER. Of course I'll drive you home. When would you like to go?"

"Now?"

But just as they walked through the automatic door and into the parking lot, Theodosia's phone began to ring.

It was Detective Riley calling back.

"Guess what?" he said.

"You closed the case?" Theodosia asked, a hopeful note coloring her voice. "You arrested Reggie Huston and he freely admitted that he murdered Beau Briggs and Marcus Covey? And that he tried to run down Drayton?"

"Not quite," Riley said. "It turns out that Reggie Huston's car was stolen this afternoon."

Theodosia's mouth dropped open. "No way."

"Way," Riley said. "Huston even called in a report at . . . let's see . . . five forty-five this afternoon."

"How convenient for him. I hope you realize that Reggie was just setting up his alibi."

"Still, the fact remains that his car is missing," Riley said. "It might have been Reggie's car that hit Drayton with somebody else driving it. Or it could be a different car and driver altogether. We just don't know."

"What are you going to do now?" Theodosia asked.

"For one thing we've got a BOLO out," Riley said.

"A BOLO . . ."

"Be on the lookout for."

"That's just peachy for Reggie's car, but what about Reggie himself?"

"I'm not discounting your theory," Riley said. "Huston might be your man. But the fact remains, we don't have any hard evidence against him."

"You need evidence," Theodosia said slowly.

"Yes. Of course we do."

"You can't just go cowboying over to his house and arrest him. Throw a noose over a tree limb." She was still livid over Drayton being attacked.

"Good heavens, no. Theodosia, you scare me sometimes."

"Drayton thought the car that hit him might have also clipped a lamppost. Maybe if you sent your crime scene guys over there, you'd find some paint scrapes. Something that would definitively connect Reggie's Porsche to the scene of the crime."

"Then I'll go ahead and make that call."

"Good. Thank you."

"But Theodosia . . ."

She didn't say anything.

"From now on, I want you to stay out of this investigation. Like *way* out. As in twenty miles from ground zero."

"Sure, Detective Riley," she said in her nicey-nice voice. "That won't be a problem." But what she really meant was, *Sorry, pal. Fat chance of that. Now I'm pulling out all the stops.*

26

Theodosia was haunted by strange dreams all night long. Reggie Huston roaring around Charleston in his red sports car, chewing up the road. And just when she thought she'd chased him down, he tore around a curve and disappeared out of sight. Then her dream morphed into Drayton being hit and flung to the side of the road, where he lay limp like a rag doll. Then a parade of ugly caskets flashed before her eyes.

Shaking her head vigorously, Theodosia set down her teapot. No, she told herself. *This dream flashback has got to stop right now. I'm here at the Indigo Tea Shop on a Saturday morning and everything is perfectly fine. Well, maybe not perfectly fine. But at least we're all here and functioning. At least Haley and I am. Poor Drayton is limping around like crazy.*

Theodosia watched Drayton measure out

two scoops of English breakfast tea and said, "Why on earth did you come in today?"

"I'm just here for the morning," Drayton said. "Then I plan to go home and take it easy."

"Why not take it easy now?"

"Theodosia, you worry too much."

"And sometimes you don't worry enough."

Haley strolled out of the kitchen with a plate of coconut scones. "How are you feeling, Drayton?" Her voice was filled with compassion and she looked more than a little worried. "Theo said you got roughed up pretty bad last night."

"Nonsense," Drayton said. "I'm fine. Don't I look fine?"

"Not really," Haley said. "You look kind of stiff and creaky. Maybe I should give you a hand out here. Help you reach those tea tins and stuff."

Drayton pursed his lips. "Thank you, but I don't need any help."

"Then how come you're limping?" Haley asked. "Every time you move, you kind of drag your left foot behind you all gimpy like."

"Not dragging," Drayton said. "Merely *favoring*. There's a difference, you know."

He took two steps from the counter to his wall of tea tins. Theodosia and Haley watched him carefully. Stump, drag, stump, drag.

"Did the ER doc at least give you some good drugs?" Haley asked. "Some painkillers?"

"My injury doesn't require pain pills," Drayton said. "Only the right blend of soothing tea."

"And what might that be?" Haley asked. "Black tea with a hit of cannabis?"

"If you must know," Drayton said, "I blended black tea with some rose hips and valerian root. It makes for a very effective anti-inflammatory. Good for muscle strains and sprains."

Haley didn't look convinced. "If you say so. You ask me, I like to knock back my pain the old-fashioned way."

"I'm going to pretend I didn't hear that," Drayton said.

"Kidding," Haley said. "I'm kidding. You have to take care of yourself, Drayton. You shouldn't be hobbling around here aggravating your injuries."

"I'll take it easy," Drayton said. "Besides, we're only open until one o'clock."

"I could call Miss Dimple and have her come in," Theodosia offered.

"Good idea," Haley said. "Then Drayton can go home and take a load off."

"No need," Drayton said. "Besides, the old dear easily has twenty years on me. And look, I'm getting around just fine. I'm not *that* fragile."

But from the way Drayton was hobbling, it looked like he was in pain.

Thank goodness the tea shop wasn't all that busy. By late morning they were still only half-full, and Theodosia had taken it upon herself to keep Drayton behind the counter, where he could perch on a stool that Haley had dragged down from her upstairs apartment.

"This is better for you, huh?" Theodosia asked.

"You're babying me," Drayton said. "No need."

"But you've been surreptitiously watching the clock. So you must be thinking of going home to rest."

"I can't say it hasn't crossed my mind," Drayton finally admitted. "But I'm here now so I'm going to stick with it."

"If it kills you," Theodosia said under her breath.

Drayton glanced up sharply. "I heard that."

Theodosia did double duty, pouring tea,

clearing tables, serving up buttermilk scones, shrimp gumbo, and roasted red pepper and Brie cheese tea sandwiches. Luckily, they weren't crazy-busy.

When one o'clock finally rolled around (none too soon for Theodosia), Haley volunteered to stay behind and close up shop. Theodosia wasn't about to let Drayton walk home by himself and told him so in no uncertain terms.

"I'm fine," Drayton said. "I've got a couple of things to finish up."

"But you need to go home," Theodosia said. "Like now. Come on, I'll drop you off and then head over to Gilded Magnolia Spa. Take them the tea you picked out for their grand opening party tonight." Drayton had selected four bags of what he called his proprietary ginger-orange tea. It was a rich Chinese black tea blended with dried ginger and bits of orange peel.

"Can't you drop off the tea and then swing back to pick me up?" Drayton asked.

"Drayton . . . I . . . yes, I suppose." There was no sense in arguing with him. The man was as bullheaded as . . . she wasn't sure. Probably a hardheaded Southern gent.

"Thank you," Drayton said.

The day was gorgeous, a cornflower blue

sky with a big bold sun lasering down, threatening to warm everything up into the middle sixties. And Theodosia, invigorated by the weather, charmed by the magnolia blooms that were twining everywhere, was lulled into a rather excellent mood as she drove along.

Until she pulled into the parking lot at Gilded Magnolia Spa, that is. Then she almost couldn't believe her eyes.

A shiny red Porsche was sitting front and center in the lot.

Big Reggie's car!

But how could that be? Theodosia wondered. Big Reggie's car had been stolen yesterday.

Unless the car thief had a change of heart and returned it?

Or maybe Reggie's car hadn't really been missing after all?

Whatever the reason, Theodosia jumped out of her Jeep and ran over to inspect the Porsche. And just as she'd feared, there was a good-sized dent in the right-front fender!

This is it, she thought. *This is the proof that Detective Riley needs in order to arrest Reggie Huston. Here it is in black and white. Or at least in shiny bright factory red paint.*

Theodosia's hands were shaking as she dialed Detective Riley's number. When he came on the line she didn't waste a single moment.

"Guess what?" she cried. "Reggie Huston's car isn't missing at all. It's sitting right here in the parking lot at Gilded Magnolia Spa."

"What!" Detective Riley sounded like a startled crow. "Are you sure it's Reggie Huston's car?"

"I'm standing right here staring at it. The car also has an enormous dent in the right-front fender. Probably from when that jack-hole Reggie tried to run Drayton down last night." Theodosia was fighting to keep her cool. To not sound too overwrought. And to not come across as gloating, either, even though she figured that Reggie had orchestrated this mess all along.

"Do you think Reggie Huston is at the spa now?" Riley asked her. "In his office?"

"Probably." Theodosia swallowed hard. "You're going to come over here, right? I mean, like, right now? You're going to question Reggie Huston and maybe even bring a search warrant?"

"I can't make any promises," Detective Riley said. "But I'm definitely coming over there and I'm bringing a squad with me just in case. Now, Theodosia, please listen to me. I want you to be very careful, okay?

336

Don't go inside where Reggie is liable to see you. Stay outside."

"I'm going to sit right here in the parking lot," Theodosia said. "And I'm not taking my eyes off his stupid car!"

Theodosia disconnected and stood there for a few moments, fidgeting like crazy. Then she decided she really should take Riley's advice and get out of sight. So she jumped in her Jeep and backed it clear across the parking lot until she was partially hidden by a large brown Dumpster. She turned off the ignition and sat there, listening to the engine tick down, feeling her heart go flip-flop inside her chest. Watching Reggie's car.

Reggie's stupid little murder car.

When Theodosia thought about how Reggie had swerved directly onto the sidewalk and slammed into Drayton . . . tears oozed from her eyes. Then she dug her fingernails into the palms of her hands until she could see pale crescents.

Probably . . . no, not probably, more like definitely . . . Reggie Huston had been the one who'd come after her and Earl Grey the night before.

What a despicable man! She was going to enjoy seeing him taken down. Hopefully taken into custody.

Detective Pete Riley showed up some forty minutes later. He came in his dark-blue unobtrusive-looking Buick accompanied by two black-and-white cruisers, each containing two uniformed officers. Both police cars immediately tucked in tight behind the Porsche, effectively blocking it from leaving.

Theodosia jumped out of her car and ran across the parking lot to meet up with Riley.

"Thank goodness you're here," she called out.

Riley turned, saw her running toward him, and waved a piece of paper in the air.

"Is that what I think it is?" Theodosia asked.

"Search warrant," Riley said. "It allows us to take an actual paint sample from Huston's Porsche and match it against the scrapes we found on the lamppost. It also gives us permission to look inside his car as well as inspect his office and domicile."

"That is so excellent," Theodosia said. "But what about . . . ?"

"Reggie Huston himself? We're going to take him downtown for questioning."

"When?"

"Right now." Riley turned to one pair of cops and said, "You guys go ahead and take

338

this car apart. Use a crowbar if you have to." Then he turned to the other set of officers. "You officers have the pleasure of coming with me."

Detective Riley marched into the spa, flanked by the two officers in uniform. They whipped past the startled-looking woman at the reception desk and headed straight for Reggie's office. Theodosia trailed the trio, anxious to see how this confrontation would play out.

Not very well, it turned out.

Sally, Reggie Huston's secretary, saw them bearing down on Reggie's office and stood up to try and block them.

"You can't go in there," Sally cried. She came around her desk, looking a little discombobulated, a lot frightened. "Mr. Huston's on an important phone call and gave strict orders not to be disturbed."

Detective Riley held out a hand to fend her off. "Police business," he said. "He can hang up and call back."

At that exact same moment, Reggie Huston threw open his office door. He stopped abruptly in his doorway and gazed at the huddle of people. Then, when he recognized Detective Riley standing there, he said, with a halfway grin on his face, "Police, huh? I bet you guys found my car."

"I'm afraid we did," Riley said. The two officers crowded up behind him along with Theodosia.

Reggie's face immediately scrunched up with worry. "Oh jeez, don't tell me it's been totaled."

"Nothing quite that drastic," Theodosia said. "Since it's sitting right outside in the parking lot."

"What?" Reggie gave them all an incredulous look. "Wait a minute. Are you telling me the car thief brought it *back*?"

"If it was ever stolen in the first place," Theodosia said.

Reggie cocked his head and glared at her. "What are you talking about? Better yet, why are *you* even involved in this?" He waved a hand dismissively. "Get out of here. This is between me and the cops."

"That's a real smart observation," Theodosia said. "Since Detective Riley has something special for you."

Now Reggie was really confused. "Say, what's going on here? Did Dickie Duncan over at Pokey's Bar put you up to this? Because if he did, it's not very funny."

Detective Riley showed Reggie the search warrant.

Reggie's eyes practically popped out of his head. "Search warrant!" he screamed. "Are you serious? What are you looking for? Just tell me and I'll try to point you in the right direction."

"Let's start with your financial records," Theodosia said.

Reggie looked ever more puzzled. "What are you talking about?"

"You've been skimming money from the business," Theodosia said. "Living the high life. I'm guessing that Beau probably caught you with your hand in the cookie jar."

"And that's why you killed him," Riley said.

Reggie took a step backward. "Are you crazy? I didn't kill Beau Briggs. He was my business partner, for crying out loud."

"Detective Riley?" someone called out.

They all turned. The two officers who'd been tasked with going through Reggie's car were standing there, looking serious.

"We found something," one of the officers said. His name tag read CHAPMAN.

"What is it?" Riley asked.

Chapman held up a small brown vial, the kind you'd get from a pharmacy. Only there was no label and it contained a small amount of white powder.

"Very nice," Riley said. "Drugs?"

"Could be, sir," Chapman said.

"That's ridiculous," Reggie snorted.

"That . . . that . . . whatever that crap is, it had to have been planted. My car was *stolen,* for cripes' sake. I reported it missing."

"So you say," Theodosia said. "Besides, I don't think it's drugs. I think it's some form of poison."

"Holy smokes," one of the officers muttered.

"Poison?" Reggie cried. He gave Detective Riley a sick smile. "Don't you see what's going on here? This is a setup, plain and simple. Some nutjob is trying to make me look like a crazed killer. And it's probably . . . probably the *real* killer."

"You're the killer," Theodosia said. "You're a dangerous predator who killed Beau Briggs and Marcus Covey."

Reggie Huston looked like somebody had just tossed a bucket of ice cubes in his face. "What are you talking about? And who the Sam Hill is Marcus Covey?"

"The man you murdered," Theodosia said. "The server from the rat tea."

"Are you people insane?" Reggie's voice rose up in a ragged squawk. "Are you making this up as you go along or are you following some kind of ridiculous script?"

"Not when the evidence points to cold-blooded murder," Detective Riley said.

Big Reggie started bellowing like an angry

bull. "Are you serious? You can't do this to me!" He whipped his head back and forth, his eyes finally landing on Sally, his secretary. "Sally, don't just stand there like a statue, get on the horn and call my lawyer . . . call Eddie Banister. Tell him to get his ridiculously high-priced butt over here."

Riley shook his head at Sally. "Not here. We're leaving, and your boss is coming with us. Any lawyer Mr. Huston retains can meet us at the police station."

The two officers who'd come in with Riley whipped out a pair of handcuffs and put them on Reggie.

"Sally, at least tell Banister what's going on," Reggie shouted back to her as he was led away. "Tell him I'm being royally framed!"

"I will, I will," Sally called after him. "But what about the grand opening party tonight? What are we supposed to do about that?"

But Reggie was already out the door. Followed by Detective Riley and the two other officers. Theodosia watched their departure with a good deal of satisfaction.

"Is Mr. Huston really under arrest?" Sally asked. She was quaking like a Chihuahua that had been kicked outside in a snowstorm.

"I don't think those handcuffs are exactly

343

party favors," Theodosia said.

"What did Mr. Huston do, anyway? I mean . . . yes, he's loud and abrasive. And he's always screaming orders at people. But what did he actually *do*?"

"For starters, he has two first-degree murder charges hanging over his head."

Sally looked stunned. "Murder? Big Reggie?"

"Along with a couple of assault charges. Vehicular hit-and-run, to be exact."

Sally's eyes grew even larger. "I can hardly believe it."

"Believe it," Theodosia said.

27

"I'm calling a meeting of the executive com-
mittee," Theodosia yelled out the minute
she arrived back at the Indigo Tea Shop.
Reggie's arrest was way too important to
keep under wraps.

Haley poked her head out of the kitchen
like an inquisitive prairie dog. "Huh?"

"That's us," Drayton said to her. "Come
out here and sit down. I'm getting a little
tingle that tells me Theodosia might have
big news for us."

Haley came out, wiping her hands on a
tea towel. "Are you sure you don't just have
nerve damage?"

"No," Drayton scoffed.

"Then what's up?" Haley asked. She sat
down at the table with Drayton and faced
Theodosia. "Please tell me we're not shut-
ting down the tea shop or anything horrible
like that."

"Nothing like that," Theodosia said. "I

give you my word, Haley, your job is safe and secure."

"So it's all good?" Haley asked.

"Not exactly." Theodosia paused. "I just wanted to tell the both of you that Reggie Huston has been arrested for murder."

"What!" Drayton said.

"Seriously?" Haley said.

"The police discovered what might be a vial of poison in the trunk of Reggie's car."

"And . . . ?" Drayton said, twirling a hand, eager for more information.

"Pending laboratory tests, the police will probably be able to connect that poison to the poison that caused Beau Briggs's death."

"Wow," Haley said. "Creepy."

"And I'm guessing they'll be able to connect Reggie to the hanging death of Marcus Covey as well," Theodosia said. She peered carefully at Drayton. "And to your hit-and-run accident last night."

"Holy cow," Drayton said. "So it was Big Reggie all along. Not Doreen or Starla or crazy neighbors or anyone else."

"Whatever Reggie's reason — envy, jealousy, money, hatred — he was the man behind it all."

Haley gazed at Theodosia. "And you figured all this out?"

Theodosia lifted a shoulder. "There were

a number of clues that pretty much led to Big Reggie. Especially after he tried to run down Drayton last night. And the fact that his car ended up with an enormous telltale dent in the front fender. After that it was a matter of connecting the dots."

"The weird thing is," Haley said, "you'd think Big Reggie would have taken his car to one of those quickie dent shops and gotten his fender pounded out right away. Or at least ditched the car."

"Killers aren't always careful linear thinkers," Theodosia said. "They operate with certain disadvantages."

"Such as?" Haley said.

"Well, most of them are sociopaths," Theodosia said. "They're people who don't feel as if they're bound by the same rules that you and I are."

"We've got to tell Doreen right away," Drayton said, sounding almost elated. "Before the police notify her. She's going to be absolutely thrilled."

"I wouldn't count on it," Theodosia said. "Considering that Reggie Huston was her husband's business partner, the one he pretty much handpicked, I'm guessing she'll be more upset than anything."

"Still," Drayton said, "we should be the ones to break the news to her."

"Okay," Theodosia said. "I guess you're probably right. Do you want to call her and let her know we're coming over?"

"Let's just pop over to Doreen's house right now," Drayton said. "Surprise her with the news. Whether she views it as good news or not, she did promise us that grant."

"Grant or no grant," Theodosia said, "she will be surprised."

Opal Anne answered the door. She studied Theodosia's face for about one second and then looked at Drayton's face. "Something happened," she said. "Something big."

"The nightmare is over," Drayton announced. His voice sounded somber, but he was fairly dancing on the balls of his feet, his aches and pains seemingly forgotten. "The police have taken Beau's killer into custody."

Opal Anne clapped a hand to her chest. "Oh, thank goodness." She drew a deep breath, then let her cheeks puff out as she slowly exhaled. "Who?" she asked.

"Reggie Huston," Drayton said.

"Big Reggie," Opal Anne said in a sad, almost accepting, manner. "Of course it was him. We should have known all along." She took a step back and said, "Please come in. Doreen's going to want to hear this news in person. And *I* want to hear every single detail."

Opal Anne led them into the library and then quickly rounded up Doreen and her son, Charles.

Theodosia gave a quick recap of last night's hit-and-run assault on Drayton, and then told them about how she'd discovered the red Porsche brazenly parked in the lot at Gilded Magnolia Spa.

"The dent was the final piece in the puzzle," Theodosia said. "It was enough evidence for the police to get a search warrant."

"And they've already started their search?" Doreen asked. She looked stunned, but not as upset as Theodosia thought she would be.

"Right then and there," Theodosia said. "They started digging in Reggie's car and found a vial of what they suspect might be poison."

"Eeeeiii!" Doreen cried. She flung herself back in her chair and banged the chair's arms with her fists. "Reggie! Reggie killed my poor dear Beau!"

"I'm afraid that he probably did," Theodosia said.

"We're so sorry," Drayton said.

Doreen was shaking her head slowly from

side to side. "It's awful, but at least now I know. At least now I have a definitive answer." She waved both hands in front of her face in a rapid fanning motion. "My poor, poor Beau. Will he ever rest in peace?"

"Of course he will," Drayton murmured.

Theodosia waited a few minutes, letting everything sink in for Doreen. Then she said, "I'm sure the police will want to speak with you. To explain everything and confirm our suspicions."

"Particularly Detective Riley," Drayton said. "He worked very hard on this case." He gave a quick glance in Theodosia's direction. "As did Theodosia."

"You're a wonder," Opal Anne said with open admiration in her voice. "Both of you."

"We thought it was important to come here and break the news in person," Theodosia said. "Since we feel a connection to everyone here."

Doreen reached out and fumbled for Drayton's hand. "You are such dear, sweet friends." She gripped his hand and pulled him closer to her. "And Drayton, to hear that you were practically run over last night . . . my heart just aches."

"I think we all need to do some much-needed healing," Opal Anne said.

"Thank you, Theodosia," Charles said.

"You've done so much. You've helped our family and gone above and beyond the call of duty."

"And we won't forget it," Doreen said. "I told the two of you that I'd double my grant to the Heritage Society if you helped me find an answer, and I meant it."

"Dear lady," Drayton said. Now he was the one gripping Doreen's hand.

"I'm going to write a check on Monday," Doreen said.

"So generous," Drayton whispered.

"There's just one problem," Doreen said.

Drayton eyed her carefully. "What's that?"

"Gilded Magnolia Spa," Doreen said. "I know it's not your problem, but who's going to run it now?" She looked around, searching the faces of each of them as if hoping to find an answer.

"Perhaps hire a general manager from the outside?" Theodosia said. "Somebody with experience in the fitness or hospitality industry?"

"I had another idea," Doreen said. She glanced sideways at Opal Anne. "What if we asked Opal Anne to step in and try to run things?"

"Me?" Opal Anne's voice rose in a surprised note and then cracked. "Are you serious?"

"I think it's something you could do if you put your mind to it," Doreen said.

"I think it's a wonderful idea," Charles said.

"So do I," Drayton chimed in. "I think she'd be a natural."

But Opal Anne was the only one who seemed completely unsure. "I don't know . . ."

"Is running the spa something that you'd consider doing?" Theodosia asked. It seemed like an awfully big job for someone who'd just recently graduated from college.

Opal Anne gave a nervous shrug. "I don't know. I never thought much about it before. I mean . . . I certainly enjoy working out and all."

"You sure do," Doreen said.

"And it's . . . well, Gilded Magnolia *is* in the family," Opal Anne said. Now she seemed to be considering the idea. "So who knows? Maybe running a spa could turn out to be my passion after all."

"Then I think you should go for it!" Doreen said.

Opal Anne ducked her head shyly. "Do you really mean that?"

"Of course I do," Doreen said. "And I hate to spring this on you at such a late date, but you could start with the party tonight."

Opal Anne looked startled. "What?"

"You can deliver the welcoming speech at the grand opening party," Doreen said.

"Do you really think I should?" Opal Anne asked. "The plan was always to have Reggie give the speech. Or Starla, since she was so active with all the publicity."

"No," Doreen said. "I think you should be the star of the show tonight."

"I think Gilded Magnolia Spa is really the star," Opal Anne said. "But I promise I'll try to do my absolute best."

"Then I think congratulations are in order," Theodosia said. She hadn't been much older than Opal Anne when she'd gotten her first job in marketing. She'd been so confident and carefree back them, un-afraid to fail. Perhaps that was the exact same attitude and chutzpah that was needed here.

"Then you're all going to be there tonight, aren't you?" Opal Anne asked. "I mean, if this is supposed to be my debut, I need to have all of you around me. For luck?" She ducked her head shyly. "And for love."

"Of course we'll come," Theodosia said, her heart going out to the girl. It looked as if Opal Anne might really have found her niche after all. "We wouldn't miss your big night for anything in the world."

28

Gilded Magnolia Spa looked like even more of a showplace this Saturday evening. Searchlights raked the dark sky overhead as red-jacketed valets hustled to park Audis, Mercedes-Benzes, and even the occasional Bentley. Inside, the lobby throbbed with energy and excitement. Hundreds of toned and tanned ladies hung on the arms of well-heeled gentlemen, champagne and chilled white wine flowed freely, gorgeous magnolia and orchid plants blossomed everywhere, and a tuxedo-clad string quartet played jazz versions of pop tunes.

Drayton had begged off, pleading a sore knee, and Theodosia was glad that he had. He could definitely use the rest. And because Delaine's date was a no-show for the second night in a row, Theodosia had offered herself up as a consolation prize.

"Isn't this all quite lovely?" Delaine asked. She gave an excited little shiver as they strolled through the crowded lobby. "It looks like everybody's here tonight. Ooh, and paparazzi, too." She aimed her face at the first available camera lens and smiled broadly as a photographer moved in to snap their photos. "Maybe we'll make the society pages."

"Maybe Gilded Magnolia Spa will luck out with a feature," Theodosia said.

Delaine nodded. "That, too. This party looks like it's shaping up to be quite an event."

Theodosia smiled to herself. She knew there was no way this party could ever be as strange and eccentric as all the events leading up to it.

"Too bad Drayton couldn't make it tonight," Delaine said. "He's going to be okay, isn't he?"

"I'm fairly sure he'll recover."

"And it was one of the spa's *owners* who tried to run him down? That Reggie person?"

"Don't look so nervous," Theodosia said. "He's behind bars now."

"But the show must go on." Delaine glanced around. "And what a show it is."

Theodosia and Delaine had worn cocktail dresses tonight, and so had many of the other women. But some of the ladies, mostly the younger ones, were dressed in the hip new athleisure style. Body-con dresses in bright colors, designer yoga pants and crop tops, and long, flowing skirts worn with skimpy bandeau tops.

"Lots of skin showing," Delaine said, sounding just this side of catty.

"It's the grand opening for a spa," Theodosia said. "A certain casualness is to be expected."

"So where's this poor little rich girl you've been telling me about? The girl who took over the spa as of today?"

"Opal Anne? I'm sure she's floating around somewhere. She's certainly got her work cut out for her."

"Oh my goodness, what's going on over there?"

"It looks like a fashion show," Theodosia said.

"Then we absolutely have to go over and have a look."

Theodosia and Delaine strolled into a large lounge that featured leather sofas and chairs, a floor-to-ceiling stone fireplace, and French doors that led out to a large outdoor swimming pool. Tiki torches surrounding the pool flamed against the dark sky and were also reflected in the shimmering water. Inside, rock 'n' roll music blasted loudly over the loudspeakers as a DJ played tunes and models strutted their stuff on a white vinyl runway.

"Are the clothes they're modeling all from the spa's gift shop?" Delaine asked.

"Have to be," Theodosia said.

"Hmm." Delaine, ever the fashion maven, observed the models with a keen eye. "This athletic look has really caught on, hasn't it?"

"You see it everywhere. Even out on the streets."

"I wonder if I should stock up on this type of clothing at Cotton Duck?"

"You'd certainly be right on trend," Theodosia said.

"Maybe I could even work some of these athleisure pieces into my spring fashion show." Delaine reached out and accepted a glass of champagne from a passing waiter. "That show is coming up awfully soon."

"Go for it."

Delaine watched the show while she sipped her champagne. "So what else is going on here?"

"I know there's a health food demonstration."

Delaine wrinkled her nose. "Wheat grass shooters and sprouts? I'll pass on that if you don't mind. What else? Is there any . . . ?"

"Theodosia!" an excited voice suddenly called out.

Theodosia spun around to find Opal Anne practically running toward her.

"You came," Opal Anne exclaimed. She clapped a hand to her chest. "Thank you so much!"

"I wouldn't miss your party for the world," Theodosia said. "Neither would Delaine. You two know each other, right?"

"We met briefly last night," Opal Anne said. "At your Candlelight Tea."

"Briefly," Delaine said. She put a hand on her hip. "I understand congratulations are in order. You're going to be managing Gilded Magnolia Spa from now on?"

"I'm going to *try*," Opal Anne corrected. "That's not to say I won't be hiring outside consultants when I need them."

"I think that's wise, dear," Delaine said. "Considering you're still quite young and inexperienced."

"Have you heard anything more about Reggie Huston?" Theodosia asked.

Opal Anne shook her head. "No. I thought the case was kind of closed."

"Detective Riley called me just before I left to come over here," Theodosia said. "He's promised a full-scale investigation."

"As well there should be," Delaine said.

"Especially with two murder charges hanging over Reggie Huston's head." She smiled at Opal Anne. "But you shouldn't have to worry about that. Tonight, it's all about the grand opening."

"Have you visited our gift shop yet?" Opal Anne asked, practically bubbling over with excitement. "It's absolutely stocked to the rafters with the most gorgeous things. Spa robes, aromatherapy candles, yoga gear, you name it." Opal Anne was dressed in a very glam sequin top paired with sleek black leggings. With her big brown eyes, she looked, Theodosia decided, like an adorable elf.

"So far we've just been taking in the music and the fashion show," Theodosia said. "You've got a lot going on here tonight."

"This isn't even half of it," Opal Anne said. "You have to visit our juice bar and then wander back to the spa treatment area. We're giving free manicures and pedicures tonight. And we have gift bags for everyone, too."

"That sounds divine," Delaine said.

They wandered back to the juice bar then. Where Theodosia was more than a little surprised to find Sally, Reggie Huston's secretary, manning the counter. She quickly introduced Delaine and then said, "I hope you're in better spirits after this afternoon's shocker."

"I guess I'm okay," Sally said. "The upside is that Opal Anne is taking over, so I get to keep my job."

"Job security is so important," Delaine said. "Especially in this day and age."

"Tell me about it," Sally said. She put both hands on the counter and leaned forward. "So what can I whip up for your amusement? The waiters are serving champagne, of course. But we're also offering samples of our special juices and smoothies." She smiled at Theodosia as she lifted a silver pitcher. "I think you might like this. We whipped up a wonderful iced chai drink and laced it with coconut milk."

"I'll give it a try," Theodosia said.

"What else have you got?" Delaine asked as Sally poured the iced chai into a tall glass for Theodosia.

"We also have what we're calling our blueberry crush," Sally said. "It's fresh blueberries blended with protein powder, a scoop of frozen yogurt, and almond milk. Really terrific."

Delaine wasn't impressed. "No, I think I prefer champagne."

"How do you like the iced chai?" Sally asked Theodosia once she'd had a taste.

"Not bad," Theodosia said. And it wasn't.

"You know," Sally said, "I still feel bad about Big Reggie. He was a pretty good guy."

"Even though he was always yelling at you?" Theodosia asked. *And will probably be convicted of murder?*

"I know," Sally said. "People are whispering terrible things about him. And particular aspects of Big Reggie's personality aren't so great. But it always felt like the man had a good heart. I know he worked very hard to make a lot of this happen tonight. He hired the musicians and put together the fashion show and even merchandised the gift shop. It's a pity he can't be here to mingle with the guests and enjoy some of the fruits of his labor."

"Perhaps sitting in a jail cell will make him reconsider his motivation," Delaine said, helping herself to a second glass of champagne from a passing waiter.

"You think so?" Theodosia asked. She didn't think so. Big Reggie had proved himself to be a cold-blooded killer. Which probably meant he was unrepentant.

"And I suppose there'll be lots of changes now," Sally said. "With Opal Anne running the show."

"How could there not be?" Delaine said.

"What some of us are thinking," Sally said, "is that, on the positive side, she'll bring a younger perspective to Gilded Magnolia Spa."

"Youth can be so overrated," Delaine said.

"When we spoke with Opal Anne earlier," Theodosia said, "she seemed extremely upbeat. Maybe a little dazed because all of this is happening so fast, but excited at the prospect of being a spa manager."

"I'm happy for her," Sally said. "Especially since she just broke up with her boyfriend."

"Men can be overrated, too," Delaine said.

"You know what?" Sally said. "You ladies should run down to the spa and get a free pedicure. If you go right now, before they make a big announcement about free treatments, you won't have to wait in line."

Sally was right. When Theodosia and Delaine walked into the spa treatment lobby, there were only a couple of ladies ahead of them.

"You're here for a pedicure?" the woman behind the front desk asked.

"That's right," Delaine said. "And maybe a manicure, too?"

"We're not doing manicures right now," the woman said. "But our pedis include an exfoliating sea salt rub."

"Be still my heart," Delaine said.

"And my toes," Theodosia echoed.

"If you'll come this way?" the spa worker asked.

Theodosia and Delaine followed her down the hallway and into a plush treatment room.

"Make yourself at home," the woman said. "I'll send in one of our technicians as soon as she's free."

"Oh," Delaine said. "You only have the one Pedi Lounger?"

"That's right."

"Not to worry," Theodosia said. "You can go first."

"You don't mind?" Delaine said. She had already crawled into the chair and kicked off her gold, high-heeled sandals.

Theodosia sat in a small leather club chair opposite her. "Not really."

"Knock knock."

Theodosia glanced up with a smile, expecting to see the nail technician. Instead Opal Anne was standing in the doorway.

"I come bearing gifts," Opal Anne said. "At least gift bags anyway."

"Ooh, I absolutely adore swag," Delaine cooed.

"Now, don't tell anybody," Opal Anne said, "but these are *special* gift bags." She handed a red-and-gold gift bag to Theodosia and a blue-and-gold gift bag to Delaine. "Along with the perfume samples and spa socks and rubber exercise bands that everybody else is getting, I loaded up these bags with lots of extra goodies."

"Thank you," Theodosia said.

"Very kind of you," Delaine said as she immediately dug a hand inside her bag.

"As you can see," Opal Anne said, "I tossed in some makeup, a bunch of handmade soaps, and a pair of flip-flops."

"*Rubber* flip-flops?" Delaine asked. She looked horrified. As if she'd been asked to surrender her Manolo Blahnik heels and wrap dead animal skins around her feet.

"The flip-flops are just to wear temporarily," Opal Anne explained, smiling, and slightly amused by Delaine's reaction. "You know, post-pedicure. So you don't smear your freshly polished toes."

"Of course," Delaine said. But she still looked unhappy.

"Well, enjoy," Opal Anne said. "I've got to go mingle with the guests and introduce myself to a whole bunch of people."

"Good luck," Theodosia said. "Have fun."

Then the nail technician arrived in a flurry of towels and loofahs, turning on the water to fill the basin, handing them a color chart to show which polishes were available.

"I've got one more pedicure to finish," the technician said, "and then I'll be right back. In the meantime, maybe you ladies could choose your color."

"Sure thing," Theodosia said. But Delaine was already busily perusing the color chart.

"I'm going for the Paradise Peach nail polish," Delaine declared. "What about you, Theo? What color are you going to choose?"

Theodosia glanced at the chart. "Maybe the Nearly Nude?"

Delaine made a face. "Don't you think that's awfully safe and boring? Why not live it up and pick something with a little more pizazz?"

"Then you pick," Theodosia said.

"Okay, I will. How about . . . Red Raspberry?"

"Perfect. It's exactly what I wanted but didn't realize it."

Delaine stuck her feet in the bowl of sudsy water and leaned back. "You know," she said, trying to sound casual, "your swag bag looks a lot more interesting than mine."

Theodosia gazed at Delaine, thinking, *Now, there's the Delaine I know and love.* "Do you want to switch bags? Is that what you're really asking me?"

"If you don't mind, Theodosia," she said

in a small voice.

"I guess not." It was probably all the same stuff, right? She handed her bag over.

"Thank you."

And now another person was peering into the treatment room. Only it wasn't the nail technician, it was Starla Crane!

29

"Starla!" Theodosia cried out. All the while thinking, *Oh dear, what does she want? Is she going to come sashaying in here and make a great big stink?*

"I suppose you're happy as a pig in a pit full of mud," Starla said. She hovered in the doorway, halfway in, halfway out, delivering her words in a grudging tone of voice.

"What are you doing here?" Delaine snapped. "Have you come to spread your vitriol once again?"

But Theodosia held up a hand. She was going to let Starla say her piece. Whatever that might be.

"I dropped by Doreen's house this afternoon," Starla said. "To try to do some damage control. Hopefully retain her as my PR client." Starla shrugged as she stared at Theodosia. "But all she did was talk my ear off about *you.* Bragging about how you figured everything out about Reggie Huston. And how you even got her money back from some venture capital guy."

"Don't you wish you were as clever as Theodosia?" Delaine asked.

Theodosia silenced Delaine with a loud *shush.* Then said, "It wasn't just me, Starla. The police were on Reggie's trail, too."

"Sure they were," Starla said. "Just like they were on my trail." She stood in the doorway, shifting from one foot to the other. She was obviously here for the grand opening, but it was clear that her role had been severely marginalized.

"I'm sorry things turned out the way they did," Theodosia said. And for some reason, she really meant it.

"Yeah, whatever," Starla said. "Still, I suppose I at least owe you a grudging nod. Thank goodness the police aren't breathing down *my* neck anymore." She shook her head, looking pensive yet distracted. "It's hard to believe that Big Reggie was the killer all along."

"A double murderer," Delaine said, smiling. "He poisoned Beau Briggs and hanged that poor boy, as well."

"I guess you never know what secrets are buried deep within the human heart," Theodosia said.

Starla made a motion to leave and then

turned back. "I'm still having trouble wrapping my head around Reggie. He always struck me as being a fairly levelheaded guy. I mean, Reggie was completely crackers, of course. He was totally ADD and was always yelling his head off at people. But he was good with finances. And he always seemed *decent.*"

"I guess looks can be deceiving," Theodosia said.

Starla remained perplexed. "I'll say."

"Okaaay," the nail technician said as she hustled back into the room. "Let's get started with your sea salt scrub and then move on to a hot stone massage."

Delaine slid down in her chair even more. "A massage, too? That sounds positively blissful."

"You know what?" Theodosia said. "While you're getting your pedicure and massage, I'm going to take a walk out to the pool." She pulled her flip-flops out of her gift bag and slipped them on. They were bright pink and felt soft and spongy. Kind of nice after wearing high heels, even if it had only been for less than an hour. "I'll see you in a little bit, Delaine."

Delaine barely lifted a hand to wave goodbye.

Theodosia padded down the hallway, headed in the direction of where she remembered the pool was located. She turned left, saw a locker room on her right, and figured she was definitely in the vicinity.

She was. But it was for the indoor pool.

Hot steam and the smell of chlorine drew her closer. And so did the sound of jazzy music.

What's going on here?

As Theodosia stepped through another door onto a damp, tiled floor, all was revealed. A crowd of people were watching some sort of pool demo. Blue swimsuit–clad ladies were bouncing around with paddleboards, mimicking the antics of a playful otter. Or maybe they were re-creating the sinking of the *Titanic.*

A woman moved in close to her as she watched.

"Do you think you have the stamina for that kind of exercise?" the woman asked in a low voice.

Theodosia glanced to her right and found that Honey Whitley was standing next to her, favoring her with a slightly snarky smile.

"I don't know," Theodosia said. "It looks awfully high energy."

"Water exercise is always tough," Honey said. "Lots of resistance to get your heart rate up and burn off a good ten calories a minute. But it's easy on the joints." She eyed Theodosia with suspicion. "Though your joints still look pretty good."

"I hope they are."

"You're a runner, aren't you?" Honey said. "I see you going by all the time with that big floppy dog of yours."

"We try to log two or three miles a couple of times a week."

"Running is hard on the knees," Honey said.

"Hasn't bothered me so far." Sometimes Theodosia's knees *were* sore after a run, but she wasn't about to admit her aches and pains to Honey.

"What do you think about Opal Anne stepping in to run Gilded Magnolia Spa?" Honey asked suddenly. "Do you think she'll be able to keep this place from going off the rails until she can hire a good general manager?"

"You think she needs a manager?" Theodosia asked.

"Most definitely," Honey said. "This is a brand-new business, after all. One that's still trying to attract clients and gain traction in the market."

"I realize that," Theodosia said. "But Opal Anne should have some practical know-how.

After all, she graduated with a major in business."

Honey frowned and shook her head. "No, I don't think she was a business major."

"Excuse me?" Theodosia said. She'd been busy watching the ladies in the pool. Now they were doing some kind of bouncing exercise that looked like a cross between drowning and jumping jacks.

"It seems to me that Doreen was always yapping about what a brainiac Opal Anne was," Honey said. "How she excelled in math and science."

"But that wasn't her major," Theodosia said.

Honey gazed at her. "I'm fairly sure Opal Anne's major was chemistry."

"Chemistry?" Theodosia said. Without fully realizing why, her stomach suddenly dropped out from under her. "Are you sure about that?"

"I'm almost positive."

Theodosia didn't respond. Her head was suddenly filled with images of periodic tables, molecular structures, chemical compounds, and an insider's know-how about toxicity. Without a word to Honey, she turned and ran.

"Theodosia," Honey called after her. "What's wrong? Why are you running away?

Theo-*do*-sia!"

Theodosia sprinted through the locker room, past a row of bright-pink lockers, and then down a hallway. As she ran, her flip-flops made loud *thwack thwack thwacks* against her heels.

Chemistry? Opal Anne was a *chemistry* major? That meant she knew all about organic matter and chemical reactions and how they might affect the human body.

But, no, Theodosia thought as she huffed along. Maybe Honey had gotten it all wrong. Honey was a ditz who talked way more than she listened.

On the other hand, Opal Anne had admitted that she spent almost all of her free time here at Gilded Magnolia Spa. So it would have been no problem at all for her to grab Reggie's car keys. And steal his car. And then . . . oh no!

Doreen had said that Opal Anne had just broken up with her boyfriend? The idea felt far-fetched, but what if her boyfriend had been Marcus Covey, one of the rat servers? What if he'd been in on Beau's murder, but Opal Anne hadn't trusted him completely? Feared that Covey might spill his guts to the police?

Of course, the final kicker was that Opal Anne hadn't really had much of an emotional connection with Beau Briggs at all. He wasn't even her father, for goodness' sakes, he was her *step*father!

Theodosia crashed her way through the lobby of the treatment area. Somehow, with all the subdued lighting and plush corridors, she'd gotten hopelessly turned around.

"Delaine!" she called out. "Delaine, where are you?" She was in such an excited state that she couldn't remember which room Delaine was in.

She peeked into a room on her right. Nothing.

Finally, in the third room down, she found Delaine sitting in her lounger. The technician was bent over her feet, about to begin a hot stone massage.

"Delaine," Theodosia said, practically out of breath. "I think I just figured this out. We've got to call . . ."

Delaine glanced up at her. "Isn't it strange?" she said blithely. "Jemma never mentioned to me last night that Glam Baby Cosmetics changed their packaging. But look at this." She held up a bright-red lipstick that she'd just uncapped. "Their lipstick tubes were originally square-shaped copper tubes, but now they're silver and round." She swiveled the lipstick up and aimed for her lips.

"Delaine!" Theodosia screamed. "Don't! Stop what you're doing immediately!"

Delaine stopped, the bloodred lipstick hovering a mere inch from her lips. "Why?" she asked querulously, a tiny wrinkle suddenly intersecting her forehead. "What's wrong?"

Oh no, that gift bag had been intended for me. Opal Anne still wanted to stop me from investigating.

"Give me that lipstick," Theodosia said. "And for goodness' sakes don't touch it to your lips!"

Delaine looked perturbed as she screwed the red lipstick back down into its tube and handed it to Theodosia. "Why not?" she demanded. "What's wrong?"

"That lipstick is . . . it's tainted." Theodosia decided that *tainted* sounded better than telling Delaine it was probably dripping with poison.

30

Lipstick clutched firmly in hand — the lipstick that had surely been intended for her — Theodosia stormed back down the hallway. A nearby door stood partially open and she could see some kind of warming stove in the room, similar to a sauna box. It was where the masseuses heated the flat, black stones they used for hot stone massages. Theodosia grabbed a black mesh bag and tossed in a dozen of the hot stones. Then she took off again.

Theodosia figured she looked like a crazy lady as she loped down the corridor, flip-flops thwacking as she clutched a lipstick in one hand and a bag full of hot stones in the other.

She didn't care.

She had one goal in mind.

Find Opal Anne.

She darted past the juice bar, where a gaggle of people barely gave her a second look. Then out through the lobby, where two spa employees in matching gold jackets, kind of like an upscale Chinese waiter might wear, were handing out pink gift bags. The real gift bags.

But there was no Opal Anne in sight.

Theodosia raced into the lounge where the fashion show was enjoying a second showing. Marilyn Manson's cover of "You're So Vain" was blasting from the speakers as the models strutted and bounced their way along the makeshift vinyl runway. At least fifty people were crowded into the lounge, enjoying the spectacle.

And there, at the far side of the room, with her back pressed up against the French doors, was Opal Anne.

Theodosia fought to push her way through the room, but it was jammed tight with people. Lubricated by more than a few glasses of champagne, they seemed oblivious to her efforts to brush past them.

Without hesitating, Theodosia stepped onto the vinyl runway and headed in the direction of the far wall. And Opal Anne.

The young woman who was walking the runway just ahead of her turned, and with a toss of her long dark hair, said, "Hey, you're not supposed to be here. Models only."

"Change of program," Theodosia said.

She elbowed her way around the girl and then jumped in front of a curly-haired blond who was wearing a tiger-striped leotard and carrying a neon-pink exercise noodle as a prop. "Excuse me," she said.

"What?" said the girl, dipping aside.

Theodosia set her jaw and kept moving fast. Her bag of hot stones banged against her leg. The *thwack* of her flip-flops could barely be heard above the wall of sound that enveloped everyone.

When Theodosia was twenty feet from Opal Anne, she yelled out, "Opal Anne!"

Opal Anne, who'd been focused on the runway models, heard her name being called and glanced around, looking mildly curious.

"Opal Anne!" Theodosia called again, much louder. She was closing in on her.

Opal Anne surveyed the crowd again, this time finally homing in on exactly who was shouting her name. Then her gazed landed directly on Theodosia and her eyes widened.

Even at a distance of fifteen feet, Theodosia could see Opal Anne's involuntary twitch.

Theodosia powered ahead faster, pushing her way past the models. She ducked around a woman in a purple jumpsuit, shoved a girl in denim leggings completely off the runway.

But when she reached the French doors, one of the doors stood partially ajar and Opal Anne had disappeared into the darkness.

But not for long!

Slipping outside, finding herself on the patio that led to the outdoor pool, Theodosia could make out a shadowy figure running away from her.

"Opal Anne!" Theodosia called out.

The figure ran along the full length of the pool and slid to a stop at another set of doors. She tried to tug them open but they were locked tight.

Theodosia was about to dart ahead when someone grabbed her by the arm. She jerked, twisted about, and found herself staring at Bill Glass.

"What's going on?" Glass asked her. He wore his same photojournalist vest, but this time he'd added a pair of camo pants. Nice touch.

"Would you like a juicy story?" Theodosia asked him.

"Always," Glass said. He wasn't stupid, just rude.

"Then follow me."

Theodosia sprinted down the length of

the pool, past blazing tiki torches, jumping over a wicker lounge chair in the bargain. "Opal Anne!" she yelled out again.

Opal Anne, now in a blind panic, was still rattling the handle of the locked door. Probably hoping for some kind of miracle.

The heavens did not smile down upon her.

As Theodosia closed the distance, she dug her right hand into her bag of hot stones. She grabbed one, angled it just right, and let it fly.

Crash!

She didn't hit Opal Anne but her tiny missile smashed a hole in the glass door that Opal Anne was struggling with.

"Why'd you do it?" Theodosia called out. She grabbed another rock and let it fly.

Smack.

This time the rock hit the doorjamb and bounced off.

Opal Anne turned and shrank back against the door, as if hoping to find protection.

"I didn't," she cried out. But her face was crumpled in fear and her pupils had contracted. Theodosia took this as a sure sign she was lying.

"Of course you did," Theodosia said.

She chucked another stone, a larger stone. This one smacked hard against a metal planter, knocking it over completely.

Clang.

Dirt and green plants spilled out onto the slippery patio stones.

"Stop it!" Opal Anne cried. "It's not what you think."

"How do you know what I think?" Theodosia called out. She dug deep into her bag and found a smaller rock. She winged it sideways at the girl, striking her in the hip. She was a modern-day David going after her Goliath.

"Ouch! You hit me!" Opal Anne cried out.

"Are you ready to talk yet?"

Opal Anne had had enough. Her eyes blazed, her hands bunched into rock-hard fists, and her mouth twisted into an angry grimace. "Leave me alone before I call security," she screamed.

"Go ahead. Call them," Theodosia said. "It'll save me the trouble."

Opal Anne's eyes darted sideways toward Theodosia, as if intending to rush at her and make a break for it. Then she noticed Bill Glass standing right behind Theodosia.

"No, you don't," Theodosia said, moving a step forward.

Like a terrified rabbit desperately trying to escape a fox, Opal Anne leapt to her left. Hoping to make it around the far side of the pool, she took three giant strides, almost making a clean getaway. Except for the fact that her left foot got tripped up on the fallen planter. She started to fall, stumbled and caught herself, and hung there midflight for a few moments. Waving her arms in a frantic swoosh, she fought to regain her balance. It didn't work. Instead, she crashed to her knees.

"Ouch," said Glass, watching her.

Down on the ground, scrambling in desperation, Opal Anne fumbled and struggled and completely miscalculated. One leg churned uselessly in the loose dirt and slippery plants. When she finally pushed herself up on one arm and tried to regain her footing, she wobbled awkwardly. Then, screeching like a scalded cat, she lost her balance and fell sideways. A split second later she tumbled headlong into the pool.

Down she plunged like an anchor on a chain. She hit bottom, hovered like a startled starfish for a few moments, and then kicked her way to the surface. The water churned and bubbled as Opal Anne, caught in the grip of panic, gasped for breath.

"Help!" Opal Anne cried out. Her voice gurgled hoarsely and then rose in a high-pitched, bloodcurdling scream. "I'm in the deep end!"

"You certainly are," Theodosia called out

to her. Opal Anne was dog-paddling like crazy now, going around in circles like a boat with a broken rudder.

"Holy Christmas!" Bill Glass gasped as he lifted his camera. "I gotta get a shot of this."

"Take all the shots you want," Theodosia said as she pulled out her cell phone and dialed the police.

Opal Anne continued to scream as she thrashed haplessly about in the pool. Which meant her ungodly noise also attracted a huge crowd. Guests and some of the fashion models streamed out onto the patio and surrounded the pool, lining the sides like gawkers at the scene of an accident. They gasped in shock as they watched Opal Anne flounder and scream.

"What's going on?" a man called out as the tiki lights around the pool continued to hiss and blaze, creating a strange, ethereal atmosphere. "Did somebody take an unscheduled swim?"

"Is she drowning?" a woman asked.

"What the heck?" cried Sally, who'd come running out from the juice bar. "Is that who I think it is?"

Opal Anne turned onto her back and kicked her way tiredly toward the edge of the pool. With the underwater lights shining, her sequined top glistened like fish scales.

"Help me," Opal Anne cried weakly. She made a horrible choking sound and spit out a stream of water.

"Somebody help her," a woman called out.

Theodosia grabbed a long lifesaver pole and held it out.

But when Opal Anne's flailing arms tried to grab hold of it, Theodosia pushed her gently back into the middle of the pool.

"Stop it!" Opal Anne screeched. "You're killing me! You're drowning me!"

"Are you ready to talk now?" Theodosia asked.

"No!"

Theodosia gave her another shove. "You will."

31

By the time Detective Riley showed up, flanked by two uniformed officers, Opal Anne was as bedraggled as a drowned rat. She was clinging to the edge of the pool — Theodosia had at least let her do that — but she hadn't been allowed to crawl out yet.

"How long has she been soaking in there?" Riley asked.

Theodosia checked her watch. "About twenty minutes."

Riley stood there with his hands in his pockets, bouncing on the balls of his feet. "Is what you told me on the phone really true?" He wore a pale-blue crewneck sweater and a pair of jeans. Casual-like, since he'd come from home.

"I'm pretty sure most of it is true. And I do have a lipstick, which I'm guessing has been dipped in cyanide." Theodosia handed him the lipstick, which Bill Glass had helpfully placed inside a clear plastic baggie. "But, of course, your lab techs will need to analyze it."

"Poison," Riley said. He gazed at Opal Anne, who was hanging on the edge of the pool, looking bitter and resentful, sniffling from the chlorine. "Has she said anything yet?"

"She said she was sorry," Theodosia said. "But I don't think she was sincere."

Riley glanced around. At least forty curious people still had their eyes riveted on Opal Anne, as if she were a two-headed rattlesnake.

"I think we should probably fish her out now," Riley said.

Theodosia gave a thin smile. "Be my guest."

Two uniformed officers knelt down and hoisted Opal Anne out of the pool, each one firmly grasping a wrist. They hauled her up onto dry land, but held on tight.

"I'm cold," Opal Anne complained. Her lips were blue and her teeth were chattering.

"Too bad," Theodosia said.

"Put the handcuffs on her," Riley said.

The two officers pulled Opal Anne's arms behind her back and snapped on a pair of silver cuffs.

Sally crept up slowly, holding a blanket. "Can I put this over her shoulders?" she asked.

Riley nodded. "Go ahead. Then please step back."

Opal Anne stood dripping in front of them. Her hair hung down in wet tendrils, her clothes clung to her, and her eye makeup had melted into a goopy mess. She was missing one shoe.

"Poison?" Riley said to her. "Why?"

Opal Anne stuck out her chin. "He was going to run this place into the ground anyway. What did it matter?"

"What did it *matter*?" Theodosia said. "You took a human life."

"Two human lives," Riley said.

"Yes, tell us about Marcus Covey," Theodosia said.

Opal Anne pouted. "All Marcus had to do was knock over a lousy candle — was that too much to ask? I was the one who took care of the rest." She shrugged. "Then he chickened out on me. He didn't want to follow the playbook, so he had to go." A tiny smile insinuated itself on her face. "What's another dead rat?"

"Dear Lord, she's cold," Riley said. He turned abruptly as a door banged open and someone came clattering across the pool tiles.

It was Delaine.

"Theo," she said, looking surprised. "There you are. I've been looking everywhere for you." She was duckwalking, leaning back on her heels because her toenail polish was still wet. "Do you know if they're still serving . . . ?" She saw Opal Anne standing there, wet, handcuffed, and sullen, and said in a drawling voice, "Good gracious. What happened to her? She looks like she's been flushed down a sewer."

"Opal Anne just found out that confession is good for the soul," Theodosia said. "She just admitted to two murders and was about to tell us why she tried to run Drayton over with a stolen car."

"You're the one I was really after," Opal Anne sneered, her eyes seeking out Theodosia. "You were the one who was snooping around and getting too involved for your own good. I tried to track you down, but you and that stupid dog of yours were always flitting down those narrow alleys. Then, when I finally saw Drayton, I figured he'd be just as good. If I put him out of commission maybe you'd get scared and back off." She shrugged. "So I just went for it."

Delaine stretched an accusing finger toward Opal Anne and said, in her most wilting tone, "How *dare* you attack my friends, you nasty little fiend. I'd say that prison isn't nearly good enough for you, you ought to be horsewhipped." She leaned down, ripped the flip-flops off her feet, and tossed them at Opal Anne. "And you can keep your crappy swag, too."

Theodosia couldn't help but grin. When Delaine was on a rampage, when Delaine went off script, she could slice and dice with the best of them.

"I'm going to phone Drayton immediately," Delaine screamed again. "And tell him that *you* were the one driving that car, that it was you who tried to run him down. I know he's going to want to press charges." She took a quick breath and stuck her nose up in the air. "And then I'm going to call Doreen and encourage her to seriously *disown* you."

"Somebody better make a phone call and have poor Reggie Huston released from jail, too," Theodosia said. She glanced at Riley. "Reggie's not going to be happy. Something tells me he's going to go on a tear and make us eat some serious crow."

"Maybe I could do a feature story on the spa," Bill Glass volunteered. "Give Reggie

Huston a few strokes. To help make up for everything that's happened here."

"That would be very kind of you," Theodosia said. "I think it would definitely help smooth things over."

Detective Riley glanced at the two uniformed officers who were hanging on tight to Opal Anne. "I think you'd better get her out of here before the villagers decide to break out the pitchforks and the torches."

As the officers led Opal Anne away, Riley touched a hand to Theodosia's arm and gently guided her away from the crowd. "I asked you this once before . . ."

"What did you ask me?" Even in this dim light Theodosia was surprised at how blue his eyes were. How cute and earnest he looked.

"I asked you how you knew. Where you were getting your information."

"Okay."

Riley gave her a quizzical look. "So how did you know it was Opal Anne? How did you figure out that she was the killer?"

"Oh well, I didn't really know it for a fact," Theodosia said. "I just sort of guessed. And then there was that chemistry major business, and the different gift bags, and suddenly it all came together in a gigantic rush . . ." Theodosia stopped talking as Riley continued to peer at her. Yes, he was listening to her, but she could tell he wasn't really *hearing* her. His mind was somewhere else. And, really, from the curious way he was looking at her, maybe that wasn't such a bad thing.

"I'm sorry, but I have to take off now," Riley said. He nodded in the direction the officers had taken Opal Anne. "You know . . ."

"Promise me you'll call Doreen," Theodosia said. "And let her know what happened before Delaine drops a big neutron bomb."

"I'll call her right away."

"You're going to be busy sorting through all this, aren't you?" Theodosia said. She knew she had to say her piece quickly and make it come out just right. It was now or never. "I mean, putting together the pieces on two separate murders, it's going to be fairly complicated and confusing. So you'll probably be busy for the next couple of days. And maybe tonight as well?"

"I'm afraid . . . Well, what exactly did you have in mind?" Riley asked, smiling at her, his eyes crinkling at the corners.

For some reason, Theodosia felt as if they were standing in their own private little bubble. Apart from the crowd, Delaine, the swimming pool, all the bizarre events that had just unfolded.

"Are you too busy to, um, get together?" Theodosia asked. There, she'd done it. She'd made the first official move.

Riley leaned in close to her. "What exactly are you asking?"

Theodosia gazed at him, a hopeful look lighting up her face. "I thought maybe you could stop by the tea shop. I could fix you a cup of tea and a bite to eat?"

"You mean right now?" Riley lifted a hand and touched it against Theodosia's face in a tender gesture.

"We could do it some other time if that would be more convenient." *Please don't disappoint me.*

He didn't.

Riley leaned in closer to Theodosia, his lips just inches from hers. "No. I think that sounds wonderful." His arms crept around her waist as he pulled her tight. "I think you and I have quite a lot to talk about."

"I think we do, too," Theodosia whispered into the darkness.

FAVORITE RECIPES FROM
THE INDIGO TEA SHOP

Lemon Tea Bread
6 Tbsp. butter
1 cup sugar
2 eggs
1 1/2 cups flour
1/4 tsp. salt
1 tsp. baking powder
1/2 cup milk
1 lemon (grated rind)
Whipped cream or Devonshire cream
Sliced strawberries

Preheat oven to 350 degrees. In large mixing bowl, cream together butter, sugar, and eggs. Add in flour, salt, baking powder, and milk. Stir in lemon rind. Pour batter into a 9-inch-by-5-inch greased and floured bread pan. Bake for 55 to 60 minutes until toothpick comes out clean. Serve with whipped cream or Devonshire cream, and sliced strawberries. Yields 1 small loaf.

Raisin Scones

3 1/2 cups flour
1/2 tsp. salt
3/4 cup butter
1/2 cup sugar
1/2 cup raisins (or Craisins)
1 egg
3/4 cup cream

Preheat oven to 350 degrees. In mixing bowl, add flour and salt, then cut in butter. Stir in sugar and raisins. Make a well in the center and add the egg and half the cream. Mix and add the rest of the cream as you go along. If mixture is too dry, add a little more cream. Roll dough out on floured board to about 1/2-inch thick. Cut into wedges and place on greased baking sheet. Bake for 12 to 15 minutes until golden brown. Yields 6 to 8 scones.

Haley's Banana Muffins

2 cups flour
1 cup sugar
1 tsp. baking powder
1 tsp. baking soda
1 cup mashed bananas
1 cup sour cream
1/2 cup chopped nuts

Preheat oven to 350 degrees. In large bowl

mix together flour, sugar, baking powder, and baking soda. Stir in mashed bananas and sour cream until mixed. Add chopped nuts. Pour batter into well-greased muffin tins and bake for 20 minutes. Yields 8 muffins.

Strawberry Cream Cheese Tea Sandwiches

3 oz. cream cheese, softened
2 Tbsp. strawberry preserves
4 slices thin white bread

Combine cream cheese and strawberry preserves in a bowl. Spread mixture on 2 slices of bread. Top with plain bread, trim crusts, and cut bread diagonally into triangles. Yields 8 small tea sandwiches.

Apple Nut Squares

2 eggs
1 1/2 cups sugar
1 tsp. vanilla
1 cup flour
2 tsp. baking powder
1/2 tsp. salt
2 cups apples, chopped
1/2 cup walnuts, chopped

Preheat oven to 350 degrees. Combine eggs, sugar, and vanilla and beat until light and fluffy. In a separate bowl, sift together flour, baking powder, and salt. Add egg mixture to flour mixture and combine. Stir in apples and nuts. Spread mixture into a greased and floured 8-inch-by-12-inch pan. Bake for 30 minutes. Let cool and then cut into squares. Yields about 12 squares.

Peanut Butter Blossom Cookies
1/2 cup butter
1/2 cup granulated white sugar, plus extra
1/2 cup brown sugar
1 tsp. vanilla
1 egg
1/2 cup peanut butter
1 tsp. baking soda
1 1/2 cup flour
Milk chocolate or Hershey's Kisses

Preheat oven to 375 degrees. In large bowl, cream together butter, white sugar, brown sugar, and vanilla. Add egg and beat well. Stir in peanut butter, baking soda, and flour until well mixed. Using a spoon, form mixture into small bowls, then roll in granulated sugar. Bake for approximately 8 minutes. Remove from oven and quickly place a piece of milk chocolate in the center of each cookie (chunk of milk chocolate or

Hershey's Kiss). Let cool and serve. Yields 12 to 15 cookies.

Avocado and Chicken Tea Sandwiches
1 avocado, ripe
1 Tbsp. chili paste (or hot sauce)
1 Tbsp. lime juice
6 slices of rye bread
Roast chicken slices

Mash avocado in bowl and add chili paste and lime juice. Spread avocado paste on 6 slices of rye bread. Top three of the slices with roast chicken slices. Add top slices to the sandwiches and trim off crusts. Cut into squares or triangles. Yields 12 small sandwiches.

Cranberry Iced Tea
1 quart tea, brewed and cooled
2 cups cranberry juice
Juice of 1 lemon
2 Tbsp. sugar

Combine all ingredients in a pitcher, then serve over ice in tall glasses. Yields 4 to 6 servings.

Quickie-Not-So-Picky Chicken Tetrazzini
3 Tbsp. butter
1 (4-oz.) can sliced mushrooms

1/4 cup chopped green pepper
1/4 cup diced onions
1 (10-oz.) can chicken gravy
1/2 cup Cheddar cheese, shredded
1 cup diced, cooked chicken
2 cups cooked spaghetti noodles
1/4 cup chopped tomato

Melt butter in saucepan and add mushrooms, green peppers, and onions. Sizzle until tender. Stir in chicken gravy and Cheddar cheese. Heat until cheese is melted. Add chicken, spaghetti noodles, and tomato. Stir until heated. Yields 4 servings.

TEA TIME TIPS FROM
LAURA CHILDS

Silk Road Tea Party
The Silk Road was the ancient trading route from China to the Mediterranean, and it brought many of China's treasures to new lands. For this tea consider serving gingered pineapple and sultana raisin scones, Chinese chicken salad tea sandwiches, Chinese noodles (Marco Polo's gift to the West!), and tea bread with plum jam and Devonshire cream. Set your table with Chinese or Middle East–inspired tablecloths, blue-and-white dishes, Chinese lilies or peonies for a centerpiece, and lots of chinoiserie. Yunnan or Lapsang souchong tea would be perfect.

Harvest Gold Tea
Use a patchwork quilt as a tablecloth and add pots filled with late-blooming yarrow and bittersweet. Scatter a few autumn leaves on your table and use simple, homespun crockery. For your food offerings, consider

apple scones, corn chowder with cranberry bread, pear and Stilton cheese tea sandwiches, and gingerbread bars for dessert. Serve Keemun tea, a rich, full-flavored tea often referred to as the Burgundy of teas.

Strawberry Tea

Served indoors or out, this Strawberry Tea motif is sure to please your guests. Use a white linen tablecloth, as many pink dishes as you can round up, and decorate your table with pink flowers. Tie your white linen napkins with pink ribbon and add a tiny strawberry charm. Serve strawberry and white chocolate scones, chicken salad tea sandwiches topped with sliced strawberries, a small sliver of cheese quiche, and strawberry tarts for dessert. Floral teas, such as jasmine, or a black tea flavored with strawberry and vanilla, would be perfect.

Sweet Summer Herb Tea

Toss a linen tablecloth on your picnic table and lay out your best china. (Yes, you're serving tea outdoors!) Dress up your tea table with colorful ceramic pots overflowing with bunches of fresh herbs and give each guest a packet of seeds as a favor. Start your three-course tea with herbed cream scones, then move on to tea sandwiches of cream cheese with chives and egg salad with dill. Herbed bread with crab salad would also be delicious. For dessert, think mint ice cream. A black tea with peppermint would be a perfect accompaniment, as would any type of tisane (French for *herbal infusion.*)

Japanese Tea

Keep your tea table simple and Zen-like. Decorate it with a Japanese bonsai, a single, lovely orchid, or a miniature water fountain. Small candles, lacquer trays, bamboo place mats, and handmade ceramic plates or bowls contribute to the atmosphere. Serve shrimp tempura with steamed rice — or sushi, if you and your guests are adventurous. You can also grill skewers of scallops and chicken on a tabletop hibachi. Poached pears and almond cookies make a simple but amazing dessert. Your *ocha* (tea) of choice should be Gyokuro, Japan's finest green tea.

TEA RESOURCES

Tea Magazines and Publications

Tea Time — A luscious magazine profiling tea and tea lore. Filled with glossy photos and wonderful recipes. (teatimemagazine .com)

Southern Lady — From the publishers of *Tea Time* with a focus on people and places in the South as well as wonderful teatime recipes. (southernladymagazine .com)

The Tea House Times — Go to theteahouse-times.com for subscription information and dozens of links to tea shops, purveyors of tea, gift shops, and tea events. Visit the Laura Childs guest blog!

Victoria — Articles and pictorials on homes, home design, gardens, and tea. (victoria mag.com)

Texas Tea & Travel — Highlighting Texas and other Southern tea rooms, tea events, and fun travel. (teaintexas.com)

Fresh Cup Magazine — For tea and coffee professionals. (freshcup.com)

Tea & Coffee — Trade journal for the tea and coffee industry. (teaandcoffee.net)

Bruce Richardson — This author has written several definitive books on tea. (store .elmwoodinn.com/brucerichardson.aspx)

Jane Pettigrew — This author has written sixteen books on the varied aspects of tea and its history and culture. (janepettigrew .com/books)

A Tea Reader — by Katrina Ávila Munichiello, an anthology of tea stories and reflections.

American Tea Plantations

Charleston Tea Plantation — The oldest and largest tea plantation in the U.S. Order their fine black tea or schedule a visit at bigelowtea.com.

Table Rock Tea Company — This Pickens, South Carolina, plantation is growing premium whole leaf tea. Target production date is 2018. (tablerocktea.com)

Fairhope Tea Plantation — Tea plantation in Fairhope, Alabama.

Sakuma Brothers Farm — This tea garden just outside Burlington, Washington, has been growing white and green tea for almost twenty years. (sakumamarket.com)

Big Island Tea — Organic artisan tea from Hawaii. (bigislandtea.com)

Mauna Kea Tea — Organic green and oolong tea from Hawaii's Big Island. (maunakeatea.com)

Onomea Tea — Nine-acre tea estate near Hilo, Hawaii. (onomeatea.com)

Moonrise Tea — Organic teas grown on Hawaii's Big Island and packed in rice paper pouches. (moonrisetea.com)

Tea Websites and Interesting Blogs

Teamap.com — Directory of hundreds of tea shops in the U.S. and Canada.

Afternoontea.co.uk — Guide to tea rooms in the UK.

Cookingwithideas.typepad.com — Recipes and book reviews for the bibliochef.

Seedrack.com — Order *Camellia sinensis* seeds and grow your own tea!

Friendshiptea.net — Tea shop reviews, recipes, and more.

RTbookreviews.com — Wonderful romance and mystery book review site.

Adelightsomelife.com — Tea, gardening, and cottage crafts.

Theladiestea.com — Networking platform for women.

Jennybakes.com — Fabulous recipes from a

real make-it-from-scratch baker.

Cozyupwithkathy.blogspot.com — Cozy mystery reviews.

Southernwritersmagazine.com — Inspiration, writing advice, and author interviews of Southern writers.

Thedailytea.com — Formerly *Tea Magazine,* this online publication is filled with tea news, recipes, inspiration, and tea travel.

Allteapots.com — Teapots from around the world.

Fireflyvodka.com — South Carolina purveyors of Sweet Tea Vodka, Raspberry Tea Vodka, Peach Tea Vodka, and more. Just visiting this website is a trip in itself!

Teasquared.blogspot.com — Fun, well-written blog about tea, tea shops, and tea musings.

Blog.bernideens.com — Bernideen's tea-time blog about tea, baking, decorating, and gardening.

Possibili-teas.net — Tea consultants with a terrific monthly newsletter.

Relevanttealeaf.blogspot.com — All about tea.

Stephcupoftea.blogspot.com — Blog on tea, food, and inspiration.

Teawithfriends.blogspot.com — Lovely blog on tea, friendship, and tea accoutrements.

Bellaonline.com/site/tea — Features and

forums on tea.

Napkinfoldingguide.com — Photo illustrations of twenty-seven different (and sometimes elaborate) napkin folds.

Worldteaexpo.com — This premier business-to-business trade show features more than three hundred tea suppliers, vendors, and tea innovators.

Sweetgrassbaskets.net — One of several websites where you can buy sweetgrass baskets direct from the artists.

Fatcatscones.com — Frozen ready-to-bake scones.

Kingarthurflour.com — One of the best flours for baking. This is what many professional pastry chefs use.

Teagw.com — Visit this website and click on Products to find dreamy tea pillows filled with jasmine, rose, lavender, and green tea.

Californiateahouse.com — Order Machu's Blend, a special herbal tea for dogs that promotes healthy skin, lowers stress, and aids digestion.

Vintageteaworks.com — This company offers six unique wine-flavored tea blends that celebrate wine and respect the tea.

Downtonabbeycooks.com — A *Downton Abbey* blog with news and recipes. You can also order their book.

Auntannie.com — Crafting site that will teach you how to make your own petal envelopes, pillow boxes, gift bags, etc.

Marktwendell.com — Mark T. Wendell is the U.S. distributor for Davison Newman & Co Ltd of London, original suppliers of tea for the historic Boston Tea Parties of 1773–1774.

Victorianhousescones.com — Scone, biscuit, and cookie mixes for both retail and wholesale orders. Plus baking and scone-making tips.

Svtea.com — Contact Simpson & Vail to order their teas and gift sets.

Harney.com — Contact Harney & Sons to order their *Titanic* Blend loose leaf tea or their RMS *Titanic* tea sachets.

Englishteastore.com — Buy a jar of English Double Devon Cream here as well as British foods and candies.

Stickyfingersbakeries.com — Scone mixes and English curds.

TeaSippersSociety.com — Join this international tea community of tea sippers, growers, and educators. A terrific newsletter!

Teabox.com — wonderful international webzine about all aspects of tea.

Purveyors of Fine Tea

Adagio.com
Harney.com
Stashtea.com
Republicoftea.com
Teazaanti.com
Bigelowtea.com
Celestialseasonings.com
Goldenmoontea.com
Uptontea.com
Svtea.com (Simpson & Vail)

Visiting Charleston

Charleston.com — Travel and hotel guide.

Charlestoncvb.com — The official Charleston convention and visitor bureau.

Charlestontour.wordpress.com — Private tours of homes and gardens, some including lunch or tea.

Culinarytoursofcharleston.com — Sample specialties from Charleston's local eateries, markets, and bakeries.

Poogansporch.com — This restored Victorian house serves traditional low-country cuisine. Be sure to ask about Poogan!

Preservationsociety.org — Hosts Charleston's annual Fall Home Tour.

Palmettocarriage.com — Horse-drawn carriage rides.

Charlestonharbortours.com — Boat tours

and harbor cruises.

Ghostwalk.net — Stroll into Charleston's haunted history. Ask them about the "original" Theodosia!

CharlestonTours.net — Ghost tours plus tours of plantations and historic homes.

Follybeach.com — Official guide to Folly Beach activities, hotels, rentals, restaurants, and events.

ABOUT THE AUTHOR

Laura Childs is the *New York Times* bestselling author of the Cackleberry Club, Tea Shop, and Scrapbooking mysteries. In her past life she was a Clio Award–winning advertising writer and CEO of her own marketing firm. She lives in Plymouth, Minnesota.